PLASTIC JESUS

WAYNE SIMMONS
PLASTIC JESUS

SALT

CROMER

PUBLISHED BY SALT
12 Norwich Road, Cromer, Norfolk NR27 0AX

© Wayne Simmons, 2013

The right of Wayne Simmons to be identified as the author of this work
has been asserted by him in accordance with Section 77 of the Copyright,
Designs and Patents Act 1988.

This book is in copyright. Subject to statutory exception and to provisions
of relevant collective licensing agreements, no reproduction of any part may
take place without the written permission of Salt Publishing.

First published by Salt Publishing, 2013

Printed in Great Britain by Clays Ltd, St Ives plc

Typeset in Paperback 9/12

*This book is sold subject to the conditions that it shall not, by way of trade
or otherwise, be lent, re-sold, hired out, or otherwise circulated without the
publisher's prior consent in any form of binding or cover other than that in which
it is published and without a similar condition including this condition being
imposed on the subsequent purchaser.*

ISBN 978 1 907773 63 1 paperback

For Dug, Jerry and Ty.
Thank you for the music.

'People think that I have come to cast peace upon the world.
They do not know that I have come to cast conflicts . . .'
The Gospel of St Thomas

PROLOGUE

Becky looked so fragile.

Johnny watched her twisting and turning on the bed, sheets gathered at her feet like crumpled foil.

She'd been zoned out for the last week. She was lucid now, no longer wired, the VR coil hanging by her bed like a dead snake.

There was a nurse in the room with them. She was pretty and Johnny felt awful for even thinking that at a time like this.

A doctor was there too. His arms were folded, the watch on his wrist horribly visible. Yet part of Johnny still waited for a miracle cure: some new and radical medicine to be sucked into a needle and injected into Becky's bloodstream, saving the day. It wouldn't happen.

The nurse bent over the bed, wiping Becky's forehead with a damp cloth. Johnny could see her face now. She wasn't as pretty as he had thought and he felt slightly better for knowing that. Becky was the only one allowed to be pretty. Valiantly fighting for each breath on the bed before them, patchy hair peppered over her skull like ash. Her bones sharp and brittle, her skin like a veil, freckles all but gone. But her eyes . . .

A sharp gasp escaped her mouth.

The doctor whispered something to the nurse and Johnny realised it was time.

He felt a sudden rush of blood. His pulse was racing.

He hadn't prepared anything. Sure, he'd spent the last thirty-six hours at her bedside, but he wasn't ready for Becky to die. Not now. Not here: in this metal bed with the not-so-nice doctor and the (not-so?) pretty nurse.

He reached for Becky's hand.

Her nails, still sharp, dug into his moist palm, breaking skin. She made a noise that Johnny would never forget; a high-pitched whine as air escaped from her frayed lungs. Her arms suddenly spread out wide as if some part of her was trying to crawl out from this ravaged little body, to be set free after weeks of fighting and struggling and suffering.

She was fading fast.

Her eyes swelled, damp but still beautiful. The whining noise was softer now as her breathing paled. And then, after one final gasp for air, Johnny Lyon watched and held on and cried as his wife gave up and died.

Silence.

Johnny kept hold of Becky's hand. Her arm had fallen limp but he wouldn't let go.

The whining noise returned; Johnny realising it wasn't coming from Becky, now, but the machine in the corner. He barely noticed it anymore. It was just another part of the room, like the metal bed or the tall windows or the plastic curtains. But now the machine's sound was changing, as if the damn thing had been recording this whole scene for him and was now playing it back. *A little something to remember her by*, he expected the not-so-pretty nurse to say before syncing a vid marked 'Becky' to his cell.

But she didn't.

She simply looked to the doctor, who looked at his watch before saying something that Johnny didn't hear and didn't want to hear.

It was finished.

ONE

Ms Liberty stood on the edge of Lark City harbour, lips pouting, star-spangled breasts pointing out to sea. At just over one hundred and fifty feet tall (in heels), she was a crude parody of New York's classic landmark.

Her face was legendary, one baby blue winking across the water, as if to goad the former US of A. Her right hand pointed to the sky, the left pressed against the hip curve of her garter belt. Shimmering from head to toe, she made a feisty welcome for sea and air traffic alike. *An' it harm none*, her inscription read, *Do what you will.*

This was Maalside, the New Republic. Lark City was its capital, sprawling across the west coast like a neon jungle. Once part of the US colonies, Maal now stood alone in the Pacific, separated from the heartland by 200 miles of salty ocean and a devil-may-care attitude.

Kitty McBride turned up Tomb Street, Lark's Red Light District. She was everything Ms Liberty was *not*, drifting through the city like a ghost, freak shows and peep shows dancing around her like marionettes.

She moved past the Penny Dreadful.

Kitty knew girls who worked there, knew the work was good. Penny was a reputable place, popular with

4

the suited and booted; men with wedding rings in their pockets who'd pay top dollar for a young thing like her.

But Kitty's turf was the street, her Johns from clubs and bars where stuck-up broads from Penny wouldn't be seen dead.

She found Vegas, Tomb's busiest bar. Converted from an old church, Vegas sat nestled between two strip clubs: the infamous Route 66 (*where the boys get their kicks*) and another dive called Swingers.

Kitty entered, nodding at the Bar Man.

He returned the nod, poured her a glass of water and passed it across the bar.

She grabbed her drink then took her usual seat in Vegas; a red plastic sofa in the corner. Chequered cushions littered the sofa but she removed them, as she always did, taking each cushion in turn and stacking them out of sight behind her.

It was warm inside, the heat overbearing.

Sweat coated her body. The New York Dolls shirt was sticking to her skin.

She scanned the room, looking for Johns.

The décor was so familiar: faux newspaper cuttings on the walls; framed snapshots above the bar, mostly punk bands that Kitty was too young to have even heard of. Bands like Sex Pistols, Blondie, Sonic Youth. Bands like New York Dolls. The irony was lost on her.

The door opened and Kitty looked over.

A tall, thin man entered, eyes darting around the bar. He looked young, desperate. Totally Kitty's type when it came to earning potential. A quick shuffle would sort him out and, more importantly, sort *her* out with some cash.

Kitty needed dope.

She hadn't had a hit in almost as long as she hadn't had a shower, and it was beginning to show. Her fingers started drumming on the table. She licked her lips. Started to itch but didn't know where to scratch.

Kitty watched the new guy make a beeline for the bar.

The Box was playing a live feed from the Barrenlands, the former Middle East, countries such as Israel, Iraq and Iran. But these were only names to Johnny Lyon, victims of a Holy War that ended badly. The Barrenlands were nasty, known as The Hole in the World for good reason. At their centre an *actual* hole ran far into the ground, an unchartered abyss leading to hell itself. Scientists reckoned it was the earth's deepest tear. But tonight, Johnny knew something deeper.

The hole in his heart.

He grabbed a seat, ordered JD and coke then sank it in one. His throat was almost numb from the hammering it had been taking lately. The drinks tasted softer by the day, tonight's like straight coke.

Johnny banged his glass on the bar to signal a refill.

The Bar Man raised an eyebrow. He looked at Johnny suspiciously.

'You good for it?' he asked.

Johnny nodded.

He pulled a credit card from his wallet and inserted it directly into the bar's old chip-and-pin.

That seemed to placate the Bar Man.

'Bottle or shot?' he asked.

Johnny took the bottle.

The Bar Man typed the bill into the chip-and-pin.

Johnny punched his code in; four simple digits. Easy. He waited until the card was debited, knowing his credit was almost maxed but not caring. As long as he had enough for tonight, all was fine and fucking dandy.

He lifted the bottle, poured a healthier dollop of JD into his glass, this time adding only a little mixer.

Johnny downed the contents in one swig.

He surveyed the bar, confidence brewing now he'd had himself a couple of drinks. He saw the regulars that every night would hold in a place like this: broken men, staring at their drinks.

Johnny wondered if he was somehow transmitting his own misery to them, if maybe they were that little bit more melancholic due to being in the company of his sorry ass. He thought of his day-job, coding VR. How some folks would pick up on others' feelings or memories when wired, as if every user, every person plugging into the system and interacting with the environments and scenarios created by code, left a little piece of themselves behind.

'Four more beers when you're ready, boss.'

'Need a tray?'

'Sure thing.'

Johnny turned, finding a younger guy stood at the bar beside him. The wiretap was pulled down from his face but his eyes were still dead. Johnny knew that look: kid had been zoning for hours.

'Alright, bud?' the kid asked.

'Couldn't be better,' Johnny said.

He watched the wirehead carry his tray over to where his buddies were sitting. They hardly noticed as he sat their beers down, wiretaps and coils running to their cells, bodies shaking as the code flowed through, drowning their brains in whatever VR release was doing the rounds.

Johnny poured another shot.

He noticed some kid in the corner staring at him. Skinny little thing with peroxide hair and a New York Dolls shirt. Couldn't have been old enough to drink. Typical of this fucking place.

His eyes moved back to the bottle. He could see his own silhouette in the dark brown glass; his head swollen up like something from a funhouse mirror. Dark rings circled his eyes. His hair was unkempt and long. The bottle was his mistress and she weren't keeping him like she should.

Becky.

He drained another glass then slammed it on the table, burping obnoxiously.

The Bar Man glared at him.

Johnny glared back.

He reached for the bottle, his hand seeming lighter than before. A little JD spilled on the bar as he poured another glass but Johnny didn't care. He didn't bother with the mixer this time, downing the JD straight. Shook his head, like some old dog, as the golden liquid worked its way down his throat.

A stupid, sloppy smile spread across his face. He looked at the reflection in the bottle again, expecting to see himself grinning back like a goddamn Cheshire cat. But it was too dark and his eyes were failing him, everything now blurred and faded like some old movie on the Box.

The Bar Man returned, unfurling the white towel from over his shoulder and mopping the bar where the JD had spilled.

Johnny beamed at him, 'Yeah, sorry about that.'

But the Bar Man wasn't amused.

'Think you've had enough,' he said.

But Johnny wanted more.

He stood up from his stool, a man meaning business. The stool fell over, crashed to the floor.

Johnny reached for the JD, flipping it to his mouth. He glugged heavily. The booze ran down his neck, his shirt, his coat, spilling onto the floor around him.

He gagged, felt something rise up from his insides. Puke, dark and bloody, surged from his mouth like lava.

It spat across the bar.

The Bar Man unfurled his towel, like a matador, deflecting the spray.

He looked up, appalled.

Johnny dropped the bottle. It smashed on the floor.

He grabbed the side of the bar to steady himself, spurts of puke still heaving from his mouth.

Every eye present (and unwired) stared back at him.

What are they all looking at, the fuckers?! Johnny wanted to say, but the world was swaying around him, blurring.

The Bar Man moved towards him, but someone else got there first: the kid in the New York Dolls shirt .

'Leave him,' she said.

9

Then grabbed Johnny, led him to the door.

Johnny could hear the Bar Man shouting at him. He heard himself growl some kind of retort.

Then he was out of there.

TWO

Kitty lived in an apartment just off Tomb Street, an old dive full of decay and damp. Electro music whirred obnoxiously from every other window. The sweet smell of Marijuana hung heavy in the air. A clatter of activity, glass breaking and shouting, came from somewhere close by.

Kitty moved through the doorway.

'Watch the step,' she said to the John as he stumbled.

A couple of yahoos pushed past them.

One of the doors on the ground floor had been kicked in. An old woman with a bust lip called out from within but Kitty ignored her, grabbing the John by the elbow and guided him up the stairs.

It was a three-floor climb, the lift having failed long before Kitty had ever lived here. With the weight of the John to bear, it took much longer to get up the stairs.

A handful of kids, hooded jackets and wiretaps covering their faces, lined the approach to the third floor. Kitty dipped her head low as she passed them, expecting the usual smartass remarks. But they said nothing, lost in their VR world of gaming, and narcotics. Wired in all senses of the word.

She reached her apartment.

Slid one hand into the pocket of her drains, retrieving her keycard. She let go of the John, watched him slump against the wall. Unlocked the door.

Once inside, the John seemed to get some balance back. He stood by the bathroom door, eyeing the place up.

It wasn't much to look at.

A single, fold-down bed took pride of place in the centre of the room. A scabby mattress with *You-Know-What* stains sat on top. Small piles of clothing, mostly tees and pairs of drains, littered the floor. A few posters on the wall. A dressing table, with an old sheet draped across its mirror like some lazy pantomime ghoul.

'Christ,' the John said. 'This place . . .'

'Is a shit hole,' Kitty said. 'I know that. But it's *my* shit hole.'

The John didn't reply, instead stumbling over to the bed and collapsing face-down onto the *You-Know-What* stains.

'Great,' Kitty muttered.

And she meant it.

An opened carton caught her eye from the other side of the room. She walked over, retrieved it and glanced out onto the Tomb Street nightlife, swigging absently on warm day-old milk.

Once drained, she crumpled the carton and dropped it out the opened window.

It struck the head of a stumbling old drunk, singing his way down the street. He stopped, seeming to think about what had happened before moving on again, chorus resumed at full decibel.

That amused Kitty.

She stood for a moment, drinking up Lark City's sounds, sights and smells.

Then she returned to the bed.

The John was still flat out, arms and legs akimbo.

His wallet poked out from the back of his baggies. Kitty reached for it, flipping it open.

Inside was a picture, no doubt a girlfriend or wife. *Typical*, Kitty thought.

She took his credit card before sticking the wallet back into the John's pocket. She slid the card into the back pocket of her vinyl drains.

Easy money.

Kitty retrieved her cell from a small pile of clothes in the middle of the room. She flipped it open, muttered a name, made the call.

'Geordie, I've got the cash. Bring us the usual.'

Kenny stood in the living area of an apartment on Titanic Quarter, cold sweat running down his back.

The corpse of the apartment's owner lay on the floor beside him.

The man's killer stood right in front of Kenny. His name was King. He held a blood stained brass figurine in one hand.

A cell was in his other hand. It was ringing and King answered it, talked for a moment, like nothing had just happened, then snapped it closed.

His eyes found Kenny.

'That was just some junkie calling his cell,' he said. 'Silly bitch thought she was talking to *him*', and here King nudged the body on the floor with his foot. 'She wants her dope.' He bent down, addressed the dead man: 'Now where would you have stashed it, pal?'

'Holy fuck,' Kenny breathed, still in shock. 'He's dead. You fucking *killed* him!'

'Shhh, I'm thinking,' King said.

He looked around the room, drawn to the Box in the corner. It was synced to that new Reality Extreme program, DEATHSTAR. King stared at it for a while, hangdog expression on his face.

On screen was the show's host, Kal, all diamond earrings and veneered teeth.

Kal spoke through a clear breathing mask: 'A sad day for viewers everywhere following the departure of last week's favourite, ex-model, Cynthia Lazar.'

The cam zoomed in on Cynthia's body, lying at the bottom of a mountain, her face frozen in a look of fear.

The words ROCKFACE CHALLENGE ran along the bottom of the screen.

'Thirty eight year old Cynthia brought in a record number of hits with her exciting demise.' Kal's voice lowered momentarily, 'Our thoughts are with her friends and family at this time,' then brightened with: 'Of course, viewers can still catch Cynthia's trial at the usual places. Hit it up on the Net. Wire to the VR replay or catch the Box reruns right here on our special catch-up show later today!'

'King!' Kenny cried. 'Did you hear me?'

The other man waved his hand.

'Shhh. I'm watching this.'

The vid switched to Val who looked so similar to Kal that she could have been grown in the same vat tank.

A man stood beside Val. Jet black hair fell over his smooth forehead. He'd used so much Botox that his lips hardly moved when he smiled. But his eyes betrayed him, set within his face like hardened jelly. Old, tired and scared.

'Thanks, Kal!' The co-host's voice echoed around her fishbowl-like mask. 'We're delighted to introduce our newest contestant, veteran of the movie world, star in over two hundred features, Mr Tom –'

Kenny synced his cell with the Box, switched it off.

'Hey, what did you do that for?' King protested. 'I told you, I was watching that!'

Kenny pointed at the body on the floor.

'Forget the fucking box!' he barked. 'I can't believe you just killed a man!'

But King remained unfazed.

'Kenny-boy,' he said, shrugging, 'this is what we do.' He kicked the body, checking that the man was definitely dead, then asked, 'Do you know who this is?'

Kenny didn't. He'd just come along for the ride, up for some wallet or purse grabs. Fishing for cells, maybe, passing them onto Charles 7 for hacking. He was even game for the odd break-in or two, but *this* was never part of the plan.

'Geordie Mac. Biggest fucking dealer in Lark. Likes to think of himself as a service to the community and all that bullshit. Yet look at where he lives?' King drew one hand across Geordie's plush Titanic Quarter apartment. 'Capitalist pig!' he spat. 'Dirty bastard's servicing himself, no one else. He ain't no friend of King's!'

Kenny hated this kind of talk. But King was on a roll, referring to himself in the third person. Now he had killed a man and Kenny was accessory to it. And Kenny knew exactly how that would roll: they would both be executed, if caught – regardless of who caught them, the goons or McBride. This shit would attract a lot of attention.

Kenny suddenly felt very unwell. He began to retch, clammy hands reaching to cover his mouth. He stooped and, still retching, pushed his way through the door leading to the hallway.

Kenny bolted down one flight of stairs, left the apartment block, ducked around the corner into an alleyway.

Another retch, the puke now heavy and warm in his mouth. He released it in the direction of an old, neglected skip, rubbed his mouth, then let himself slide down a nearby wall.

He blew some air out, looked up.

Geordie's apartment was one of the newer skyblocks. Similar blocks surrounded it, their plastic and aluminium exteriors pointing to the sky, casting shadows as far as Kenny could see. It was hard to know whether it was night or day with most of the sky secluded. And that was a good thing.

He stood up, looking to both exits from the alleyway. Apart from a scraggy old street cat, there was no one around.

Thank fuck, Kenny thought.

This wasn't Tomb Street; a man puking 'round these parts was something you'd remember.

'Where are you?' It was King's voice.

Kenny left the alleyway, finding his partner standing outside Geordie Mac's block.

A large silver billboard drifted by, its screen completely filled by the face of a woman. Kenny froze, thinking it was some new SLAM cam patrolling the streets, seeking out crims. But then the face smiled, a brand name running across the screen. Just a billboard running an ad for cigarettes.

King smiled, showing off some bag he'd found.

'What the fuck's that?' Kenny asked.

'Goodies,' said King. 'Found a stash under the bed. First place I checked.' His eyes widened, his voice now a hoarse whisper, 'Man, the street value of this shit will keep us sweet for the next fucking decade!'

Kenny's brow furrowed.

'You're going to sell it?'

'*We're* going to sell it,' King corrected him. 'Remember, we're partners now, bud!'

How could Kenny forget?

'We'll start by offloading some to that junkie whore who was calling Geordie on his cell.'

'Oh God, you can't be serious,' Kenny lamented.

An ad for DEATHSTAR was running on the billboard now. It showed a list of casualties and their popularity percentages. Kenny half-expected his own name to be added to the list.

'Easy money,' King said. 'She'll probably not even notice

we aren't her usual guys. She'll just take the dope, no questions asked.'

'But what if she *does* notice? And what if she wants to make something of it?' Kenny was thinking of McBride. Of what would happen if she squealed on them, maybe hearing Geordie's murder reported on the Box.

'Well then,' King said. 'We'll just have to make something right back at her.'

THREE

He didn't know how long he'd been awake. He could have been lying for hours, half in and out of sleep, maybe too scared to fully wake up. Either way, Johnny felt like shit. His tongue was dry and scratchy, his mouth tasted like a sewer.

The piercing drone of techno filled his ears.

Johnny sat up, ventured a look around the room. A merciless light burned his eyes, bleeding through the crudely hung blinds. He'd been lying on a mattress, in a tiny studio apartment that he vaguely remembered entering. There were clothes everywhere, as if the place had been ransacked while he slept.

A small, blonde girl sat by the open window. She was smoking, her cigarette hand shaking. She looked over as he pulled himself up.

'Hey,' she said, reaching to turn her Box down. 'You're awake.'

'Who *are* you?' he asked.

'I get that a lot,' she said. Her voice was flat, monotone. She flicked her cigarette out the window. 'But it's okay. Your wife or girlfriend don't need to know 'bout last night.'

'Last night?'

Johnny squinted against the light.

'Or your boyfriend. I get a few fags. It *is* Tomb Street, after all.'

She didn't seem old enough to be talking like this: that was the first thing that struck Johnny. The second thing, and this hit him like a knee to the groin, was that she seemed to be talking to him as if they had *done something* last night. And what was worse, Johnny couldn't for the life of him remember a single fucking thing to contest that.

'I've got to –'

'Go?' she asked. 'Not before you cough up.'

He looked at her as if she was joking, but her cell was flashing, ready to sync.

She wanted payment?

Johnny pulled himself up.

The girl stood in front of him, blocking his way. For a second Johnny thought she was going to touch him, maybe try and rekindle whatever it was they had supposedly done last night.

'I need to use the bathroom,' he said.

'First door on the right,' she said, as he stumbled past her.

Johnny closed the door behind him and locked it quickly, afraid she might try to follow him.

The bathroom was even more of a mess than the rest of the apartment. Towels lay strewn across a sparsely tiled floor. What appeared to be blood . . . *and maybe shit* . . . stained the walls. Last year's calendar hung from a nail on the wall. A toothpaste tube lay in the sink, next to a syringe.

Johnny swallowed hard.

Oh God, he thought to himself, running his hands through his hair.

He fell back on the side of the bath. He noticed a mirror and lifted it, checking his appearance, making sure that it was still Johnny Lyon's face there; that he hadn't somehow jumped into someone else's body like some real-life VR blip. He looked awful. He couldn't remember the last time he'd shaved, changed his clothes or washed. He could smell himself.

His eyes welled up. Johnny stifled his sobbing with one hand. He couldn't believe he was here: hardly two weeks since Becky was laid in her grave.

Johnny pulled himself to his feet and reached for the bath tap to clean his face, but no water came from it.

He heard knocking.

His body tensed.

He thought the knock came against the bathroom door but it was from outside the apartment.

Johnny listened. He heard the girl go to the door, opening it. He heard male voices. They seemed to enter the apartment.

Johnny quietly checked the bathroom door finding it locked tight. He breathed a sigh of relief. He didn't want anyone to find him here; he wanted to leave, like a thief in the night, and forget all about this place.

He could hear the voices more clearly, now in the main living area.

'You're late. And where's Geordie?' (her voice).

'Anyone else here?' (one of the male voices, ignoring her question).

'No,' she lied. 'Just me.'

Silence then a rustling noise.

'That all?' she said.

'Are you kidding me?' one of the males said. He spoke in a lazy southern accent. Koy Town, maybe.

'This isn't what I normally get.' Her voice again.

'Well, you should have synced us cash, sweetheart, not given us plastic,' Southern replied. 'This card will need hacking and that means Charles 7. And Charles don't work for nothing, you know.'

The other man's voice came quieter, less aggressive: 'Johnny Lyon,' he said, as if reading the name.

It took Johnny a moment to realise that was *his* name. He checked his back pocket, finding his wallet. There was no card in it.

Fuck!

'I want to talk to Geordie,' the girl said.

'Geordie's not working tonight,' the quieter male replied.

'He'll talk to me. Call him now and ask him. He'll tell you what I normally get. We have a deal.'

'No can do,' came Southern.

'I ALWAYS GET –' she started, her voice suddenly furious.

But she wasn't allowed to finish. There was a hard slap, followed by the sound of her body falling to the floor.

'You'll get what's coming to you,' Southern sneered.

Silence followed. Johnny heard a sniffling sound, probably her, but nothing else.

'Maybe you need to bed more Johns,' Southern goaded.

The other man mumbled something, his voice nervous. There was commotion as the men moved back towards the door.

'And clean shit up,' Southern shouted. 'Who'll want to fuck you in a dive like this?'

The door opened then closed, Johnny listening as the voices faded down the corridor. He waited a few moments until he could hear nothing save the quiet sobbing in the main room. Then, gently, Johnny undid the lock and stepped out of the bathroom.

He found her still on the floor, her mouth bleeding. Tears were running down her face, diluting the blood. She suddenly reminded him of Becky in the hospital; her washed out face; the stifled breathing. Johnny felt a sting across his heart.

'What are you looking at?' she barked.

Her tiny hands gathered the spilled contents of her plastic bag. Johnny went to help, but she pushed him away.

'No!' she cried, glaring up at him.

Her eyes were dead. They passed through Johnny like he wasn't really there; like he was a figment of her imagination or some persistent ghost.

She brushed the remnants of brown powder into the bag. Found an old cardigan on the floor and retrieved it, wrapping her stash in it, pulling the whole lot against her chest.

She looked up again, challenging Johnny.

'I –' he started.

'Just fucking *go*,' she ordered.

He paused, not quite sure what to do. Then he turned, made his way through the debris on the floor, opened the door, and left.

FOUR

Charles 7 was just closing up for the night when two faces appeared at the door of his tech repair shop. He recognised them both; couple of yahoos named King and Kenny. Mostly harmless, save a little card swiping. Easy money for little work.

He was zoning but that meant nothing: a tech hack like Charles was *always* zoning. He didn't even need a wiretap. Three coils were permanently attached to his head, their plastic wires entangled within his dreads, jacked into his very brain.

Charles unlocked the door with his cell, letting the two men in.

The older yahoo, King, threw a card across the counter.

'Need it swiped, Charles. You good for it?'

The VR was rocking. Charles could feel its doll run a hand through his hair. She was beautiful; a Latino girl wearing nothing but a short latex skirt, legs wrapped around his hips like two lithe snakes.

An involuntary gasp escaped the tech hack's mouth.

The two yahoos looked at each other.

'What is it?' King said. He pointed at the card. 'Something wrong with it, bro?'

Charles shook his head, smiled.

The doll was loosening his belt now and he felt a slight tingle rise up his thighs.

He lifted the card from the table, ran it through his fingers then slid it into the tech bleed next to him. The keys of the device immediately lit up.

Charles allowed one hand to reach under the counter, finding the doll's hair, working her as she gave him head.

With the other hand, he began tapping various combinations of characters on the tech bleed keyboard, battling against the card's security.

A small screen showed him the account details of the card.

Charles read the name: Johnny Lyon. He was good with names. Didn't know *this* cat, though. Not that it mattered. Wouldn't be the first time he'd hacked one client as a job for another.

Charles bled the card within minutes, but left it in the device until the VR ran its course, ending in a light but enjoyable orgasm. As the two men watched on, Charles raised his hand to his mouth, chewing his knuckle until the moment passed. Then he pulled the card from the tech and handed it to King.

He wiped a little perspiration from his brow.

'Synced the usual sum . . . including my fee,' he said, still recovering. 'Set up a temp account for you . . . It'll close within an hour so . . . be sure to grab the cash ASAP.'

'Will it trace?'

It was Kenny speaking. Charles suddenly felt a real bad vibe off the kid.

'It's clean. Once the cash drains from the temp account, it'll bleed the trace automatically. Little bit of viral wizardry that I created. Don't ask.'

'He wasn't going to,' King said. He reached his hand across the counter. 'Charles, pleasure as always.'

The bag around his shoulder shifted as King's hand extended, a sizable package slipping from its open zip and landing on the floor.

Charles peered over the counter. The package had split, brown dust spilling out.

King stopped to sweep the dust into his hands, Kenny falling to his knees to help.

'You boys dealing?' Charles asked.

King looked up.

'Might be. Want some?'

'Jesus, King! How many people we gonna tell?!' Kenny protested.

Charles shook his head.

'Don't do drugs. Never have.'

King laughed.

'Says the man with three wires in his head.' He stood up, leaving Kenny to finish scooping. 'Charlie-Boy, you're every bit as hooked to *that* shit,' he swung his hand, pointing out the many pieces of tech hanging from the ceiling of Charles' shop, 'as any junkie I've met. So don't go preaching to me, Padre.'

'Will that be all today, boys?' Charles snapped.

'Sure is. But we'll see you again, Charlie Boy. You can bet on it.'

'Can't wait,' Charles said.

King moved towards the door, paused, looked back at Charles.

'And go easy on that VR shit,' he said. 'Can't be good for you.'

Kenny pulled at King's sleeve.

'Come on!' he said. 'And shut the fuck up, would you?!'

Yeah, thought Charles. *Shut the fuck up.*

FIVE

Johnny lived in the south eastern part of the city, known as the River Quarter. It ran alongside Lark's River Lag.

Alt, the corporation Johnny worked for, employed many of the folks who lived nearby. Its water plant provided hydropower, generating heat and electricity for a good part of Maal's population. As he neared home, Johnny could hear the low hum of turbines, the hiss of water as it bled through the plant's system.

He lived in one of Alt's economy blocks. It was a cheap and cheerful perk of his job. It would normally be a thirty minute walk from Tomb Street but took a little longer when feeling as delicate as Johnny did. He could have taken the underground, done it in five, but he needed the walk to clear his head.

He arrived at his apartment, opening the door. The lights came on, automatically syncing to his cell.

He suddenly remembered the credit card.

Johnny flipped his cell open, spread its screen. He inputted his security details, accessing his bank's website. Called up the relevant statements. There had been a withdrawal via his card to the tune of three hundred dollars. Today's date. Funds had been transferred online.

The fuckers had hacked him.

Johnny searched for details of the receiving account, finding it had been swiftly closed after the transfer. No account, bar his own, could be traced. Johnny cursed, banging his fist on the nearby wall.

He cancelled the card. Damage limitation. Shouldn't have had the fucking thing anyway. Cards were bad news: everyone knew that. Handy if you lost your cell but risky all the same. At least with a cell, you had security: most would only respond to pre-set fingerprints or voices; shutting down if a different user tried to interact. Cards, on the other hand, were simple, basic, archaic, little bastards.

Johnny set his cell down, walked through the living area and entered the kitchen.

His fan immediately kicked into action, its whirring motion making him a little dizzy.

A bunch of flowers lay dead and unwrapped in the sink.

The smell of decaying food was overbearing and Johnny covered his mouth before opening the fridge. A plastic bottle of milk, the most likely culprit. Johnny lifted it out of the fridge and poured its thick, pungent contents down the sink.

He went to toss the empty carton, then realised his trash can was full to overflowing. It wasn't smelling too healthy either.

Johnny sat the empty carton on top of the fridge and went to leave the kitchen.

He spotted the bottle of JD. An empty glass sat on the bench nearby, taunting him. Johnny lifted the bottle, quickly pouring a small helping of JD. *Just something to take the edge off*, he thought to himself. He downed the contents. It ran down his throat like acid. A sharp pain hit his stomach, doubling him over. It dulled within moments.

His cell beeped from the other room.

He walked through, retrieved the damn thing, flicking it open.

'What?!'

'Hallo? Johnny? Is that you?' *Christ*, Johnny mused. *This is the last thing I need.* 'Hallo?' the voice persisted.

'Yeah, Sarah. It's me. I've just had a bad morning. Sorry for snapping.'

There was a pause, then: 'Are you okay, Johnny? We're all worried about you. Did you get the flowers?'

Johnny thought of the dead stalks lying in his sink, now covered in sour milk.

'Yeah,' he said. 'It was very thoughtful. Tell everyone thanks.'

'I will.'

Another pause. Johnny had tired of the call already.

But just as he went to make his excuses and hang up, Sarah spoke again: 'Everyone's wondering when you're coming back.'

Johnny laughed. It wasn't a good laugh.

'Everyone? Or just Garçon?'

He heard Sarah sigh.

'Look, he told me to call you,' she whispered. 'I think he's going to fire you, Johnny. You need to call him. Talk to him. Please.'

'Let him fire me. I don't need him or his poxy job.'

'But Johnny –'

'Goodbye, Sarah.'

Johnny snapped the cell closed then stood, for a moment, staring at the wall. There was a framed photograph, hanging on a nail right opposite him. It was crooked. He went to steady it, pausing to examine the image.

He'd taken the pic last summer. It was Becky. The sun had burned her skin a little and a fresh sprinkle of freckles had broken across her forehead, just below her hairline. Her lips were slightly twisted, as though she'd been stifling a smile.

Johnny ran his finger over the picture, wanting her mouth to open, to nibble at his finger the way she sometimes would.

Yet Becky's lips remained closed.

She wasn't smiling properly and Johnny knew why. She had a slight gap in the middle of her front row of teeth. It was endearing, one of the things Johnny had first noticed about her. But Becky hated it.

Johnny wondered if he had any photos where Becky *was* smiling properly, with her teeth showing.

He went into the bedroom, ignoring the mess of scattered clothes. He rummaged through the drawer of his wardrobe, finding an old box of prints. He dug through them, finding pictures of Becky with the same stifled grin.

Johnny dropped the box to the floor.

He flicked open his cell, searched its image files. Every picture of Becky had the same expression. There were no photos of her smiling.

With horror, Johnny realised that he had forgotten what her smile looked like. Her *real* smile, not her photo-smile.

He tried to picture it in his mind but couldn't. She was becoming a stranger to him. He was losing more of her with each passing day.

Johnny sat down on the edge of the bed, allowed the heavy wave of remorse and sorrow to wash across his chest.

He had no tears left. He had no pictures of Becky's smile and he had no tears.

His eyes were as dry as his mouth.

SIX

Rudlow stood by the docks, looking out across the ocean. He wore a long trench coat, glad of the shelter it offered against the downpour of rain.

It was dark and a thick blanket of cloud hid the stars. Yet, in the distance, Rudlow could still see the pyramids, circling the island like ships, their glow starting to fade without the sun. The pyramids collected solar and steam, their three-sided glass walls and m_5 piping said to be the most effective energy drain around.

Two cranes loomed over the harbour. To Rudlow, they were like giant robots, guarding the city from some fantastical alien invasion. Once upon a time they were used to lift and lay loads coming on and going off shore. But now, a time when pretty much all tech was code-assisted, the old cranes simply rotted in the salty air.

A clatter of uniforms busied themselves around Ms Liberty's toes. The old girl was her usual perky self, standing tall and proud on her pedestal beside the cranes, rain-battered face still smiling. On the ground before her was a split polystyrene case of cuddly bears. It had come from Total America. Rudlow suspected that the bears held something more sinister than fibre in their fluffy bellies:

Grade A Heroin, the last drug to remain illegal in Maalside.

He had received the call twenty minutes ago. Made it downtown fast enough to find a trickle of what had clearly been a big haul. Tyre tracks, discarded goods, a hint of gasoline in the air: it suggested a sloppy getaway, but a getaway nonetheless.

Rudlow knew too well where he'd find the rest of the stash. But tonight he was tired, and a shakedown at Paul McBride's place down in Koy Town wasn't appealing. It would inevitably end with a stand-off; Rudlow and his men on one side with McBride and his on the other.

Retrieving a small penknife from his pocket, Rudlow lifted one of the bears then carefully cut a small hole around its belly. Acrylic stuffing showered the dock's cold, damp tarmac.

He eased his gloved hand through the hole, piercing a thin lining of plastic. It returned coated in brown powder.

Rudlow dropped the bear to the ground. Peeled the glove off fast, like it was coated in acid. He'd known what to expect, but it still bit him every time he came into contact with this shit. This wonderfully, addictive, electrifying and destructive . . . *shit*.

He rubbed his mouth then pulled the collar of the trench coat up to his neck. A sudden chill rose through his body.

He turned to walk away.

'What do you want done with it?' one of the uniforms asked him as he passed.

'Just clean it up,' Rudlow said. 'Then go home.'

∼

Downtown was a banal city block over on River Quarter.

Since Lark's secession, and its repeals, Rudlow found himself with so few men he hardly could keep the building staffed at night. Tonight there was only one guy on the desk; an Irishman by the name of Jones.

Rudlow was tired. He wanted to get in, write up that fiasco at the docks then get the hell home.

But Jones called as he passed.

'Sir?'

'Not now, Jones.'

'But sir, there's –'

'I said not *now*, Jones.'

Rudlow pushed through the double doors leading into the open plan.

He moved through to the bathrooms, banged open the door and entered, finding the sink.

He pressed the blue button, waiting until a little water had poured before scooping it up and throwing it around his face.

He looked in the mirror, finding his worn-out stubbled face looking back. God, he needed some sleep.

He cupped some more water into his hands, sipped it, swilling a little around his mouth before spitting it out. He watched it swirl, disappearing down the plughole. It was pink and Rudlow realised his gums were bleeding. Seemed to be a stress thing. That or not brushing his teeth too much, the night seeming to blend into morning, all sense of routine lost.

Rudlow left the bathrooms, heading back through the open plan towards his own office.

Jones spotted him once more, this time leaving the desk to approach him. Boy couldn't take a hint.

'Didn't you hear me? I said to leave it, Jones. Whatever this is can wait until morning.'

'But sir –'

Rudlow opened the door to his office, reaching his hat towards the nearby coat stand.

He froze.

There, at his desk, *in his chair*, sat another man.

Rudlow looked to Jones.

'I tried to tell you, sir.'

'It's okay,' Rudlow said, waving the desk cop away.

He closed the door, sized up the man at his desk. Joker was leaning back in Rudlow's chair, wiretap on his face, coil running to his cell. He was zoning. Right here in Rudlow's office, this no-mark was hanging loose and zoning.

'Can I help you?'

The VR trigger kicked in, alerting the man to Rudlow's question. He shook once, twice, before a hand reached to remove the wiretap.

His eyes opened.

'Ah, Mr Rudlow,' he said, a wide smile spreading across his tanned and perfectly toned face. Rudlow figured him as forty-something. Fairly well-to-do company guy. Bit of work done for sure; he'd maybe pass as thirty to some folks.

'Chief Rudlow, actually.'

'Forgive me if I'm intruding,' the company guy said,

jumping to his feet and coming around to the other side of the desk. Standing, he seemed taller. He wore a sheen jacket and strides. PVC shoes on his feet; probably size nines.

'You *are* intruding,' Rudlow said. 'This is *my* office. Waiting room's out there.'

The other man smiled again, seemingly undeterred.

'I've been watching you, Chief Rudlow,' he said. 'Keeping tabs on you.'

'Now look here, Mr –'

'While City Hall goes to hell, and the Mayor couldn't give a damn, you soldier on. And that takes courage.'

With that he had Rudlow's attention.

The company guy buttoned his jacket, straightened his tie.

'I can see that you and I are on the same page,' he continued. 'You see right and wrong as black and white, easily laid out in perfectly good legislation. Legislation, of course, that has been repealed in the name of so-called *progress*.' He leaned on the side of Rudlow's oak desk. 'But *we* know that progress isn't only about dollars. Progress needs moral fibre and moral fibre's something you have, Chief Rudlow, by the bucket load.'

Rudlow raised his hand.

'Look, who are you?' he asked.

'Forgive me,' the company guy said, extending his hand. 'My name is Philip Garçon and I'm here to make you an offer you won't be able to refuse.'

SEVEN

Thursday night in Cathedral Quarter.

The Old Crusader church stood on a corner, damp, breezy and in need of some serious renovation. In a heathen gaff such as Lark City, it was nothing but an eyesore, bitterly reminiscent of a God no one liked anymore.

Its curator, Reverend Harold Shepherd, stood in the car park, watching a truck pull up. The acrid smell of gasoline wafted from the truck's exhaust.

Several gasheads, with calloused skin and oil-stained slacks, jumped out and prepared to offload their stock.

'Where do you want it?' one asked.

Harold was about to tell the man where he could shove his stock when he noticed an all-too familiar face looking out at him from the driver's cab.

'Take it around the back,' Harold said, bitterly. 'And be discrete about it, for God's sake. It's Outreach night and I don't want any of those poor bastards getting a sniff of this. Christ knows, it's all but destroyed their lives already.'

'Good thing you were there, then, Padre,' came McBride's voice.

He climbed down from the cab, walked towards Harold,

smiling. Paul McBride was a well-built man with rounded shoulders and sun-baked skin. There was nothing remarkable about him; looked like any other Koy Town boy, if you didn't know better. But Harold *did* know better.

McBride drew a pack of cigarettes from the breast pocket of his oily shirt, offered one to the preacher. Harold took it without saying thanks. Accepted the light in the same way.

'You know, I can't keep doing this,' McBride said, then lit up, himself. 'If word gets out that Paul McBride has gone soft, it'll be bad for business.'

Harold drew in some smoke then exhaled.

'You always say that and I've never once known what you mean. It's not like I'm getting special treatment, is it?'

McBride shrugged.

'So, what do you want this week?' Harold asked.

'The usual seven hundred. Not bad considering how much you owe me.'

Harold didn't flinch.

'And *that*?' he asked, nodding in the direction of the truck where the gasheads were working, unpacking a pallet.

'The Good Stuff,' McBride said. 'I need you to keep it under wraps for a while.'

Harold turned away, appalled at the irony of those words on so many levels. 'The Good Stuff,' he mused. 'It's Outreach night, you know. We have a lot of people in the church right now, doped up on The Good Stuff.' He tipped some ash from his cigarette, looked at Paul McBride, 'When will you leave us alone?'

Paul met his gaze.

'When you're all paid up, old friend' he said calmly, then put his hand on Harold's shoulder. 'And when you're not of use to me, anymore.'

McBride dropped his own cigarette, stamped it into the tarmac.

Harold watched as he moved towards the truck, calling after him, 'And close that gate behind you when you leave. You hear me?'

There was no reply.

Harold entered the church, taking care to close the doors. He stood for a moment, collecting his thoughts, trying desperately to calm himself down. *This is madness! What the hell am I doing?*

He stubbed his cigarette out hard in the nearby font then made his way inside.

It was the usual crowd in tonight, a ragtag assortment of vagrants, drop-outs and people who called themselves 'volunteers'. They'd *all* been volunteers at one stage or another, offering help to look after the others when Harold really knew they were looking after themselves. Loneliness, he had learned, was the worst affliction of all.

Most of those gathered were users, or had been users, and it was obvious that the experience had blown their minds in the worst way possible.

It wasn't unheard of for the Thursday nights to turn into Friday mornings, but Harold didn't mind everyone staying the night, maybe sleeping on the pews. He'd be sure to give the place a good clean out in the morning: personal hygiene wasn't top of the average user's to-do list.

'Is he still there?'

The voice came from the shadows. Harold found a small girl nestling a cup of coffee, sitting on her own. To her left, along the pew, she had stacked a pile of cushions, peeling them away from the faux wood. A plate of sandwiches, mostly untouched, sat on the floor next to her.

'What are you talking about, Katherine?' Harold said, hoping to God she hadn't heard anything she shouldn't have.

'My dad.'

'How did you know?'

'I heard his voice. Was he looking for me?'

Harold sighed. His eyes found the cross above the pulpit. 'No, he wasn't looking for you, Katherine.'

'Good,' Kitty said. 'I don't want to talk to him right now.'

Her words came even slower than normal. Harold figured she'd taken a hit before coming in tonight.

He turned towards the door as the sound of voices bled in from outside. Then a truck firing up, pulling away.

Harold listened for the gate closing and nodded approvingly.

EIGHT

Titanic Quarter, ten past nine on Friday night.

Most of the skyblocks had emptied, office staff pouring onto the streets, hungry for the weekend.

Some were already kicking back at the smoky jazz clubs and burlesque shows over on Cathedral, or hanging loose at Vegas on Tomb Street. A few lingered around Route 66 or the Penny Dreadful, while others chose to zone, perusing VR for something to take their minds off the daily grind. Lark folks played as hard as they worked, squeezing every inch of life they could from their four score and ten.

Rudlow was still working.

He moved through the thickening crowds, jostling with the revellers; the troupes of girls in plastic or silk or lace courting business for whatever show they worked, syncing fliers to receptive cells.

He approached one of the newer skyblocks over on the residential side of Titanic. Rudlow found the block he needed, made for the first floor.

There had been a homicide.

Stiff had been lying for days. Might have been a few days more only the smell put next door off their caviar. That didn't surprise Rudlow in itself; people got killed, usually unsavoury people that nobody cared about, McBride being the usual suspect. Most of them lay for days, maybe weeks, no one giving a damn about them.

But this particular homicide *did* surprise him, because it looked like a drugs killing. These were rare in Lark. While Rudlow hated to admit it, he knew that McBride was good at one thing: maintaining order. Even within the disorder of Lark's drug trade, legal and illegal alike, McBride brought structure, unwritten rules that needed strict adherence. And he covered the entire market; every small-time operator having to literally beg McBride's permission to deal.

The deceased's name was Geordie Mac. He was one of McBride's most respected dealers, known best for the rehab programmes he would run when his clients got too hungry.

Ironically, Geordie was one of the biggest benefactors to the 'Clean Up Our Streets' initiative. The programme hoped to bring the more sober of Maalside together against drug-related crimes and Lark's increasingly popular sex trade.

Even the Mayor spoke highly of Geordie.

But now Geordie lay on the floor, his bath robe strewn to the side, tiny cock peeking out next to a sizeable belly.

Rudlow looked around the room. For a man so giving, Geordie wasn't too bad to himself. His apartment was decked out in fur carpet. Ivory ornaments stood regally on mahogany shelves.

His Box played the latest episode of reality programme, DEATHSTAR.

It was a rerun; Rudlow had caught the live episode last night.

An older man with jet black hair was negotiating his way through a patch of desert. The cam homed in on a sign warning of landmines in the area. A timer ran along the bottom left of the screen.

Rudlow knew how the sequence would end, yet found it hard to turn away.

There was a sudden flash, the poor bastard's left leg turning to pink mist, his body falling to the sand, shaking as the cam swooped in to record the latest kill.

Then Kal, one of the show's hosts came onscreen, dancing with excitement.

The older man's face appeared as his name was crossed off the list of contestants. The timer on the screen was stopped at 5.36. The numbers were flashing, a new icon showing gold coins flowing from a slot machine. Winners' names scrolled along the bottom of the screen.

'Rudlow,' came a voice from nearby.

An overworked and underpaid detective stood by the bathroom. His name was Furlong. A stalwart of the force, Furlong had a killer instinct in all senses of the word. Clean but heavy-handed, it was worrying to think what this man would do were he not a cop. He munched on a sandwich, coffee in his other hand. Stepped aside, allowing several uniforms to move through to the bathroom.

'You finally made it,' he quipped.

Rudlow ignored the jibe.

'Inside job?' he asked. It was meant as a question, not a statement of fact but his voice remained even.

'Don't think so,' Furlong said. 'McBride was on the Box this morning. Seemed genuinely shocked.'

'Maybe he's bluffing.'

The other man shoved the rest of the sandwich into his mouth, chewing as he watched the Box. DEATHSTAR was still running, the show's host now introducing a new contestant; some washed out baseball hitter.

'We have our boys studying the vids now,' he said, 'but it's unlike McBride to be so messy.' Furlong tipped the last of his coffee down, crumpled the cup and papers and shoved them into his coat pocket. Rubbed his mouth then studied the back of his hand. 'No, I'd bet this was someone else.'

Rudlow's eyes swept the room again.

'Find any narcotics?' he asked.

'Kind of . . .' Furlong said.

'What do you mean, *kind of?*'

'There are traces of heroin in the bedroom,' Furlong explained. 'Floorboards were ripped up. Lab boys are doing the maths on it, but I'd reckon you had a pretty big stash in there until recently. Lot of brown dust amongst the cobwebs, shall we say.'

'So, whoever did this has killed Geordie and taken his stock? *All of it?*' This time Rudlow's voice wasn't even. 'Would take some balls to do that.'

'You're not wrong there.'

'Any prints?'

'Dusting the place as we speak. Not sure if we're likely to find anything that'll help us.' Furlong sighed then continued, 'Geordie, as you know, was something of a playboy.

Lot of parties. Celebs, tycoons, you name it and they've been here for a posh knees up. Half of City Hall's been cam'd creeping out of this place. The Mayor was a personal friend.'

Rudlow shook his head. He wasn't a fan of the Mayor and made no secret of the fact. His mind travelled back to the other night; the company guy who came downtown to visit him, talking of his own disdain for the Mayor and making Rudlow an offer he couldn't refuse

Rudlow went to the window, looked out across the revellers moving through Titanic towards Tomb Street.

He turned, noticed something on the carpet. Bent down slowly, retrieving a clear plastic bag from his pocket with one hand and a small plastic knife with the other. Carefully, he scratched the carpet, releasing a pale, hard chalk from the fibres. He dropped it into the plastic bag.

'What is it?' Furlong asked.

'Puke. I think.'

'Puke? Hardly much to go on. Like I said, Geordie was a party man. Puke comes with the territory.'

'Well, I've never seen anyone puking at a wine and cheese. Have you?'

'Good point,' conceded the detective. 'What're you thinking?'

Rudlow stared into the space ahead.

The cogs of his brain were still turning and as he spoke, the words came out slowly:

'I'm thinking that someone, whoever did this, maybe hadn't the stomach for it. Could be someone who'd sweat it in a chair. Break easily.' He looked up at the detective. 'So we have to find them before McBride does.'

NINE

Monday morning at Alt Corp.

A pretty, young blonde stared at her screen.

'Good morning Sarah,' a voice interrupted.

'M-morning, Mr Garçon,' the girl said, standing up as if to attention.

Garçon regarded her thinly. He probably noticed that she'd been ten minutes late this morning. Sure, she looked the part, smartly dressed in a figure-hugging skirt, her white blouse buttoned down low to give the boys a view. But she felt like shit. It'd been a heavy weekend and Sarah Lee was struggling to stay on top.

She removed her glasses, rubbed her eyes. Lifted her coffee and took a sip, watching as Garçon led his two visitors to the lift opposite. There was the usual loud talk and revelry between the three men. Backs were slapped, bravado rolled out. The lift reached 20 and they were sent on their way.

Good riddance, Sarah thought.

This particular pair had been in a lot, lately. Sarah hated how they stared at her: Goldsmith, the more flamboyant of the two, seemed to have developed something of a fondness for her cleavage.

Garçon made his way back through the office.

Sarah called as he passed.

'Sir, I need to talk to you.'

Garçon stopped.

'What is it?'

'It's about Johnny.'

Garçon walked on as if the topic held no interest for him.

'You've got to give him another chance, sir,' Sarah called, following him through the open plan, hot coffee still in hand.

'I've *got to do* nothing of the sort,' Garçon warned her, waving his finger.

He started walking again.

'But, sir,' Sarah persisted, bobbing along after him on her high heels, 'the man lost his wife. The tragedy of –'

'All death is tragic, my dear' Garçon said, cutting across her. 'Take Mrs Lewis over there,' he pointed to an older woman in the open plan whose ears suddenly pricked up, hearing her name mentioned, 'lost her husband of forty years barely a week ago. Back at work today.'

Sarah cringed as Mrs Lewis crumbled at her workstation. But Garçon walked on, oblivious.

'Give him one more chance, sir,' she pressed, smiling weakly at Mrs Lewis before following Garçon into his office.

A billboard drifted by the window, its spectral smile ever alluring. The neon glow was killing Sarah and she was glad when Garçon dimmed the blinds.

He dropped his cell to his desk, sighed.

'Sarah, this is not the –'

'Please!' she insisted.

Her impudence surprised her. It surprised Garçon too. He paused, fixed his eyes upon her, waited.

'A-after all,' she continued, voice now shaking, 'If we've got a new project on the horizon, there's no better code guy on the books.'

Garçon considered this for a second. His gaze lingered on the secretary, trying to read something from her. But Sarah kept her face straight.

'Close the door, please,' he said.

Sarah was taken back.

'S-sorry?' she stuttered.

'The door, Sarah. Close it.'

Oh, Christ, she thought. Had she gone too far? Was she too pushy?

Sarah did as Garçon asked then gingerly sat in the empty chair across from his desk. She put her coffee down slowly.

'You've met Mr Goldsmith and Mr Flynn,' he said. 'They're part of a new VR project I'll be heading up. Something very,' and here Garçon searched in his mind for the appropriate words, 'cutting-edge, shall we say.'

'Johnny's all about the VR,' Sarah said quickly. 'That's all I was trying to say. I didn't mean any harm.'

She stopped, noticing that Garçon wasn't listening to a word she was saying. He leaned back in his chair, eyes fixed on the wall behind her. There was a slight twitch building in one eye. A mere flicker but definitely something.

'Sir, are you feeling alright?'

He lifted his hand to shush her, went to speak then smiled instead. It was a guilty smile; as if unsure whether to say whatever was on his mind. Then he leaned forward, head tipped to one side.

'Sarah, I'm on thin ice,' he said. 'But this project, this new VR we're working on could save my bacon.'

Sarah went to say something but again Garçon interrupted her.

'My wife,' he said, 'she put me out of the house last week. I've been sleeping here. In this office. On that couch right there.' He pointed to the plastic sofa. 'Pretending I was working late, working early. I'm telling you all this, but I don't want anyone out there to know.' He nodded to the window looking out onto the open plan. 'Do you hear me?'

Sarah nodded.

'I mean it, Sarah!'

'Yes, sir.'

She felt very uncomfortable, now.

Garçon smiled faintly.

'You've picked a good time to ask about Johnny Lyon,' he said. 'Right now, I really need a code guy. Really, REALLY need a code guy. One who can work around the clock. One who knows VR like Johnny does.'

Sarah raised an eyebrow.

'I've been foolish, you see.' A naughty look drew across his face. Skin-crawlingly creepy. 'Very foolish.'

Sarah felt like a deer in headlights, unable to even blink.

'What have you done?' she asked.

Garçon cupped both hands around his mouth, whispered his next words, as if they were top secret: 'I've lied.'

Still Sarah didn't blink, *couldn't* blink.

'I've lied,' he said again, 'to people you wouldn't believe

you could lie to; people whose whole raison d'être is *against* lying.'

'Lied about what?'

'Time. I told them we could have the project finished within a week. It was the only way.'

'Oh.'

'Oh, indeed.'

Something of his old swagger was coming back.

'Sarah, I need you to bring Johnny Lyon to me. Take the rest of the day off, and go find him. Tell him I need him back. Can you do that?'

'Yes, sir.'

She picked up her coffee. Noticed her hands were shaking.

Garçon stood up from his desk.

She didn't know why, but weirdly Sarah found herself perform a curtsey as she backed out of the office. The coffee slopped from her cup, spilling over the floor and Garçon's perfectly polished shoes.

'Sorry,' she whispered as she scrambled for a tissue, bending down to wipe his feet. 'I'll just –'

But Garçon's eyes were on the door now, head tipping to indicate she should leave now.

Sarah hurried out of his office, into the open plan area.

Across the way, Mrs Lewis was still crying, several of her colleagues trying to console her.

TEN

Sarah took the underground out to where Johnny lived. She could have walked, his apartment on the edge of River Quarter only being a twenty minute stroll from Alt, but the rain was starting to come down.

Being an employee of Alt, Sarah got her ticket for free. Lark's underground system was one of the company's first projects and it was still a good money-spinner for them. Functioning on air compression alone, it remained one of the cheapest and most reliable forms of transport around.

Sarah jumped off at her stop, calling into a nearby store for a bunch of flowers. She wasn't sure if it was the done thing to offer flowers to grieving men, but it would give her some reason to call around. He seemed to like the ones sent by the company. And appearing empty handed would seem odd. She added milk and some biscuits to her bag, thinking that picking up groceries was likely to be something Johnny had neglected of late.

Sarah found the front entrance to Johnny's block and hit the buzzer.

No answer.

She wondered if he had gone out. Chose another buzzer at random

A grumpy woman answered.

'What'd ye want?'

'I'm a friend of Johnny Lyon,' Sarah said.

'Who?'

'Apartment 43. Johnny Lyon.'

The voice didn't return, but Sarah heard the sound of the door opening.

She pushed through, entering the hallway.

Darkness greeted her. A stairwell light suddenly flickered on, spilling across the landing.

It was a typical inner-city economy block. River Quarter was full of them. Sarah wondered why Johnny and Becky had chosen to live here. They could have afforded much better on his wage alone, not to mention their combined earnings.

Sarah found herself thinking about getting her own place again. At the moment, she was still living with her folks out of town, just north of Lark, near the airport. She'd even convinced herself it was all she could afford, but in many ways it was a false economy: the underground didn't stretch out as far as her folks' place meaning she had to get the train into town. And even though the train was one of Alt's, a tourist attraction with its hydrosteam turbine and locomotive style engine, their generosity knew some limits. Hydrosteam wasn't cheap; riding the train into work each day cost almost as much as renting a place in the city.

Sarah climbed the stairs, avoiding the lift.

Tonight, the block was deathly quiet. The pale light cast

a cold shadow over the stairs. It seemed empty, vacant, like a long-deserted building.

She arrived at the fourth floor, finding Johnny's door.

His Box was blaring. Sarah could hear it from the other side of the door.

She tried the buzzer several times, still receiving no reply.

Exasperated, she tried the door. To her surprise, it opened without resistance.

Sarah inched her way into the apartment.

'Hallo?'

No reply.

Sarah moved further inside.

She synced her cell to the apartment's lighting, a soft warm glow filling the space around her.

She noticed the kitchen door open, the pungent smell of out-of-date food wafting through. She closed the door, waving the smell away with her hand.

'Johnny? You in here?'

Still no reply.

Sarah travelled into the living area, her eyes finding the Box. It was playing a doc about The Barrenlands, the aftermath of the Holy War.

The footage drew her in.

Bloodstained survivors wandered through the smoke, a red, damaged sky in the background. There were children crying, women keening over bodies. There was an old man, his face getting larger as the cam focused on his ranting.

'This . . . this is what your God has done,' he said, voice strained as if it were painful for him to talk. Blood was running down his nose, unchecked. His clothes were torn, charcoaled. Sand stuck to his face as if glued on. 'Look at them all!' he said, waving one arm behind him, the cam filming more scenes of broken people in the dirt, wailing as they held the limp bodies of family in their arms. 'This is what your God has done.'

The cam followed the old man as he too fumbled about in the dust, searching for something which seemed important to him. Important, yet lost amongst the bodies and the debris.

Sarah looked away from the Box.

'Hallo?' she called.

Still no reply.

The programme flipped to a commercial break.

Music began playing over some advert, its tempo building. It was an old rock tune, the band's lead singer squealing like a strangled cat as high end guitar screeched in a different key. The visual had a family sitting down to enjoy breakfast. A familiar voiceover was saying something nostalgic about how bread used to be fresh, how butter used to be something to enjoy, before focusing in on the orange juice and announcing, proudly, how it had *always* been the same great, natural taste.

Sarah killed the sound.

She took a seat on the sofa, pushing some clothes away to make room. Placed the flowers and groceries in the space beside her.

Where are you, Johnny?

The floors were messy. Drawers had been pulled out, their contents scattered everywhere.

But Johnny was nowhere to be seen.

He'd maybe gone out, door left akimbo, Box blaring. It would be like Johnny, scatterbrain that he was.

Sarah stood to leave.

A pile of pictures caught her eye, scattered just under the coffee table. She bent down to lift them, flipping through the first couple in her hand. They were all pictures of Becky and Johnny on holiday. Sarah smiled. Probably their honeymoon. They looked so happy, so young. She remembered Johnny coming back into work afterwards, how tired and hungover he'd been. Yet still upbeat. Content.

Sudden sounds of movement from the other side of the hall.

'Johnny?'

Sarah rested the pictures on the coffee table. Slowly, she walked back down the hallway past the kitchen.

The bathroom door was closed. She hadn't noticed it earlier, even though it was the first door she would have passed.

She pushed it open. Inched her head through the crack.

In the far corner she could see the bath. It was full, still hot. Steam gathered around the open window. But there was something else: the bath water was stained... a light pink or red. Sarah was drawn to it, moved closer to get a better look.

Is that ... blood?

Her heart rose into her mouth.

'Johnny?' she managed before a hand drew across her mouth and pulled her back.

ELEVEN

The blood drew a thin line across the side of the needle. The needle lay on the edge of the bed, barely out of her arm as she fell back. But Kitty was already coming to, the sad taste of sobriety flowing through her mind like muddy water.

She sat up quickly, almost jabbing her hand on the needle's sharp tip.

Her cell lay on the bed, next to the needle. It was beeping. She picked it up, noticed it was her dad on the other end, decided to ignore it. Mere seconds later, it started to beep again. She answered this time.

'What?'

Her voice was slow, groggy.

'Are you doped?'

'No,' she said, defiantly, like he was stupid for even asking.

'Well, you *sound* doped.'

A moment passed.

'How are you, anyway?'

'Fine,' she said. 'Did Harold tell you to ring?'

A sigh from the other end.

'Do you need anything?'

'No.'

More silence.

'Geordie looking after you okay?'

She could script their conversation. He was checking that she was getting her dope. Kitty knew that her dad was too embarrassed to let her get what she needed elsewhere. It would bring shame to his door. More shame than usual.

'Yeah. Geordie's looking after me.'

'Did he bring you your package?'

'Yeah,' she lied. 'He did.'

'Well, it's funny that,' her dad mocked, 'because Geordie was found dead the other day. So, either you're seeing ghosts around there or you're lying to me.'

This wasn't part of their script. It threw her. Kitty thought for a moment, tried to get her shit together.

'Who did you get your gear from if it wasn't Geordie?'

She said nothing.

'Katherine, tell me who you got it from?'

'I called Geordie's cell,' she said.

'Who answered?'

'Sounded like Geordie.'

'Well, *it wasn't* Geordie, Katherine. Not unless –'

'Yes, I heard you,' she snapped. She hated it when he patronised her like this. It made her feel really stupid. She may be a junkie whore, but she weren't stupid.

'Well, tell me who it was then, sweetheart.'

She'd have liked to believe that the slip of his tongue was intentional, that beneath all of the resentment he *did* love her. But no part of her *really* thought that.

'Tell me,' he pressed, and she could hear a certain anger building in his voice.

He still scared her. He'd only hit her once, shortly after her mom had died. Used an old chain that had been hanging over the banister, a dog chain, maybe. Kitty didn't remember a dog, but she remembered the chain

'There were two of them,' she said, answering his question. 'Mouthy guy with a southern accent. There was a taller one with him. He was younger, quieter. That's all I know.'

'That's all I need,' her dad said, and hung up.

Kitty sat for a moment, cell still in her hand, mind drifting. She always thought of her mom after talking with Paul McBride.

Kitty was only three when her mom died. They used to play together in the house, in her mom's bedroom. Hide and seek in the cupboards, under the bed, between the folds of the duvet. The bedroom was her mom's whole world. Young, beautiful and dressed in a long, silk nightdress, she had seemed like a real-life princess to Kitty.

In their games, the pillows had been clouds, the duvet a thick coating of snow in her fairytale kingdom.

A sudden noise from outside. Kitty's eyes found the window.

The curtain moved.

But it was nothing, just the breeze from outside.

TWELVE

'Jesus, I'm sorry!' Johnny said, removing his hands from Sarah's mouth.

'What the hell are you doing?!' she yelled at him.

Sarah pulled away, stepping back through the doorway. She could see Johnny more clearly as he followed her out of the bathroom, away from the steam. He was wearing a large towelling dressing gown. His normally floppy hair was wet and greased back off his face.

'I . . . well, I had some trouble with some people,' he said, sheepishly. 'They got my card, hacked it. I thought you were maybe one of them'

'Well I wasn't! And if you're worried about security, you should lock the damn door!'

Sarah leaned one hand against the wall, steadying herself.

The steam from the bath was now in the hallway, moving through the apartment.

Johnny spoke next: 'So, what *are* you doing here?'

'Garçon sent me. He wants you back, Johnny. There's a big project on the cards and he needs you.'

'I told you, I'm not –'

'Johnny, I'm worried about you. Everybody is.'

Sarah pulled her best little girl lost face, one part sincere and one part faked. She knew all about being fake. Her work with Garçon demanded insincerity every day of the week.

'Well, you shouldn't be. I'm absolutely fine.' He smiled as he said the word 'fine', as if that might convince her.

It didn't.

'Well, why is the water red, then? Johnny, were you . . .' she left the sentence hanging, hoping he would get her meaning quickly.

'I cut myself shaving,' he said.

She watched as he pressed a finger against a spot on his neck, straining and making as if it were sore.

'That much blood from a little nick?' she pressed.

'I couldn't get it stopped!'

Sarah wasn't convinced.

'Honestly!' he protested.

She shook her head, moved towards the living area. Perched herself on the arm of the sofa, too freaked to sit down properly.

Johnny followed her, sat on the other arm.

'Honestly,' he said. 'I'm okay.'

'You promise?' She stared at him intently. 'I mean *really* promise?'

'Yes. I *really* promise.'

'Well, come back to work, then,' she said.

'I'll think about it.'

'Don't just *think about it*, Johnny. *Do it*. Because if you don't . . . Well . . .' Her eyes moistened. 'Well, I worry about you, that's all.'

He moved across the sofa, reaching his hand to her cheek to catch a tear. She allowed him, even dipping her head as he drew closer.

'I *am* okay,' he said, maybe trying to convince himself as well as her.

'Well, then prove it,' she said, pulling back a little and looking up at him. 'Come back to work,' she repeated. 'Tomorrow.'

THIRTEEN

Bordering the nearby Queen's Quarter, the Village was a place that was always busy; a motley crew of students, yahoos and hard-faced locals constantly moving through its grey paved streets. It sat opposite the hospital, endless rows of housing running parallel with the train station. Steam filled the air, creating a thin veneer from which stores and cheap diners appeared like two-dime tricks.

Janice got off the train.

The rain beat down, puddles gathering like black holes at her feet.

It was almost 4.30 p.m. and Janice realised she'd stayed longer at work than she'd intended. But she'd been enjoying herself, chatting to Billy the doorman. Talking to Billy took her mind off things.

Janice struggled daily with real life, and real life was winning. She lived with her son, Kenny, tried her best for them. But her part-time cleaning job didn't cut it when it came to paying the bills. Janice was behind with her landlord, the bank and just about anyone else silly enough to lend her money.

She was even behind with Paul McBride.

Her heart sank as she saw his truck parked outside her house, growling like a rabid dog, smoke pouring from its rusty exhaust. The engine was still running, McBride, himself, behind the wheel, two of his boys beside him.

He gave her a big wave.

Janice nodded solemnly, moving to the door of her house and unlocking it quickly.

'Terrible weather,' McBride said as he climbed out of the truck. 'You should be wearing a coat, Janice.'

'Hello Paul,' Janice replied, curtly.

She moved into the house, leaving the door ajar as she went.

'Not going to ask me in?' McBride said, moving on through despite the lack of invite. 'Look, what do you want?' Janice asked.

McBride lit up, took a long drag then said, 'Right down to business, Janice? Just like old times.'

But Janice didn't want to revisit any 'old times' with him. Paul McBride was one night she had tried damn hard to forget. That was twenty years ago and not one of those years had been kind to her.

'Got a new shipment in,' he said. 'Can you stash some of it for me?'

'Are you asking me or telling me?' Janice said.

Paul stubbed his cigarette out in a crystal ash tray by the door.

'Telling you,' he said. 'Unless you've got seven thousand dollars handy. Plus interest.'

Janice took her pinafore off. Reached for her housecoat, hanging from a peg on the nearby wall, and pulled it on.

She moved through to the kitchen, busied herself with some dishes steeping in the sink. They were still dirty, remnants of food ground in.

'Stick it under the stairs,' she said, hands sinking into the lukewarm water.

'Christ,' McBride said. 'Bit of an obvious place, that.'

He tutted, shaking his head, picked up a photo from her mantelpiece. It was one of Kenny and Janice in happier times, before he started going off the rails. He was wearing a baseball jersey.

'We need to be more creative. Thought I'd get some of the boys to pull up the carpet, maybe do a little floor refurbishment, then relay the carpet for you. In the bedroom, maybe?' He was still looking at the photo. 'You wouldn't mind that, Janice, would you?'

She said nothing, her hands shaking and rubbing the dishes furiously.

'Good girl,' McBride said.

He picked up another photo, this one taken only a couple of years ago. Kenny sat in the stalls of some stadium. Janice had taken him there for his birthday. He was smiling in the picture. She hadn't seen him smile like that in quite a while.

'This your boy?' McBride asked.

'Yeah,' Janice answered, uncomfortably.

He stared at the photo, studied it carefully.

'Tell him to come down and see me,' he said. 'I want to talk to him.'

FOURTEEN

Over the years, Chief Rudlow had spent a lot of time in the Penny Dreadful whorehouse, chasing leads, pressing suspects, working the joint over. A place like this represented everything he hated; every bad smell that crept up his nose and lingered for days; every speck of dirt that embedded itself into his skin, no matter how hard he scrubbed in the shower.

Yet after his wife had left him, Rudlow found himself here in a different capacity: he found comfort in the arms of a forty-something chain-smoker called Dolly Bird.

Tonight, Dolly was working the desk.

A typical throwback, she wore a dark wire corset, elbow length satin gloves and a black lace skirt. Bright red hair hung shoulder length. Her make-up was heavy, an ever-present cigarette dangling from royal blue lips.

'Chief Rudlow,' she said. 'Business or pleasure?'

He dressed as he always did after the sex: swiftly and with a familiar sense of regret. From somewhere close, a single beep sounded, a reminder that his hour was up, that Dolly needed to get back downstairs, maybe relieve that twelve year old that was covering front desk for her.

But Rudlow wasn't done.

'New shipment got through,' he said, pulling his vest on, still with his back to her. 'Probably hitting the streets tonight. You can expect trouble.'

He could hear Dolly patting the pillow down, rolling the spent plastic off the bed and binning it in a tub at the door.

'I'll keep an eye out,' she said

Rudlow slipped his shirt on, started to button it.

Dolly came behind him, reaching around his waist, her long, slender fingers moving his hands away and finishing the last few buttons.

Rudlow shrugged Dolly away, reaching for his holster, retrieving the charge gun, checking then sheathing it.

He reached for his cell. Waited for his money to transfer. Found his coat, slipped it on.

'McBride,' he said. 'If I can get McBride, I've got Lark's central source. And I'm on to him, Dolly. Closer than ever.'

Dolly laughed.

'You'll never get McBride, sweetheart.'

'But I've got this deal going. Some guy named Garçon.'

'No matter how many leads or deals you have, or how many men you post at the docks, or the airports or the border.' Dolly smiled, reaching her hand to his face. 'Sweet stuff, McBride will *always* find a way in. Hell, he wouldn't think twice before paying your men a year's wage, just to let *one* shipment through. You can't compete with that kind of maths and you know it.'

Rudlow felt his fists clench.

'There was a murder. Geordie Mac, McBride's main man. Seems drug-related. Killer got away with Geordie's stash and they'll be running the streets. So I want to know about any new blood coming in, Dolly, spending money like there's no tomorrow. Or maybe someone scared. *Real* scared. God knows, they should be.'

Dolly finished with one cigarette, lit another from its end.

'I hear anything, babe, you'll be the first I call,' she said.

Rudlow looked at her. It was a lingering look and she shifted uncomfortably.

'What?'

'Nothing,' he said. 'Just . . . well, just be careful, hear?'

'You know it, babe.'

Her words were confident yet the voice was anything but.

FIFTEEN

Johnny decided to come in early, to avoid preying eyes and the creeping silence he'd face walking through a busy office.

For some reason, he expected the place to have changed in the short time he'd been away. But the open plan on 20 looked the same as always. Lines of acrylic hot-desks, like tiny little prisons, filled the main office space. A single glass wall looked out onto the skyblocks opposite. The familiar Alt logo stared down at him from the office screen. The screen was Alt's soul. Synced to Lark's sister offices; from Berlin and Prague, right through to Tokyo; it captured the deals, trends and styles of Alt right across the globe.

Sighing, Johnny set his cell on the desk, synced to his touchscreen and the company Net. The welcome logo appeared. APPS were presented in 3D layers across the concave screen.

Johnny moved through to the e-mail APP. He began to sift through his inbox, flicking unwanted mails away with one hand, opening or filing some with his other.

He hadn't looked at his inbox since Becky and it was jam-packed. Messages from pretty much everyone he worked with, saying how sorry they were and if there was anything they could do, anything at all. This was exactly the sort of thing that Johnny hoped to avoid. He thought of how many conversations he was destined to have over the days and weeks to follow, not only with staff but the many, many clients he would deal with on a daily basis.

And then he saw it.

At first it was just one of many unopened PMs; a request for this code or that file; status updates on half-completed projects; costings, statements or invoices. But amongst all the shit was something important. Something that at one stage would have seemed routine, insignificant, but was now magical: there, right below a PM from cleaner Janice, requesting staff to place all used cups in the dishwasher and sync the damn thing to their cells, was an e-mail from Becky.

Johnny stared blankly at the icon for a while.

Someone grabbed his shoulder.

Johnny jumped, turning to find Sarah Lee.

He pressed a hand against his chest.

'Jesus, you scared me!'

'Now you know how I felt,' she said, smiling.

Johnny felt his face redden.

'Look, I still feel terrible about that.'

'You don't need to, silly.'

Sarah pulled up the chair from a nearby desk, sat down next to Johnny. Her coat was wet, little beads of rain running down its lapels. Blonde hair fell on her shoulders.

'How does it feel, being back and all?' she said.

Johnny minimised the e-mail alert.

'It feels great,' he said.

'I'm guessing Garçon isn't in yet, then.'

'Nope.'

She gave a little wink.

'It really *is* good to see you, Johnny.'

Her face was close to his. Her eyes lingered for a while.

Johnny coughed, muttered something about needing to get back to whatever it was that he wasn't doing. Sarah fumbled some more words herself then stood up.

Johnny watched her walk away.

She turned, catching him looking at her, and he felt embarrassed.

He maximised his screen, the layers opening.

There it was, still calling him. Becky's e-mail, unopened. The word 'tonight' was written in the subject line. He checked the date. It was the day she was taken into hospital. He had not been in the office since then.

Johnny closed the screen down without opening the e-mail.

He needed a drink.

Kenny downed the last of his bottle, dropping it into a nearby hedge as he made his way through the hospital grounds, coming out onto the Village district.

It was still quite dark.

His vision was blurred, his whole body feeling light and unstable.

He heard a noise, looked behind finding only the hospital's billboard high in the air; nestled within the steam from the latest train. A pretty girl with a blue stripe across her eyes looked out from the digital foil. The words MORNING GLORY ran below her impossibly white teeth.

Kenny walked on.

He drew close to his mom's place, noticing the light on in her bedroom. His heart sank, thinking about the grief he would face.

Kenny tried to let himself in quietly. Maybe she had fallen asleep with the light on and he could sneak into his den, in the basement, without her noticing. But he could hear her stir just as he reached the kitchen.

'That you, Kenny?' she called.

'Yeah, Mom,' he called out. 'It's only me.'

He walked through the kitchen, opened the fridge door and searched through its contents. He lifted out some eggs.

'I'm going to put some breakfast on,' he said. 'Just you go back to sleep.'

He fumbled about in the cupboards, finding a pan. He sat it on the cooker, firing up a thermo ring. He poured the oil into the pan, sat it onto the ring.

He heard footsteps on the stairs.

'Shit,' he muttered to himself.

She appeared in the kitchen, hair tied up in a net, dressed in her housecoat, pajamas and slippers. She looked tired, like she'd just woken up.

'You'll burn the house down,' she said, grumpily. 'Go and sit down, and I'll sort it out.'

He did as he was told, moving to the kitchen table and slumping into the chair.

'Where were you last night?' she asked, cracking the eggs against the side of the pan and pouring their contents.

'Out.'

'Out where?'

'Just out,' he repeated.

From the table, he watched her open a cupboard and retrieve a plate. She set it on the worktop then reached for Kenny's cup, added some coffee and filled it from the thermo tap.

He reached his hand out, taking the cup from her, then blowing at it before taking a sip.

'What are you doing today?' she said, flipping each of the eggs. She fixed him another look, waiting for a satisfactory answer.

'Nothing.'

'Nothing,' she repeated, sighing.

Kenny knew where this was going and he didn't like it.

She slapped the plate down in front of him.

He ignored her, lifted the salt from the table, sprinkled it across the fried food then added some sauce.

He took the knife and fork she handed to him next, tucked in, hungrily.

'Paul wants to see you,' she said.

Kenny stopped chewing. He glanced up from his food, watched her swipe the pan away from the thermo ring.

He set his knife and fork down, asked, 'Paul who?'

'What do you mean, *Paul who*?' she snapped back.

His face drained of colour. He forgot the food, wasn't hungry anymore.

'Paul McBride?' he asked sheepishly.

'That's right,' she said, filling the sink with hot, soapy

water from the auxiliary tap. 'Paul McBride wants to see you.'

'What for?'

'How do I know, *what for?!*'

She turned and looked at him. Her mouth was cut into a frown.

'What have you been doing out there?!' she yelled.

Kenny got up from his chair and tried to push past her to leave the kitchen, but she grabbed him with surprising strength.

'Don't you fucking dare leave here until I've finished!' she spat.

'This isn't fair,' he protested, 'I've done nothing wrong!'

'What does Paul McBride want, then?'

'How do I know?!'

She turned away from him. Curled against the fridge door, as if it might comfort her. Her eyes were heavy, drained, struggling with the effort of wringing out tears. He'd often seen her cry before, but rarely with such aban-donment. It made him feel sad. Ashamed.

It made him feel scared.

Again Kenny pushed past her, and this time she didn't stop him.

He grabbed his coat from the hanger at the foot of the stairs, opened the door and stepped outside, slamming it closed behind him.

He started walking.

SIXTEEN

Johnny knocked on Garçon's door then stepped into the office. The blinds were closed, the room lit by a single lamp in the corner.

Garçon was working at his desk.

Johnny cleared his throat.

'You wanted to see me, sir?'

Garçon looked up, smiled.

'Take a seat, Johnny. Would you like a drink?'

'Just a glass of water.'

Garçon stood up, reached for a nearby jug and poured Johnny a glass of water. Helped himself to a glass of bourbon from a rather expensive looking decanter.

'So,' he said, sitting back down at his desk and cradling his drink in his hands. 'You've been away for a while, Johnny, haven't you?' He spoke as if slightly amused by the code guy's absence.

'Er . . . yes, sir . . .'

'But you're back,' Garçon said, flashing his plastic veneers. 'And we're really glad to have you back, Johnny.'

Johnny lifted his water, took a sip.

'Feel better now, I hope?' Garçon asked vaguely.

'Yes, sir. Much better,' Johnny lied.

'Good. Because I need you at your prime, Johnny. I've got something big lined up. I'm trying to create the impossible. I'm trying to pull the biggest, legitimate heist in history.' He leaned across his desk, eyes twinkling. 'I want to raise the very dead, here, Johnny.'

'The dead?'

'I want to bring Jesus Christ back to life and you're going to help me.'

Johnny waited for the punch line but it didn't come.

'Our customers,' Garçon continued 'are ready for something more daring. More taboo. More *spiritual!*'

Another flash of those veneers.

'Jesus . . . *Christ?*' Johnny quizzed.

'Jesus Christ. The Christian God.'

Johnny laughed. He couldn't help it.

He could think of no greater commercial flop than Jesus Christ. Since the Holy War, religion, and every distant cousin of religion, was a no-no. Outside of Total America, there was no money in Jesus. And with a closed border policy, online as well as offline, there was absolutely no way to exploit the TA market.

Garçon glared at him from across the desk.

Johnny lifted his drink, nervously, took another sip, suddenly wishing it was JD instead of water

'You *do* mean VR, Mr Garçon?' he said. 'Right?'

Garçon came alive, again.

'Have you ever read any history of Jesus Christ, Johnny?' he asked.

Johnny had not.

'The story of Jesus was told in chunks. None of which

came from any official source.' Garçon waved his hand, impatiently. 'People didn't write things down back then, you see. Most of them couldn't. So these fables about the things Jesus did spread via word-of-mouth.'

He lifted his own glass, touched it with his lips, set it back down.

'And what a story! It's really quite amazing: Jesus was reported to not only be the *son* of God, but a part of God himself. Here was a man the average Joe could relate to, have a beer with, and yet, he promised the very earth to them. He promised *more* than the earth, Johnny. Don't you see? Jesus was the ideal brand.'

'I guess . . .' Johnny mused.

'Of course it took more than just a few storytellers for this new brand to catch on,' Garçon continued. 'Constantine, you ever heard of him?'

'No sir.'

'He was the Roman emperor at the time, made Christianity the state religion. Suddenly Jesus was the new black. Everyone, and I mean *everyone*, wanted a piece of him. We're talking books, merchandise, the whole nine yards.'

Garçon leaned back in his seat, looked to Johnny and smiled.

'Man,' he said in a softer voice, 'if there'd been movies back then, you'd have had one hell of a script. Some of the stories they recorded were just beautiful. His lover, an ex-prostitute called Mary, was said to have poured shampoo on Jesus' feet, washed them with her hair. Isn't that something?'

Johnny suddenly thought of the whore from Tomb Street, scrambling around on the floor in front of him, scooping up dope.

'That *is* something,' he agreed.

Garçon leaned forward again, back to business.

'Johnny, I don't believe there ever was a Jesus. Not in the historical sense, anyway. People were desperate for someone *like* him, though, someone to liberate them from an empire that thrived on hedonism, where gluttony was a sign of success, where middle-aged men took nine year olds to be their lovers.' Garçon's eyes narrowed. 'So they created their own religion, pieced it together from the myths that surrounded them. Don't you see, Johnny? These people created a crude form of *virtual reality*.'

'Okay,' Johnny said, still not sure he did see, 'so you want me to create a VR Jesus doll?'

'Yes! Lark City's out of control. There's as much demand for change now as there was back in Constantine's time. People need religion again, Johnny, a reason, a product to help rein themselves in, and we can capitalise on that.'

Johnny thought for a moment, toying over the brief in his head. It all still seemed insane to him.

'How long do I have on the beta version?' he asked. 'The usual three months?'

Garçon's face dropped.

'Johnny. I've . . . er . . . well, I've been put under some pressure by the funders. I told them we *already have* the beta version. They want to see something sooner than that.'

'Sooner as in *one* month?'

Garçon grimaced.

'Try one *week*.'

'A week?!' Johnny blew out some air.

He caught a sharp look from Garçon, cleared his throat, checked himself: that was a little expressive for a doghouse code guy. But a beta version in a week was pretty tough even for standard, off-the-shelf VR. For something like this, it would be pretty much impossible. Johnny was looking at long hours, little sleep . . .

. . . *which was exactly what he needed.*

'Okay. We can maybe do that. Beta version in your inbox for Friday week, latest.'

But Garçon still wasn't happy.

'No, Johnny,' he said, 'I'll need the *final* cut. By next *Thursday*. Otherwise, they're going to pull the plug, cut the funding.'

Garçon leaned forward again. Against the orange glow of the desk lamp, Johnny could see him a little better. A single bead of sweat rolled down his perfectly smooth forehead. His normally perfect hair was ruffled. Even his suit looked creased, the silk shirt upturned oddly at the collar.

'Can you do it, Johnny?' he asked. 'Can you?'

SEVENTEEN

Johnny's head was hurting. Words and pics danced from his touchscreen as he worked.

He paused to rub his eyes.

He was starting to really hate Jesus. Researching the guy was proving to be a royal pain in the ass.

His main source, the bible, was long out of print. You couldn't even download it. A couple of second hand stores over on Cathedral seemed to stock it, but Johnny had neither desire nor inclination to leaf through a hard copy.

Even the Net lacked interest in Jesus, and you could get all kinds of shit there. Sure, there was some data available, mostly from nut jobs still proselytising the *real* Jesus, but it varied widely concerning key facts and proved ultimately useless. Extremists were imaginative if nothing else.

Johnny tried to remember what he was taught in school. During the war, Jesus was the veritable linchpin of The West; a principled and confident leader; a model patriot. This Jesus had men and women signing up for battle in their droves. But there was little substance to be found here either: the HW Jesus was merely a symbol or flag; the soldier's muse.

Bored, Johnny leaned back from the screen and stretched his arms. One hand connected with his coffee cup and, before he could steady it, the damn thing toppled and spilled across the desk, burning him in the process.

'Shit!'

Johnny shifted in his chair, sucking on a scalded finger.

He glanced round, noticing Garçon make a beeline across the room.

He pulled his finger out of his mouth, tried to look professional.

'So how's my favourite code guy?' Garçon announced.

Several office heads turned to glare at Johnny before returning quickly to their screens.

Johnny straightened, cleared his throat, said, 'Just researching, sir.'

Garçon smiled, his eyes falling upon the spilled coffee.

'Good man,' he said. 'Let's make our Jesus *authentic!* The *Real Deal!*' And then, with a playful pat of Johnny's back, the company man was gone.

Johnny's eyes remained on the coffee, continuing its journey away from the toppled cup. He was suddenly fascinated by it. How it flowed, how it gathered at the edge of the desk before dripping down onto the floor, where it gathered again, each drip helping to spread the little pool further across the floor.

He had found since Becky's death that simple things, mundane things, became significant. Sacred. Profound, even.

He reached for a tissue and started to mop.

He paused, put the tissues down and looked at the

e-mail APP on his touchscreen. There it was; the tiny envelope in the corner with the number 4 beside it. One of those e-mails had been sent by Becky and it remained unopened.

Johnny stared at the little icon. What if Becky's e-mail *didn't contain* something nice? What if the words it held were condescending or accusatory or spiteful? What if Becky had made some declaration, some sort of statement in this e-mail which would change everything between them? Or, worse still, what if it was just a mundane message saying nothing at all about anything: a permanent reminder of how stale their lives had become towards the end.

Johnny picked out another tissue and started cleaning again. He sighed, scrunching the used paper into a ball and lobbing it into the bin.

He leaned back in his chair suddenly feeling very deflated.

'What's happening?'

It was Sarah. Her face was flushed. She chewed on her bottom lip sheepishly, like she knew she was bothering him. Johnny wished she would just go away. He knew it was unfair, but in that brief moment Sarah Lee suddenly represented everything that was wrong to him. The spilt coffee. Garçon's ridiculous brief. The e-mail from Becky still unopened.

'Nothing's happening,' he told her

'How's the "Big Secret Project" going?' Sarah made air-quotes with her fingers.

'It's slow.'

'What's it about?'

'Jesus.'

The word sounded ridiculous to Johnny. Comical.

'Jesus?'

'Yeah,' he said, 'Jesus Fucking Christ.'

She laughed, snorting a little.

Johnny smiled, despite himself.

'How am I meant to write a Jesus program?' he said, opening up to her. 'I mean, no one can agree on who or what he was supposed to be! Every commentator has defined him differently for –' he threw his hands into the air, exasperated, 'For *centuries*! And I'm meant to write his AI in a *week*?!'

Sarah had stopped laughing. Her face was serious.

'What now?' Johnny asked.

'Nothing!' But her face had a guilty shine about it, like she was holding something back.

'Tell me, Sarah.'

'Well, it's just . . .'

She pulled closer to him and he could smell her perfume. It was a familiar scent, floral yet not overbearing. He remembered Becky wearing something similar.

'This is my fault, Johnny. I convinced Garçon you could do this and now I've put more stress on you. That's the last thing I wanted to do and I'm –'

'Worried,' he finished for her. 'Well, you needn't be, Sarah. This will be good for me. You said so yourself when you came round to see me. This will keep me busy. Not to mention pay the bills.'

He thought of those yahoos and the stolen card. How empty his bank account looked.

'Just be careful, Johnny. Garçon's acting strange. You're acting strange too, I guess. I don't like it.'

'*I'm* acting strange?!'

'I'm serious,' Sarah said, and her eyes confirmed it. 'There's something about VR that I've never liked. I think it changes people, users who spend too long in their virtual worlds and not enough time in the *real* world. Don't let it do that to you, Johnny. I know you're looking for escapism right now, but too much VR could be a very dangerous thing.'

'Don't let Garçon hear you say that,' Johnny ribbed. 'Or it could be *you* he's firing, not me!'

Sarah rolled her eyes. She went to walk away, then paused. Thought for a moment, then turned to him again. .

'It's like water,' she said.

'What?'

'Water,' she repeated. 'It changes according to how you use it.'

But Johnny was still confused.

'The Jesus AI. Think about it from an energy perspective,' she continued. 'In the solar pyramids, we boil water and it becomes steam. And in the winter, it becomes ice or hail or snow.' Sarah moved back over to Johnny's desk, lifted his coffee cup and shook it, little drops of brown moisture showering the floor. 'And if we add coffee granules to it when it's hot, it becomes coffee. So, water can be anything you want it to be, Johnny. It changes according to how we use it.'

Johnny thought for a moment, digested what she was saying. Then he stood up, snapped his fingers.

He remembered reading somewhere on the Net how Jesus was referred to as the Water of Life. It was one of those weird titles they gave him, something that meant nothing.

Until now, that was.

Johnny grabbed Sarah, planted his lips on her forehead, beaming.

'You're a genius.'

He wired his cell, linking to a file named MAGIC MOMENTS. Johnny was the type of guy to have various projects on the go at once. Some were little more than random thoughts, vaguely realised before being shelved. Others were closer to being finished. MAGIC MOMENTS was somewhere in between; designed to provide the user with a treasured experience from their own memory, something they could relive over and over.

But it went beyond just a simple replay.

In today's VR obsessed world, criminal techs would employ viral code to infiltrate the files and data of users. In extreme cases, the very minds of users came under attack, on occasion leaving the user mind-wiped, or comatose. Such events put many off the VR experience. Others, perhaps less cautious or more desperate for the world that had become so central to their existence, carried on regardless, perhaps signing up for one of the many security packages that flooded the market in the wake of these threats.

Johnny's code was always straight. He never dabbled in viral code.

In fact, in many ways the code he used for MAGIC MOMENTS was *anti-viral*. Instead of infiltrating the mind of the user, the VR was *shaped* by it, a sponge to every whim, creating an experience even better than the real thing. As the user interacted with MAGIC MOMENTS, the code responded to their desires like commands, even allowing the event to become different, more elaborate or valuable than what it had been in the user's *actual* reality.

Johnny lifted the wiretap and applied it to his face. His vision gave way, sparking up the program's simulation.

The VR kicked into gear, displaying a blank, underdeveloped screen. A menu appeared right in front of Johnny's virtual eyes, the audio encouraging him to choose BEGIN when he was ready.

It was Sarah who reminded Johnny of this code. Its basic engine had evolved into the VR Counsellor program, one of several bombs Garçon had dropped on an apathetic market over the years. But Johnny wondered if in its root form, he could adapt this engine to give Garçon his Jesus.

Hell, it would save a lot of time.

The VR was stark, at first, until the code began to work its magic, interacting with Johnny's mind via the wiretap to create his own magic moment. And of course, his magic moment involved Becky.

The background filled in, slowly, creating its own vector wireframes before adding the shading and colour.

Johnny found himself in a restaurant.

In front of him, a waiter without a face was speaking, graphics evolving as he welcomed Johnny to the restaurant.

He asked to take Johnny's coat. Johnny went to remove it, helped by the waiter. It was a smart woollen coat, one he would only wear on a night out.

Underneath, Johnny wore a flecked jacket and strides, a high-collared shirt with a thin PVC tie. Grey slip-ons on his feet. It was a brand new outfit, throwback style. He'd bought the whole shebang in Cathedral that very day, knowing how much Becky liked it when he made the effort.

The waiter returned from the cloakroom, more of his face now visible. His lips were moving now. Soon, his eyes held colour. They were kind eyes. He seemed genuinely pleased to see Johnny, and Johnny wondered whether that was how the waiter had *actually* been, or whether it was how Johnny *wanted* to remember him. This was the beauty of the code.

'I'll show you to your seat, sir. Madam has already arrived.'

Johnny's heart jumped, a cold sweat breaking across his skin. His *real* skin. In the VR, only his hands were sweating, one clenched around a small plastic box, hidden in his strides pocket.

It was her hair he saw first. She'd had it cut later on, in the real world, but now, as Johnny approached from behind, it hung over the back of her chair. It reminded him of waterfalls. He felt his heartbeat racing and wondered if it had been quite as fast on that actual evening.

She turned and he saw her for the first time since the hospital bed. His chest tightened, like something had become stuck: a huge knot or lump of food. Johnny paused and the VR paused with him, the stupid, idiotic audio interrupting, asking if he wanted to continue.

Wanted to? He *needed* to, for God's sake. How could they ask him that?!

He shouted this at the audio voice, the VR kicking in again, as per command.

Johnny realised how stupid he was being: there was nothing *real* to be angry at here, nothing tangible. He looked around the restaurant. The decor, the other people, the smells of food, the waiter, the table.

Becky.

All of this was code.

But still he wanted it.

The waiter pulled out a chair for him with vector hands. But Johnny didn't notice, didn't care.

It was all about Becky now. She was perfect. A flawless imitation. No flickering graphics or uneven colour tone. Perfect.

Johnny's hands were now wringing wet, seeping through to the skin of his leg. He remembered this exact moment from the actual night; how he worried she might notice.

But for now Becky wasn't bothered.

She glanced up at the waiter briefly before dipping her head back into her menu.

She ignored Johnny.

He remembered being late that night, how she'd been angry with him.

So they sat in awkward silence for a while, Becky huffing. Johnny couldn't remember if that was how it played out at the time, or if he'd tried to talk her out of it, like he usually did. But the VR, the doll, didn't care about any of that. Perfect though it looked, the doll had no concept of reality.

It was just code, after all.

Of course, right now to Johnny, it was a lot *more* than code. This could have been Becky sitting opposite him. Even her perfume was right, that same floral scent he remembered Sarah wearing.

No, not Sarah, he thought. *Get her out of your mind.*

The VR held fast; Becky's face undisturbed. If anything, the doll became even *more* like Becky. Her eyes widened a little, subtly flipping between various shades, finding their natural colour.

'Wanna pour yourself a glass of wine?' she said, 'been working my way through the bottle. It's half gone.' She looked up at Johnny. 'You'll be late to your own funeral,' she added, and her face lifted in that way it would when she was ready to come out of a huff and forgive him.

He realised he had forgotten that about her. Johnny had forgotten a lot and it scared him.

'Sorry,' he heard himself say and couldn't be sure if it was his own voice or the code's. God knows, in the heat of VR it was pretty damn hard to tell the difference. 'Work was a killer. Garçon –'

'Garçon, Garçon, Garçon.' She reached across the table, took his hand. 'Did you tell Garçon that your beautiful girlfriend was waiting for you in Titanic's finest restaurant?'

It was the first time the VR had tripped up. Her manner seemed too precise, too perfect. Becky had always been sharp but he wondered whether she was *this* sharp.

Goddamnit! Why couldn't he just enjoy it?! Why couldn't he just go with the flow, relive all he could remember about her, about them and this night?!

Johnny reached one hand into his pocket, found the small square box. Still there. He knew that was something that *actually* happened. He had gripped that box so tight all night that his nails left little scratches on it.

'Have you ordered yet?' he asked her.

'Nope. Still looking.'

Her freckles were almost hidden, her lips bright red.

She was wearing his favourite dress, green chiffon with a silver zip.

Johnny wondered if that dress was with the others now, packed tightly into black plastic bin bags, waiting to be dumped (he absolutely couldn't face giving them to goodwill – to think of someone else wearing her clothes, making use of her things).

He couldn't take his eyes off her.

Were she real and not a VR doll, she would have probably noticed, become aware. And as soon as Johnny thought that, she *did* become aware, playing with her hair, blinking then looking at him.

'What?' she said.

'Nothing,' he said. 'Just . . . Well, it's just that you're beautiful.'

'Oh shut up.'

'Seriously. You know I love that dress on you.'

'Not so bad yourself, Johnny boy. That a new suit?'

He was getting into it now, relaxing. Soon, they were talking freely, going through the motions, Johnny giving himself over to the code, unable to stop himself, Becky playing the role more fluidly, more naturally.

At times, he would forget she was a doll; forget he was in VR, instead thinking himself actually there in the restaurant; worrying about the box in his pocket; about when he should take it out and place it on the table, and what she would say when he did.

Becky ordered the salmon with a sushi starter. She loved fish, would have eaten it every meal if she could. Johnny got the same because, whatever he had done at the time, in the VR he didn't as much as glance at the menu. The waiter took their orders, a blue square flickering in his hair, vector hands holding his notepad. He brought the food and set it on the table, but Johnny didn't touch it. And, of course, Becky only commented on this whenever he himself had clocked it. She devoured her own meal, even reaching across to dig into his. In reality, her appetite had always been good. In VR, she seemed ravenous.

They finished and the waiter took away their plates, his still untouched. When Becky asked if he wanted dessert, he could feel his guts twist. For a moment he wondered if he was going to be sick. And then he wondered if you *could* be sick in VR.

But you could be *anything* in VR.

She was still looking at him, patiently waiting for an answer, and it was then that he reached into his pocket; retrieved that little plastic box and set it on the table.

'How about this for dessert?' he said and she looked at the box, puzzlement in her face, and he pushed it closer to her as if she hadn't seen it; as if in pushing it closer, there was more chance she would accept it.

Johnny watched as her lips opened, as her eyes lifted to meet his, a mixture of fear and excitement and intrigue and . . .

But he couldn't finish.

Johnny pulled the wiretap off, switching back to his own vision.

He was back in the open-plan.

He rubbed his eyes, trying to refocus on the real world.

The office was busy now. A guy called Colin wandered by, smiling at Johnny.

But Johnny didn't smile back.

He was still thinking about the VR. About Becky and the little plastic box.

He remembered her panicking, reaching into her handbag, retrieving her cell and syncing the bill. How the waiter had come over and they had all ignored the little box on the table together, like it wasn't really there.

It was then that it clicked with Johnny.

Although he made it through the rest of the day, Johnny didn't do much. He couldn't focus, feeling sick, the fallout from the VR both heavy and light in his stomach.

At five, he left work and returned to his apartment.

He ruffled through the drawers again. He opened all those plastic bags with her stuff. He found her handbags, her purse. He opened them up, finding the picture he was looking for, the one she carried with her everywhere she went.

It was from their first holiday together.

Her hair was still long, freckles more obvious with the sun.

And she was smiling. *Properly* smiling, showing her teeth.

Johnny didn't think he had any tears left. But he cried again that night.

EIGHTEEN

Spend too long in a bar like Vegas, and it started to mess with your head. A man could be forgiven for flipping out, thinking he was in 1959. Or 1759 for that matter.

Maybe it was the beer; its suspiciously tart bite, or the ever-present smell of ganja and piss, mixing like some cheap, out-of-date cologne. But this was a place – whether by design or destiny – that looked (and smelled and sounded) like a scene from some classic Box movie.

Retro wasn't the word for it.

Take the clientele, for example: a curious mix of ages and styles; a cross section of eras and fashions that all but captured the very essence of Lark City. *Do what ye will*, Ms Liberty proclaimed. In Vegas, you could go one further; be anyone from any place or time, do whatever *they* wanted.

In Vegas, each Quarter mixed with surprising indifference towards one another; businessmen, looking for quick kicks; throwbacks with their slick hair and pressed strides, toe-tapping to the beat; yahoos under hoods, hungry eyes peeking out from long narrow faces; wireheads in blue and yellow neon, wiretaps and coils glowing in the musky light. Vegas served them all.

But then there was Kitty, sitting in her corner. A constant reminder that beyond zoning, there was a more potent addiction. A destructive vice that ripped the very soul from a person, leaving them nowhere, doing nothing, a shell without style or substance.

Tonight, Kitty had stacked the cushions by her side as always. She sat on the sofa, half in the world, half out – no wiretap attached – both hands clinging to her glass of water like it were made of gold.

Her dad, Paul McBride, sat at the bar, beer in hand.

The Bar Man stood opposite, looking how he always looked with his crisp white shirt, thin black tie and leather apron.

'Hear about Geordie Mac?' McBride asked.

The Bar Man nodded, glass and towel in hand.

'Real shame,' McBride said. He lifted his beer, sipped then sat it back down. 'And I'll tell you what's even more of a shame,' he added, 'fuckers who did it were messing with my little girl.'

The Bar Man's eyes rose quickly, found Kitty, then the glass again.

'That a fact?' he said.

'That's a fact alright,' McBride said. He leaned in closer. 'They took Geordie's gear, brought it to my little girl then sold it to her. Can you believe that?'

The Bar Man lifted his glass to the light. Examined it, twisting it round and round. He shook his head at McBride's question, began polishing the glass again with his cloth.

'And here's me thinking you were doing your job and keeping your eye on her,' McBride added.

The Bar Man's hand slipped, the glass tumbling to the floor, breaking.

There was a short round of applause from those in the bar not zoning. But the Bar Man wasn't smiling.

McBride wasn't smiling, either.

'Best clean that up,' he seethed. 'Before someone gets hurt.'

The Bar Man didn't blink. He held McBride's stare.

'I do my best,' he said, and his voice didn't waver, 'along with everything else you have me doing, everyone else you have me watching. But she's *your* little girl, Paul. Ever think of it that way?'

McBride lifted his drink, sipped again, set it down. He didn't turn the comment.

He said: 'One of them's Janice's boy. I've seen him around here. Nice kid, got himself in with a bad crowd. Pity, really.' He seemed to think on that for a second. 'The other I don't know. Word has it he's loud, talks like a redneck. I want them both. Can you do that for me?'

The Bar Man reached under the bar for a dustpan and brush, bent down to clean the broken glass. Once done, he emptied the pan in the nearby trash, brushed his hands, lifted his towel and another glass then began polishing again.

He looked up at McBride, almost as an afterthought.

'Sure thing,' he said.

NINETEEN

That Sunday, Reverend Harold Shepherd noticed one of his regulars missing.

'I didn't notice Saul in the service, this morning,' he whispered to Mrs O'Brien, pulling her aside as the church emptied.

'I heard he was sick, Reverend,' she said in a faint, nervous voice.

'Really? Did you hear if it was *something serious*?'

'Well, he's in hospital.' Harold could see the emotion building in her face. 'I'm sorry,' she added, 'but it's all very upsetting.'

'Which hospital?' Harold said, gently pressing her arm. There were a number in Lark and more across Maalside. 'I'd like to visit him, make sure he's got everything he needs.'

'Lark City Hospital,' she said. 'I must be on my way, Reverend.'

Harold nodded, releasing her.

He knew of her affair with Saul. How they had shacked up together, leaving their poorly old partners in the care home. But that was the way of things now: marriage was no longer the institution it used to be, 'in sickness and in health' well out-of-date.

As Harold watched, Mrs O'Brien ducked out into the mid-morning rain, the tails of her coat flailing behind in the wind. She lifted one hand to cover her head from the rain, using the old, paperback bible she carried.

A large billboard hung above the entrance to Lark City Hospital, playing some advert as Harold approached. But the preacher's mind was filled with other things; the memories of patients he had visited over the years, many of them now dead.

This was not a nice place. It didn't even look nice: a super-sized white cube, all plastic, aluminium and glass. From a distance, you could place your thumb and forefinger around the cube, pretend it was a dice; maybe try shaking it.

And then there was the smell. Harold had always hated the smell of hospitals; that slightly soiled sweetness that spoke of medication and white coats and long faces. Lark City's smell was particularly nauseating.

Inside was even more depressing. Soulless artwork blended into off-white walls. Forgotten patients, propped up on beds or abandoned wheelchairs, stared into space. The ancient Irish playwright, Samuel Beckett, once wrote a play about waiting, and Harold shuddered to think how horrific a setting this hospital would have made; two old men sitting in wheelchairs waiting for something or someone to take away their ills.

Visiting an old coot like Saul was unlikely to cheer

Harold up any. Saul's whole life had been about misery, a misery more clinical and disinfected than any of the floors here could boast. In fact, Harold reckoned Saul was one of those folks who *enjoyed* being miserable.

The doctors always talked about chemical imbalance when they didn't know what made someone such a bastard. Saul was *very* chemically imbalanced. As a lawyer he had taken nothing but sheer pleasure in doling out heartache to others. Home repossessions, accident lawsuits, money judgements: Saul handled them all. He was just the man to go to if someone owed you what they couldn't afford to pay back. And his rates depended on him making sure they *did* pay you back.

Harold paused at the self-serve, retrieving his cell and syncing the required cash for some fizzy drink and sweets. He didn't know whether Saul would like the flavours and brands he'd chosen, but that was hardly the point. It was poor form to turn up to a hospital bed empty-handed; that was one of the rules he'd learned.

Armed with his gifts, Harold moved towards reception.

'Welcome to Lark City Hospital,' the automated voice said, warmly. 'Which service, please?'

'Patient visit,' Harold said. 'Mr Saul J. Collins'

A slight pause, as the tech checked its records.

'Third floor. Ward 7. Will you require assistance?'

'No thanks.'

'Enjoy your visit.'

He heard his cell beep once, confirming his security clearance. But Harold checked just in case, reading: VISITOR, SAUL J. COLLINS. STABLE. Some time ago, when they'd just changed the security system and he'd forgotten to download the required APP to his cell, Harold was rushing to see a patient described as FADING by the hospital tech. He'd hurried through reception without clearance, setting the alarm off. Embarrassing to say the least.

Today, Harold moved past reception with ease. Cleaner drones quietly polished the floor on either side of him, the low hum of their tech the only sound to resemble noise. He found the elevator, called it, waited.

A young nurse appeared beside him, glancing at his clerical collar.

'Hallo,' Harold said, politely. 'How's your day going?'

'Pretty shit,' she quipped dryly. 'And you?'

The lift arrived before he could answer. It was fairly crowded, two hospital porters in blue tunics and strides standing at either end of a long wheeled stretcher. Harold and the nurse stepped in, finding space. The doors closed, and the auto voice announced which floor they would be travelling to next.

An awkward silence fell. It was Harold's worst nightmare to be trapped in an elevator, forced to share this cramped space with so many others.

'Who are you visiting?' the nurse asked, pulling him out of his thoughts.

He said the name.

'Ah,' she said. 'He's the main reason my day has been shit. Going to give him his last rites, perchance?'

Harold smiled.

'No, that would be the Catholics who do that. I'm just here to deliver some fizzy pop.'

The nurse laughed.

The lift stopped and she left, turning to him as she went.

'Tell him he can bath himself next time,' she said.

Harold nodded, smiling once more, but *she* didn't seem as amused this time. She seemed angry, affronted. And then she was gone, lost to some new emergency, cell beeping angrily at her as she stole away.

The lift doors closed again.

Harold arrived at Saul's ward, finding the crabby old bastard propped up on his pillows.

'I thought you were meant to be sick,' he said, setting the fizzy pop on the lawyer's bedside table.

Saul ignored the gift, 'And I thought you were one of the nurses. But you're uglier and a lot less useful, let's face it.'

'Just met one of your nurses, as it happens,' Harold laughed. 'She said to say hallo.'

Saul gave a dirty look.

'I'll bet she did,' he sneered.

'So, what's the matter with you, anyway?' Harold sat down on the chair by the bed. 'You seem healthy enough to me.'

He was lying of course. The old man looked and sounded awful. Folds of skin slopped around his cheeks. Tiredness softened his voice.

'I *am* healthy,' Saul protested. 'Just had a few chest pains. Temporary paralysis. Good as new now.' He chuckled, coughing a little. 'They want to keep me in for some tests.'

He waved his hand, dismissively, like Harold would

understand how stupid they were in these hospitals, with their silly tests. But there was another vibe about him, a distinct feeling that this place, with its nurses and pajamas and tests, had spooked an old battleship like Saul J. Collins. Reminded him of mortality, the all too few years left on his clock.

'Better safe than sorry,' Harold said.

He reached for the bottle of fizzy pop. He unscrewed the lid, lifted a glass from the bedside table and filled it. Offered it to Saul.

The old man tutted.

'Can't touch it,' he said. 'Too much sugar. Fucking Nazis in here won't let me have anything.'

Harold considered emptying the glass of pop into the nearby sink and refilling it with water.

But Saul was on a roll.

'They're trying to bleed me dry in here,' he spat. 'These fucking places are all about money! And God knows how much their fucking tests cost!'

He leaned back, looked away. He was shaking, his head curled against his shoulder like a wounded bird.

Harold looked at the glass of pop still in his hand, set it down on the side of the bedside table.

He reached for the old man's hand, held it.

'Mrs O'Brien seems very worried about you, Saul,' he said, softly. 'She really cares for you. You know you're very lucky to have her.'

Saul started to cry. It was a quiet sob, aimed towards the pillows, built like bags of sand behind his head. It was the first time Harold had seen any sort of vulnerability from him. He had thought Saul devoid of emotion, save anger.

He continued to hold the old man's hand. Saul didn't look at him, his face still buried in the pillows. And there they sat for a while, the quiet, disinfected air filling the space between them.

Finally, Saul pulled his hand free. He wiped his tears away with a swift, frantic movement. He sniffed a few times, reaching for a nearby tissue and blowing his nose hard.

His face returned to its usual angry sneer.

'I'm sure you've better things to be doing than hanging around here,' he said. 'Don't worry, I've told Mrs O'Brien to sync my tithe every Sunday until I'm back, if that's what you're worried about.'

Harold smiled. 'Saul, if you need anything –'

'You'll be the last fucker to know.'

Harold smiled.

He pulled himself to his feet, bid the old man farewell.

As he left the ward, Harold heard a sudden shrill cry coming from a nearby corridor. There was a flurry of activity, several nurses rushing past.

Harold continued walking.

TWENTY

Harold stepped outside. It was raining and he welcomed the coolness of the water against his face. It was a relief from the warm compressed air of the hospital.

Above him, on the silver billboard, a perfectly featured young mom tended to her cosmetically designed baby. Beside them, Dad drew close; seemingly delighted with how much the child looked like its mother. An animated Ms Liberty joined them, winking at the camera. Stats ran along the bottom of the screen highlighting the number of successful baby designs Lark City Hospital had nurtured within the last year.

Harold drew a hanky from his jacket pocket and blew his nose deeply. He wanted whatever he had breathed in there out. Damn well felt infected.

He noticed a car out front. New eco-fuel model. Harold hadn't seen one in the flesh, only ads running on the Box. It felt odd to see something move without solar panels, compression or hydrosteam. But just when you were getting used to something, they went and changed all the rules. The market demanded it, after all. Harold remembered the tagline: something about how eco-fuels gave similar performance to the old gasoline engines that Paul McBride and his boys drove around in. More burn than any PV pod or steam turbine could offer. And when it came to automobiles, folks wanted some kick to their metal.

The window lowered, revealing its sole occupant: a slick looking company man. He looked in Harold's direction, all teeth and Botox; his skin so orange that Harold thought the man to be glowing for a second.

He smiled.

Harold looked behind, expecting to see a harem of models or executives, but there was no one, save some old guy in a wheelchair toking on what smelled like his daily fix of medicinal marijuana.

'Reverend Shepherd!' the company man called.

'You want me?' Harold said, placing a hand on his chest.

'You indeed, sir. I was wondering if we could have a word.'

Harold walked over, pulling the hood of his anorak up against the rain. It was getting heavier, the sky an almost biblical shade of grey. Up close the company man looked even less human: his hair was like thick cream; his eyes a piercing neon blue. He wore a black shirt and red tie. Everything about him screamed money.

'I have a proposal for you, Reverend,' he said. 'Might just be the kind of thing needed to get you out of your current,' he cleared his throat and said the next words quieter, 'financial difficulties.'

Harold was taken back.

'What do you know about my business?'

'Please, Reverend,' the company man said, flashing those veneers again. 'If you could get in, I'll explain it all.'

He introduced himself as Philip Garçon, head of Alt Lark. Harold felt immediately on edge, not used to corporate types; their world; their language. But Garçon talked succinctly and remained polite to a fault.

First he talked about the car he was driving, pointing out its features as if part of some sales patter. At one stage, Harold thought he was trying to sell him the damn thing, going on and on about horsepower and speed and other things Harold knew or cared little about.

A mischievous smile spread across the company man's orange face.

He said: 'Do you know what Alt's new eco-fuel is made from?'

Harold didn't.

'Raw sewage,' Garçon beamed, proudly. 'That's the basic ingredient. We treat it, of course, mostly for synthetic reasons. People wouldn't like the smell.'

'No, I guess they wouldn't,' Harold agreed.

Thankfully Garçon moved on from the particulars of eco-fuels to his current work, described as 'a very different affair altogether'. He said this new project may be of interest to Harold. His next words almost gave the preacher a hernia.

'I want to bring Jesus Christ back from the dead.'

'Is this some kind of joke?' Harold barked.

'No, sir, I assure you it is not.'

'Look, I don't know what kind of racket you've got going here, Mr Garçon, but I for one am not interested.'

'Not even for fifty thousand dollars?'

Harold did not know what to say to that.

He listened as Garçon explained the particulars of the project, talking of things which Harold did not understand; things that old men like him, who watched the weather forecast on the Box and carried old fashioned functional cells in their pockets, still struggled with. Things like Virtual Reality: how it could modernise religion, make it palatable for the masses again. This scared Harold. Because, deep down, a part of Harold didn't want the masses. A part of him was quite happy with his lot, with the small, loyal flock that scuttled through the doors of the Old Crusader each Sunday morning, only to leave one hour later. Harold wondered how the Thursday night Outreach would cope with 'the masses.' He wondered if 'the masses' and 'virtual reality' would pierce the very heart of his church and leave it cold and lifeless.

He leaned back in the impossibly comfortable seat of the car, ran one hand along the glove compartment. Such affluence was alien to him. Born into a working class family, Harold was used to more base comforts. A hearty meal, good company. Little nip of gin or a smoke. Ordinary things for ordinary folks. Filling weekends, marking space between one hard graft and the next.

'And what do you need me for, exactly?' Harold asked.

Garçon drew closer: 'Reverend Shepherd,' and then, 'Harold. Can I call you Harold?' It was a rhetorical question. 'We need your church. The Old Crusader, I believe it's called? We want it as a showroom, Harold, somewhere for people to come and try our new product out. We think it would be perfect.'

It amused Harold to think of the Crusader being perfect for anything. The old girl was hardly able to stand. Were it to be situated anywhere else but Cathedral, a place well known for quaint architecture, Harold reckoned some businessman would have raised the place to the ground by now to make room for a mall or club.

But then he thought of his love for the church, his care for every little crack on its walls, every flake of paint that would float down from the ceiling when the cold drew in and the whole building seemed to shiver and shed lumps of itself, like an old hag. Harold thought of the large wooden cross behind the pulpit and realised that the Crusader *was* beautiful. *Perfect* just as this Garçon fella said.

But that was the problem.

'What's wrong?' Garçon asked, reading his face.

Harold shook his head.

'It's just that I can't see how –'

'Seventy thousand.'

'But –'

'One hundred thousand. Final offer.'

'Stop throwing your fucking money at me!'

There was anger in Harold's voice. He wasn't used to this kind of conversation. Sure, money talked, but not in a language Harold cared for.

He thought about the loans he'd taken out in order to keep the old church afloat. He thought of the trouble he'd got into over that; the clear plastic bags stashed in his back store. And then it hit home: this money Garçon was offering *really could* help him; it was more than enough to pay all his loans off. It would get Paul McBride out of his life, once and for all.

'Harold,' Garçon said, quietly, 'I'm offering you a considerable amount of money for very little inconvenience on your part.'

'I just can't see why it's so important to you. It's just an old church.'

'It's the *only* old church left in Lark. The only *real* church. And authenticity is important for this product, Harold. It's essential.'

Harold sighed, shook his head, deflated.

'If I agree to this,' he said, 'it will only be temporary.'

'Just to launch the product,' Garçon promised, 'to act as a pilot project, if you like. I can guarantee that within six months we will be out of your life altogether.'

'And out of the church?'

'Yes,' Garçon said. 'You won't see a trace of us.'

As if on cue, the car pulled up beside the old place.

Harold sighed.

He peered through the perfectly clear windshield, saddened by how tired the Crusader looked. It had been the salvation of many through the years. Yet, now if Harold didn't do something to save it, this very building could end up like every other church in Lark: a club, peddling sleaze and drugs and booze and whores.

'Okay,' Harold said, offering his hand to Garçon.

They shook.

Harold then reached for his cell.

'You can sync me the relevant paperwork.' He thought of

Saul at the hospital then added, 'But it may take me a while to get it back to you. My lawyer is, er, incapacitated, shall we say, at present.'

Later that night, Harold stood by the pulpit, staring up at the wooden cross. The windows around the cross seemed darker, somehow, as if in mourning. There was a dripping sound from somewhere, a new patch of damp building in the front wall. Money would fix it all but Harold couldn't find it in his heart to be happy.

'Sorry,' he said, eyes still on the cross, his voice echoing around the empty building.

TWENTY ONE

Almost a week had passed since Johnny had been hacked. But he woke this morning with a fresh new anger. He'd dreamt about it, how those two little bastards had taken his card and bled his account. It still riled him. And of course, the yahoos didn't do it alone.

They'd mentioned another name, Charles 7, while talking with that little whore. Charles was a tech hack who worked in Smithfield, a random little marketplace down by Cathedral. Whilst the rest of the city moved with the times, enjoying the recent surge of commerce and all that came with it, Smithfield stood still. It was like the market was stuck within some kind of time warp. Sync a random pic of the place from ten, twenty even fifty years ago and little would have changed. This was the land that time forgot.

An assortment of bazaars provided the heart of trade here. Esoteric trade that required a little privacy, a little discretion. It was a hotbed for migrants; Asian dealers with their eateries, grocers and butchers catering mainly to their own. Meat hung from hooks at storefronts, traders calling in pigeon English as Johnny passed, offering him green tea or Chinese leaf or herbal remedies to any number of ailments.

While the migrants bartered, locals moved through like ants, some catching Johnny's eye as he passed, suspiciously wrapped parcels tucked under arms or pulled tight against their bodies like parachutes.

Somewhere in the middle was Charles 7's shop. It was an amoral haven for tech freak and yahoo alike; credit cards hacking, cells syncing, APPS firing, data bleeding. Tech hung from the walls and ceiling, half stripped and half alive; sparking and jittering as if victim to some form of mechanical Tourette's Syndrome.

Johnny pushed the door open.

Charles was behind the counter. With his dark skin, silver hair and muted clothing, Johnny half-expected the tech hack to somehow merge into the wall of metal and coil behind him, maybe sync with the store itself, commanding it to scoop Johnny up and throw him back out onto the street.

Instead he found Charles zoning, two of the three coils implanted in his head connecting directly into his cell and another device which, to a code guy like Johnny, looked very much like a data-bleed.

At his hands, Charles was working at yet another device, Johnny wondering just how many cards, cells or databases the multi-tasking Charles would crack within any given hour, and how many people he was doing over in the process.

And then there was his viral work. VR was a competitive market, often aggressively so. Johnny knew Garçon had employed Charles 7 to attack rival companies' systems and products, exploiting weaknesses. This was common practice in commerce, everyone seemed to be in on it. Not least the insurance companies, viral attacks forcing consumers to take out increasingly expensive coverage to protect their VR products and data.

As Johnny approached the counter, one of Charles' eyes opened.

'Can I help y-you?' he said.

He was twitching all over, tingling with the code.

'Johnny Lyon's the name. You hacked my card. Stole three hundred dollars from me and I want it back.'

The tech hack's other eye opened. He muttered something to his cell, pausing one of the VR programs. Disconnected a coil, leaned slowly back in his chair, sizing Johnny up.

'You got any proof of this thing you accuse me of, Johnny Lyon?'

Johnny stood for a second, holding 7's gaze.

'Two yahoos were given my card by a whore on Tomb Street. They mentioned your name.'

Charles shook his head.

'Lots of folks mention my name,' he said, 'but that don't mean I know them.' He reached for his tech, added, 'My advice to you, Johnny Lyon, is to be careful who you mix with.'

7 slipped his third coil back into the cell, fired the whole lot up. He was done with this conversation.

Johnny thumped his fist hard on the counter.

'I haven't finished with you!' he yelled.

7's eye opened again.

'Get out of my store, man.'

But Johnny didn't move.

'How can you just . . .?!' he began.

His heart was racing. He would later realise that the anger was little to do with any hacking.

It was Becky.

The anger replaced his mourning, *became* his mourning; a crass protest at everything around him; at those yahoos and the junkie whore who stole his cell; at Charles 7 for hacking it, but ultimately at Becky. This pure anger, this white-hot rage, was all for her.

How could she leave him like this?

He reached for 7, grabbed the third coil, pulling it free from the cell.

Charles spun back out of the VR, both eyes opening wide, grabbing hold of the disconnected coil.

But Johnny held on, the two men struggling across the counter.

'Three hundred, you bastard!' Johnny spat.

'You're crazy, bro!' Charles countered, still gripping the coil.

But the younger man was persistent, strong despite his lean, wiry physique.

Charles climbed the counter, his stocky body pressing down on Johnny.

Still Johnny wouldn't desist, instead grabbing 7's dreads, pulling him onto the floor, both men rolling amongst the various pieces of tech and junk piled around them.

The struggle continued, Charles now on top, one hand

pressed against the floor, the other reaching for his own hair, as Johnny kept hold of his dreads and coils.

'Let go of me,' Charles yelled. His hand grabbed Johnny's neck, giving him the edge. 'You're mad, bro, MAD!'

Johnny let go.

7 pinned him on the ground.

In a last ditch attempt, Johnny leaned his head forward, sinking his teeth into Charles 7's leather clad arm.

With his free hand, the tech hack slapped Johnny's face over and over again.

Appalled, Johnny levered his foot up, kicked Charles 7 away, then rolled himself across the floor. He sat up, leaning against the nearby wall. He reached a hand up to his face. It was stinging. He caressed his cheek where Charles had struck him.

'You . . . bastard!'

'Made me do it, bro,' Charles said, still on the floor. 'Messin' with my tech like that. Could give a man a heart attack when he's zonin'!'

'But you *bitchslapped me*?!'

'You pushed me too far, white boy!'

Suddenly, Johnny's anger was gone. His heart was still thumping in his chest, but instead of the rage, he was laughing, doubled over in a way he didn't think possible since Becky.

He looked at the baffled Charles 7, 'Man, that's so *funny*!'

Charles crawled over to the counter, leaned back against it, catching his breath. By the shape of him, Johnny reckoned it was probably the most exercise he'd taken in years. *Real* exercise, anyway.

He rubbed the back of his neck, 'Fuckin' crazy-assed –'

'Oh come on!' Johnny protested. 'You didn't enjoy that? Even a little?'

But Charles wasn't amused.

'Man, you come into my store, tear coils from my head!' He threw his arms in the air. 'Get the hell out of here before I call someone, have them put a cap in your ass.'

Johnny shook his head, walked over and offered Charles 7 a hand to get up.

The other man glared at him, finally accepted.

They stood for a moment, facing each other, both men not quite sure what to do.

Finally, Johnny spoke: 'Please,' he said, 'I need that cash.'

But Charles sighed, shoved his hands in his pockets.

'No can do, bro,' he said. 'Just paid the rent. Fresh out of dollars until I get some more gigs sorted.'

Johnny shrugged. There was nothing else for it. He made for the door, finished with this man and his ramshackle of a business.

'We can trade, Johnny Lyon,' Charles called after him. 'You need a job done, or a nice new cell?'

Johnny's hand already was on the door.

'Store credit, my man. It's yours if you want it.'

'Nothing I'd want to buy,' Johnny said.

He left the store, stood at the doorway, glanced up at the plastic sign above the store, reading TECH REPAIR. He could see Charles through the window, reconnecting.

Jesus, he thought, *hasn't even given himself a minute.*

Johnny blew out some air, went on his way.

TWENTY TWO

Rudlow snapped open his cell.

'Yeah?'

Furlong's voice: 'Got something. Little no-mark that's friendly with our guy. Goes by the name of King. Picked him up round Tomb Street, heading towards Vegas. Mouthy little bastard.'

'Good. Keep him fresh 'til I get there. And Furlong?'

'Boss?'

'Go easy.'

'Sure thing, boss. You know me.'

'That's why I'm telling you to go easy.'

Rudlow snapped the cell shut, sat up.

'Trouble?'

He turned round finding Dolly on the edge of the bed. She wore a red satin garter, one stocking removed to reveal the tattoo on her thigh. It was the profile of a show-girl behind a dark blue fan, flamingo feathers in her hair.

'Lab boys came back on that puke I dug out of Geordie Mac's carpet,' Rudlow told her.

'Charming.'

'Turns out it belongs to some local yahoo named Kenny Fee. Lives with his mom over in Queen's.' He tightened the knot on his tie. 'We ran the place over, his mom squealing at us the whole time 'bout how her boy's done nothing wrong, 'bout police brutality.' Rudlow frowned, 'Didn't get nothing.' He pulled the braces up over his shirt, looked to the ground for his shoes. 'Thought the lead had gone dry, but Furlong picked up his buddy. We're putting the screws on him.'

'That's my boy,' Dolly quipped. 'Always catching the bad guys.'

She leaned forward, found her stocking, rolled it up her leg, attached it to the garter belt. Relaxed back on the four poster. An old jazz song played softly in the background and Dolly hummed along with it absently. In the low lights, Rudlow thought, she looked very beautiful.

'Dolly,' he called.

'That's my name,' she said, 'Don't wear it out.'

'You got anything on this kid? King, you call him.'

Dolly reached for her cigarettes. They were resting on the ivory bedside, next to an old bronze lamp. She lit up, inhaled, breathed out slowly.

'King, you say?' She thought for a moment, Rudlow noticing how her lipstick had stained the end of her cigarette. 'Matter of fact, one of the girls said a guy called by last night. Mouthy. Southern accent. Tried to sell her some crack. Didn't catch his name, but you know what they say,' she inhaled again, held it, exhaled. 'If the cap fits –'

Rudlow glared at her.

'And you didn't think to tell me?!'

Dolly smiled, eyelashes fluttering, cigarette poised in one hand.

She crossed one leg over the other, took another drag, said, 'You didn't think to ask.'

King looked up, face bloodied and lip torn.

He was sat on a chair in the middle of a small, dark room. Beside him was a desk made of faux wood. Above him burned a bright spotlight. There was a fly circling the light, annoying him, annoying the three men towering over him.

'Where is he?' one of them asked.

A plain clothes goon, squat and overweight. He smoked a cigarette, his voice coarse and gravelly.

'Don't know what –'

The man reached quickly, grabbing a tuft of King's hair, tilting his head then pressing the cigarette against his cheek. The burn made King grit his teeth, but he'd be damned if he was going to let this fucker hear his pain.

Goon pulled his hand away, the stubbed cigarette hanging for a moment against King's face before falling away.

'Where is he?'

'Don't –'

A punch across the mouth.

King stifled his moan, shuffled in his chair.

The fly came down from the light, settled on his cheek, flew off again.

Drool leaked from his split lip, a few teeth loose. King spat onto the grey, concrete floor.

He looked up at the man, 'Said I didn't know. You deaf, bro?'

The middle guy stepped forward. Punched him in the stomach. Followed through with a boot to the groin.

This time King did react: 'You fuck!' he moaned, falling from the chair and curling up on the floor.

The pain surged through him like electric, tearing at his groin.

'Just tell us and you can go.'

'I've already told you,' he gasped, 'I don't know what you –'

The middle guy reached for King, lifting him up by the collar, pulling him close to his face, 'If you don't tell me what I want to know, I'm going to kill you. Do you want that? Want to die for this guy?'

King spat, a thick globule of blood landing across the goon's eyes.

'Fuck!' he complained, dropping King to the floor.

The other two men moved in on the felled yahoo.

Suddenly the door opened. A fourth man stood in the light. The others froze on seeing him.

The new guy was tall, slim, wore a long trench coat.

He pulled a hanky from his pocket, handed it to the bettered goon, waited for him to wipe his eyes, steady himself.

'Thought I warned you before about this kind of thing, Furlong,' he said. 'We do NOT do this shit. Do you hear me?'

'He's a scum bucket!' countered Furlong. 'What does it matter how we treat him?'

'When we behave like them, we *become* them. That's why it matters. Now go and clean yourself up.'

The taller man glared at the other men, watching as they left the room, heads bowed. He stood for a moment, deep in thought, before looking to King. Pulled up a chair, sat down opposite him.

'You alright?' he asked.

'Yeah,' King said. 'I'm good.'

The tall man nodded, face drawn and serious.

'Chief Rudlow,' he said. 'Investigating a murder and drugs pull. You're a suspect. Simple as.'

King spat a tooth to the floor. Wiped his mouth. *Chief goon, eh?*

'Nothing to do with me.'

'We've got SLAM cams saying otherwise.'

King thought about that a while.

'Bullshit,' he said. 'They took down them cams. Invasion of privacy and all. Every kid on the street knows that, pal. Try harder.'

'Okay, here's the real deal. You've been pretty loose lipped around town, Mr –'

'King.'

'Mr King.'

'No, just King.'

'Doesn't matter to me. Might matter to the bagman, when he's thinking of something to write on your death cert, though.'

'I'm a young man. Healthy, strong.'

'You're a dead man if you keep peddling that crack.'

'What crack?'

'The crack you tried to sell on Tomb Street. The crack you were telling every Tom, Dick and whore about since killing Geordie Mac.'

'I ain't killed no one. And I didn't steal no crack, either.'

He needed to play this goon carefully. Not get too excited and start running his mouth off. They had nothing on him, save dealing. And he had been smart enough not to keep the goods on his person, stashing it somewhere safe.

He sat quietly, staring Rudlow out.

'You've a friend: Kenny Fee. Can't seem to find him on the streets. Maybe McBride's got him?'

King's face changed.

'How long you going to hold me?' he said.

Rudlow leaned forward in his chair.

'King, you know what McBride will do to you when he finds you? What he's doing to this Kenny guy right now?'

'HOW LONG?!'

A line of spittle left King's mouth, spraying across Rudlow's coat. It was pink, bloody. The fly was back now, excited by the sudden drama. It settled on the desk next to them. Waited.

Rudlow sighed.

'Tell you what, we'll forget about the murder.'

King glared at him.

'What?'

'Geordie Mac, Heroin dealing scumbag. I could forget his murder,' and here Rudlow slapped the fly against the desk, spreading its tiny remains in a red smear, 'as easily as I forget the death of that fly.'

'You're crazy, man.'

'You'd be facing a charge gun if we pinned Geordie Mac on you. Thirty years if some bleeding heart judge swallowed all that bullshit about what a bad life you've had. Out when you're sixty. How does that suit you?'

King laughed. It was a hollow, spiritless laugh.

But Rudlow continued: 'We'll put you back on the street. Stick a mic on you. Wait 'til McBride makes a move, sings to the mic, then crimp him. We'll pin Geordie Mac's murder on him. You can testify, lie, slap him with every damn thing your dirty little hands have gotten away with over the years. Won't bother me. I want McBride. I don't care about you.'

King wasn't impressed. Goon had no hold over him. There was nothing to fear from a man with his back against the wall, his hands outstretched and begging. A needy man was not a powerful man. And Rudlow seemed pretty damn needy right now.

King leaned forward and in a flat, level voice asked again, 'How long you going to hold me?'

TWENTY THREE

It was just shy of midnight.

Kenny had spent the last few days under wraps, paying cash for a small gaff on Water Quarter, keeping his head down, avoiding trouble. But guilt got the better of him. He'd heard King was still on the streets, no doubt peddling crack to anyone and everyone.

Typical, he thought. *Brother can't hold his water.*

Kenny didn't know if King was the man's real name or just some nickname he'd inherited over the years; indicative of his well-earned reputation as a bullshitter. This one time, King told Kenny he'd spent five years in the Barrenlands, trading gold and oil. Kenny didn't believe it. King was a Koy boy through and through. The wind farms and beaches up north were probably as far as he'd ever travelled.

Tomb Street.

Kenny had checked a few places already: eateries, pawn shops, Route 66. Vegas was his next stop, still buzzing despite the late hour. And it was there that he found King, stoned, propping up the bar.

He called as Kenny came through the door, both arms outstretched, a sloppy grin on his face.

Kenny shushed him, pulled up a nearby stool.

'Need to talk to you, man.'

'Have yourself a drink.' King snapped his fingers at the bored looking man behind the bar. 'Get my friend here a glass. And bring us a bottle of your finest Buckfast.'

The Bar Man sighed before reaching for the notoriously expensive drink. Previously made by monks, Buckfast wine had become something of a legend in Lark city. Vegas was the only bar that stocked it, and Kenny always doubted its authenticity. But he placated his friend, nonetheless, accepting the glass.

'You here long?' Kenny asked but the answer was obvious: King was a mess; washed-out face, greasy hair, dog breath. A sliver of light fell across the yahoo's face, a flash of neon from the bar's dated rig, but it was enough for Kenny to notice bruising. 'Hey, what happened your face?!'

But King wasn't listening. His eyes were fixed on a table of young girls sitting across the bar. The girls were giggling, syncing pics or vids to each other's cells.

Kenny grabbed him, 'You're all swollen, man. What happened?!'

King smiled proudly.

'Goons,' he said. 'Tried a shakedown. But they got nothing on me.'

A shiver ran down Kenny's back.

'Jesus, we have to –'

'We have to *nothing*!' King slurred. 'They've fuck all on us. We're untouchable, Kenny Boy. Even said they don't care 'bout Geordie Mac. In fact, they're glad he got crimped.'

'It's not the goons we need to worry about,' Kenny protested. He glanced around the bar before continuing, 'McBride's looking for me.'

King didn't say anything, still staring at the girls.

'Do you know what this means?!'

'No. What does it mean?'

Kenny drew an index finger across his own neck in answer.

'Both of us,' he added. 'So we need to lie low for a while, let this thing pass. You hear me? He'll forget us if he don't hear nothin'.'

King laughed, his wheezy little cackle drowning out the low hum of ambient trance music.

Kenny glanced around, nervously. The Bar Man stood nearby, quietly cleaning a glass, watching them.

'This is fucking serious,' Kenny said through gritted teeth. 'You need to sober the fuck up!'

But King still wouldn't listen. His eyes were on the door. Kenny followed his gaze, finding a small, punky girl enter the bar.

King was grinning ear-to-ear.

'Helllloooo, sweetheart,' he said.

She moved across the bar like a hologram, the sheen of her vinyl drains reflecting the poor, two-tone light. When she reached her table at the back corner, she set her drink down. Removed all of the cushions from the sofa next to the table, piling them up neatly. Only then did the girl sit, leaning forward in her seat, glass held tightly in both hands.

'She's hungry for it,' King said and Kenny didn't have to ask what it was she was meant to be hungry for. 'We'll give her a few minutes to settle herself.'

Kenny grabbed King by the arm, pulling him back around to face the bar.

'Look,' he said, 'this is exactly what I mean! We have to put the brakes on for a while. Keep our heads low. I've got this place over on Water Quarter.'

But King wasn't having any of it: 'You must be fucking kidding me, man. She's the biggest earner we've got! Ever since we offed that little scrotum, Geordie.'

'YOU offed him,' Kenny corrected. 'I had nothing to do with it.'

'You were there,' King said, suddenly a lot more sober. 'You held the door. Can't say you're not involved.'

'Listen you stupid fuck,' Kenny's voice was more raised than he intended, 'we need to lie low and let this whole thing blow over.' He thought for a moment, added, 'Even better, we'll get the stash, head out of town.'

'I've got the stash on me right now,' King said.

He grinned, opening his jacket, showing off several clear plastic pouches.

Kenny couldn't believe what he was seeing. He grabbed hold of King's arm but the older man pulled away, zipped his jacket, stood up and then strolled over to the girl at the back of the bar.

Jesus! Kenny thought, before getting up and following. *Jesus Fuck!*

He reached a second time but King shook him off, his step quickening. The yahoo was still a bit shaky on his feet, the booze affecting more than just his head, but he made it through without tripping, pulled up a nearby stool and sat himself down opposite the girl.

Kenny stood beside the table, still keen to get away.

'How's it going, sweetheart?' King said, his southern accent slurring.

She didn't respond.

'Got your stuff.' King reached a hand inside his jacket, retrieving a small package. 'You can have it right now, if you like.'

King leaned forward and pushed the package across the table towards her. His hand brushed hers but she didn't move, didn't as much as look at him.

'Fuck's sake,' Kenny protested, eyes darting around the bar.

But no one seemed interested. The girls were still busy with their cells. Everyone else was either zoning or staring at the Box in the corner.

'Hey, I'm talking to you, bitch!' King spat. 'Are you some kind of retard or something?'

She still didn't speak, blinking once, setting her water down and wiping her face of spit. Then she lifted the drink in both hands, continued to stare straight ahead.

'Fucking schizo.'

King went to lift the stash, but as he reached across the table, the girl pulled a needle from somewhere and brought it down squarely on his hand. The needle went deep, sliding through flesh, cartilage and bone to spear the bag the yahoo's hand was grasping. The smack burst over the table as King pulled away.

Kenny glared at her, hardly able to believe what she'd done. But her eyes were as blank as ever. There was no soul in this girl.

'You crazy BITCH!' Kenny yelled.

He swung the back of his hand, connecting with her bony jaw. She fell against the cushions stacked to the side of the sofa. Suddenly she started flailing about in panic, as if she'd just fallen onto a bag of snakes.

She was screaming. King was screaming. People were starting to get up from their seats, move towards the doors.

King eased the needle painfully from the pierced hand.

'I'm going to fucking kill that junkie whore!' he spat, pulling a switchblade with his other hand.

He stepped forward, but a sound from behind stalled him.

As Kenny watched, powerlessly, the man he'd known for years as simply 'the Bar Man' aimed a charge gun to the back of King's head. He flicked the trigger switch, sucking up power from the battery and jettisoning it out in a blinding white light. It seemed to go straight through King, the poor bastard's skull turning to pink mash almost instantaneously.

Kenny stepped back as his friend's body fell, close to where the still hysterical girl lay.

He looked up, found the charge gun aimed in his direction.

'Don't move,' the Bar Man said.

TWENTY FOUR

Two a.m. and Johnny was still working.

When he got started on a project, it was difficult to stop. He would live and breathe it. When his body fell asleep, pushed to sheer exhaustion, his mind would dream about it. It consumed him. It became his life, raison d'être, religion.

His fingers hurt, forever sifting the layers of touchscreen, burrowing through the code. But Johnny kept going. He was determined to finish this.

The MAGIC MOMENTS VR: it was good, sure, but it wasn't *perfect*. The VR would say things that Becky wouldn't say. Once, twice perhaps, Johnny's own mind had too much control over the experience, and Becky didn't seem real enough to him.

But it didn't matter.

It was something that Sarah had said which got him thinking. The real Becky was lost to him, gone forever. He knew that, he accepted it. And the Charles 7 incident helped him get over it (in a weird way). Becky's smile, her habits, her ways: these were things he would forget. She was gone and all he had was her legend. What was important was not *how* Johnny remembered her, but the fact that he *would* remember her.

Likewise, the historical Jesus meant nothing. Facts, figures: unimportant. It didn't matter a damn how he was portrayed by those who wrote about him, whether in the bible or some Netpage nuthouse. It only mattered what the user *wanted* him to be, *needed* him to be. After all, the customer was always right.

(Right?)

Johnny knew how important this Jesus project was. The Alt Corp elite were circling Garçon like hungry loan sharks, dangerously close to pulling the plug. Maybe that's why Garçon was offering him a blank cheque pay rise if he could make this thing work by the end of the week. Of course, if there was any truth in what he'd heard, that cheque was hardly worth a dime.

But Johnny wasn't doing this for the money. He wasn't doing it for Garçon either. Johnny had an entirely different reason: he wanted to be distracted. Because despite what he told himself, despite what he was feeling, Becky Lyon wasn't gone just yet.

In the corner of his touchscreen, the small envelope icon persisted. Still calling him. Becky's name was written beside it. But Johnny was afraid of that e-mail. Afraid of the many, many things it might reveal.

It wasn't that he ever thought she'd have an affair. Not since their first year, the early days when Johnny thought himself way too lucky to have a girl like Becky on his arm; when practically every man she walked past was a man who could take her from him. No, Johnny had been feeling quite secure in recent years. Complacent, comfortable, maybe even lazy. In fact, there were even days when he saw Becky as something that *wasn't* special or magical.

But that icon in the corner of his screen might say something destructive, something that poured mockery over their whole relationship.

Maybe, as Johnny had suspected, she too had become complacent, and Becky wasn't one to deal well with complacency. She feared it, like others feared death. For Becky, it was little better than death. Boredom was not something she handled well and Johnny had that small comfort in all of this: her death had been anything but boring. It was violent, tumultuous, tempestuous. But never boring.

The e-mail could change everything or it could change nothing. A flipped coin, 50/50 as it spilled across the screen, telling him exactly what was going through her head on that last day, the day before the hospital and the doctors and the (not so) pretty nurses descended upon them like vultures and ripped their lives apart.

Johnny looked to the screen, its layers spread open, a collage of colours and text and image files dancing literally before his eyes.

That e-mail.

TWENTY FIVE

Kitty opened her eyes to find herself in bed. It wasn't her own bed, the old stained mattress from her Tomb Street apartment. No, this was her mom's bed. The bed she remembered so vividly from her childhood.

Nothing had changed. The same luxurious duvet that would have wrapped her mom like white mink now wrapped Kitty.

Several pillows cradled her head, puffed up like silk clouds. Yet Kitty didn't fear these pillows, didn't feel the need to stack them on the floor like she stacked the cushions from the bar or church. She felt relaxed, comfortable, pulling the duvet tight against her naked body, the softness of the fabric making her skin tingle.

This was bliss. This was better than a hit.

Kitty rolled over, content to slip back into a long, deep sleep, to allow whatever nightmares she had experienced to drift away and be forgotten.

But something wasn't right.

Her eyes opened again, searched the room.

She could smell burning.

The duvet suddenly became less like the soft clouds

from her childhood and more like thick bellows of grey smoke. Flames rose up from the mattress. The pillows caught fire, spreading, catching Kitty's hair.

She snapped up, patting her head, but the flames kept thriving, the room now an inferno, curtains like two fiery pillars on either side of the window.

The glass blew out, its sound deafening, the fire now roaring all around her.

Kitty started to scream but where noise should have come from her mouth she heard only a deep, low moan, a sound she did not recognise as her own.

The room became silent then, even though the flames still lapped at everything around her.

Kitty screamed again, but still couldn't hear her voice, only that crackling moan; a deathly carp, a last desperate gasp, a drawing in of breath where there was no breath.

The bellow of the flames returned, furious now, and Kitty saw a figure, sitting opposite her at the other side of the bed.

It looked like her mom.

She was dressed in her fairytale gown, sitting peacefully while the flames spread across her body. But where her face should have been, Kitty saw only an old pillow. Acrylic stuffing hung from its open seams. The pillow face *wasn't* burning, somehow immune to the flames.

And then her mom spoke.

'You can change it,' she said. 'You can change every-thing, make it better again.'

But the voice wasn't her mom's. It wasn't even female, the pillow-shaped face morphing into a man's face, the fairytale gown now a blood stained white tunic, ripped and torn, deep red scars beneath its fabric.

She woke with a start.

Pulled the wiretap off, patted her hair, her face. But there were no flames.

Again, she was back in her mom's room. The look, feel, smell was familiar to her. The bed felt smaller as a grown-up; a lot more compact. Less like the landscape of endless white clouds she knew as a little girl.

The pillows were removed and the bedding unfurled; both stacked, safely, at the bottom of the open wardrobe across the room.

Kitty was still dressed in her New York Dolls tee and vinyl drains. Her flat slip-ons sat on the floor by the door.

A spent needle lay dead on the bedside table.

Her cell sat beside it, the coil running onto the bed.

An empty glass sat beside the cell. It was crystal and Kitty found herself staring at it for a second. It was the same glass she remembered from years ago, the one Paul McBride would carry up on its tray, accompanied by a plastic brown bottle with a label Kitty could never read.

The plastic bottle held her mom's pills. They were supposed to make her feel better but Kitty remembered her mom feeling worse. That brown bottle was the sign that their games were coming to an end for the day. A serious-ness would descend upon the room and Kitty would have to leave.

She remembered standing by the door watching as her mom would sit up, face solemn and suddenly drawn. Her dad, Paul McBride, would drop a single pill into her out-stretched hand. Her mom would throw the pill into her mouth, wash it down with some water, then set the crystal glass down onto the bedside table. Paul McBride would then kiss his wife on the forehead. He would pat the pillows then lift the duvet up, wait for her to lie down again.

Kitty lifted the glass with both hands, sniffed it. There was a little water left in the bottom. She downed it, paused, set the glass back on the bedside table.

She could hear something from downstairs. Shouting, crying. Kitty sat still for a moment, listening. It wasn't much different to the sounds she would hear on Tomb Street. The ugly close of night, the angry resistance to a sober, stark dawn.

But Kitty wasn't in Tomb Street now.

She pulled herself from the bed, wandered over to the window, opened the curtains. The dirt road outside was familiar; the same old house across the way; the garage on the corner with its usual cartel of gasheads, stripping old engines and cars.

Another screech from downstairs.

Kitty retrieved the glass from the bedside cabinet.

She opened the bedroom door, stepped out.

From the landing, she could hear the noises more clearly. Screams of protest. She could even make some words out: someone was begging, pleading for their life.

Gingerly, Kitty proceeded down the stairs, both hands still wrapped around the glass.

She reached the hall, allowed one hand to open the door straight ahead.

The kitchen hadn't changed much in the years she'd been away. Cabinets lined the far wall, cooker and fridge to the right alongside the sink and washer.

It was cramped.

Her mom would have talked about extending the kitchen. It seemed to be what would happen *when things got better*, when she was able to leave her bedroom and get out of her princess gown. *We'll extend the kitchen*, she would say, just before she took her tablet. *And we'll hold a party, get people round, play some music*. Her face would light up, and she would hold her husband's hand. But then Paul McBride would whisper something in her ear and she would take her tablet and her face would grow soft and empty.

Kitty walked through the kitchen, crystal glass still in her hand.

There was a man tied to a chair in the centre of the room.

The Bar Man stood over him. He wore a white, blood-stained shirt.

The man in the chair was barely recognisable. His face was torn and bruised, his eyes hidden beneath swollen folds of skin, purple and veiny like red cabbage. He struggled against the binds. Screamed at her, as she passed, but Kitty didn't pay heed.

The Bar Man punished him.

Another screech, more crying. And then the pleading.

This was familiar. As a child, Kitty remembered the same sounds drifting upstairs, her mom smiling, kissing her gently on the forehead. *Shhhh*, she would have said, then sang something they both knew, something Kitty could sing along with.

Paul McBride stood at the other side of the kitchen, his apron also bloodied. Kitty ignored him too, reaching her glass into the sink and filling it quietly. She drank deeply, wiped her mouth with the other hand, then dipped the glass for a refill.

There was another screech.

'Shut him up for a minute!' McBride barked.

He looked to Kitty.

'Sleep okay?'

'You wired me,' she said. 'Doped me out. So of course I slept.'

She drank some more, emptied the dregs back into the sink, set the glass on the edge of the draining board.

She went to leave.

McBride grabbed her arm, pulled her back.

'I'm only trying to help,' he said.

'What did you wire me to?' she snapped, pulling her arm away.

'Eh?'

'The VR. What was it?'

But McBride didn't seem to hear her. From the other side of the kitchen the man on the chair was sobbing heavily, each sob peppered with speech: 'I didn't touch him. . . I swear to God, I didn't touch him.'

'He's the one who got Geordie,' McBride told Kitty. 'Recognise him?'

Kitty drew closer and stood for a while looking at the man on the chair. He hardly seemed human anymore, like one of those vids from the Holy War where bodies would be stacked in mass graves, one the same as the next. Then he spoke, a nonsensical mess of words and tears, as if he was speaking from under water. The voice was familiar.

Kitty drew closer.

His mouth twisted, hawking up some bloody mucus.

He spat at her.

Kitty felt the gob strike her face. She blinked, reached quietly for a tissue from the nearby worktop, wiped her face then dropped the tissue to the floor.

As she went to pass, she saw the Bar Man move in again.

The bound man's screams came more strained this time. They sounded like the desperate moans from her dream.

TWENTY SIX

Kenny was in freefall.

He was light headed, the constant hum in his ears almost musical. His body felt so pathetically soft and disjointed that he believed he might just lift off and fly out the window.

A day ago, he would have given anything to do that. But now, he didn't care. He didn't feel pain anymore.

After the first few hours, his body had gone into shock, his heart beating so fast and hard that the noise seemed to lull him into a deep trance, where nothing seemed real.

A few hours later and even his heart stilled.

Now, he felt weak, sleepy.

A warm sweat coated his skin.

His mouth and nose seemed to have melted, Kenny feeling only a damp, useless mess where most of his face was.

One eye had closed over completely. He saw nothing with that one. Nothing at all. The other opened then closed sporadically, seeing everything as if through a green-tinted movie screen, like he had somehow transcended the room and the chair and was now watching the scene of his own demise unfold in some old horror flick.

Paul McBride stood in front of him. His apron was stained red. Pieces of Kenny's skin were stuck to the apron, hanging from the plastic like little scraps of meat.

McBride was holding a razor blade. Nothing fancy. Nothing hi-tech or modern. Just an honest-to-God, old-time razor blade. He was using it to peel Kenny like an overripe fruit. Slowly, carefully. Each cut measured, controlled, before wiping the blade on his apron.

At times, Kenny would watch with his one good eye as McBride worked at him, brow furrowed, choosing his spot and moving towards it with the blade, like a surgeon performing a particularly difficult procedure.

At other times, he would just rest, the procedure going on around him. A particularly rough, hard-to-get lump of flesh might jolt him awake. A sudden surge of pain (or reminder of pain) would briefly run through his body, causing him to shake all over. But then the numbness would return, settling through his body like a warm drink.

When the kitchen door was open, he watched the Box playing in the corner of the living area. He remembered an episode of DEATHSTAR, where that old guy with the dark, floppy hair and rubber skin was strapped to a chair, just like the one he was in, and the show's hosts Kal and Val were feeding him live spiders. The cam closed in just as the poor old bastard was starting to gag; a thick foam spewing through his lips. *Rather you than me, pal*, Kenny thought.

Once, during the second day, Kenny opened his eye to find no one in the kitchen at all. The next time he looked, he found that little Tomb Street whore up close to his face, studying him. When he looked again, McBride was back in the hot seat, sat across from him, carving away with that razor. Only, behind him there were more McBrides. Dancing McBrides, wearing not aprons but long, flowing dresses and little tiaras.

Kenny went to laugh, ended up coughing.

McBride paused for a moment, blade in the air, before returning to the work at hand.

Now, the girl was in the kitchen again. The Tomb Street whore. She stepped over Kenny's feet as if he was no more than some drunk, sleeping it off outside Vegas. He went to say something to her, again, forgetting about the moist, useless mess where his mouth used to be and how it didn't work too good.

But Paul McBride stopped him. He tapped Kenny's chin with the edge of the blade.

'Are you ready to talk yet?'

Kenny grunted.

He thought a moment about what he would say, about what had led up to all of this, and all of a sudden fear returned. It ran through him like VR, quickening his pulse, shortening his breath. His throat felt dry.

Suddenly the Bar Man was there and a cocktail glass with a straw was presented. Kenny sucked at the straw greedily, allowing the liquid (whatever it was; probably water but Kenny couldn't tell: his taste buds recognised nothing save the salty, coppery taste of his own blood) to dampen his mouth as it moved on through, sliding down his throat.

'Do you know why you're here?' McBride asked him.

Kenny tried to respond, but could not.

McBride reached to the nearby table, retrieving a notepad and pen. He sat them onto Kenny's lap.

'Use that,' he said. 'Write it down.'

Someone untied Kenny from behind.

He reached his freed hands out, looking them over with his one good eye. They were clean, free of blood or wounds. Kenny could see his nails, the fine hairs on the back of his hands.

He stared at each of his fingers, marvelling at how well they worked. He couldn't feel them, though, and it took him a while to notice they were shaking, at first thinking it was his vision that was wrong.

That damn Pirate's eye.

Kenny went to laugh again, but little more than blood came out of his mouth.

'Go on,' he heard McBride's voice again.

Go on where?

And then he remembered. They wanted him to say something. To write it down.

'Why are you here?' McBride reminded him.

Slowly, Kenny stretched out his hand, reached for the pen. He wrote one word on the notepad on the table, then set the pen down. He checked the word, just to make sure it was the right one. *Geordie*. The letters were off, a little shaky, maybe, but they couldn't blame him for that, could they? No, it was still the right answer. He knew this one. *Easy.*

McBride looked at the notepad.

'That's one thing,' he said. 'But it isn't the worst of it.'

Kenny stared back at him, baffled. He tried to say something, again failing.

McBride pointed to the notepad, 'Write it down.'

Kenny reached for the pen again, pausing as he considered what else McBride would want.

He wrote another word: *Dealing*. Checked it again, satisfied that it too was the right answer.

He thought back to King, stumbling around that little whore's table, blood seeping between his fingers. The needle in her hand. The Bar Man's charge gun behind King's head, firing, spreading the poor fucker's brain across the wall.

McBride checked again.

The Bar Man stood behind him, waiting then reading the notepad with McBride. It reminded Kenny of school. He was a slow learner, always last to get stuff right. He remembered the teacher working something out on the projection, hoping, praying that Kenny would give her the right answer so everyone could go home, call it a day.

'No. It's more than that,' McBride said.

He called to the girl.

She turned, looked at Kenny as if he wasn't even there.

'Do you know who she is?' McBride asked him.

Of course he did. The junkie whore. The reason why King's brains were spread across the wall in Vegas and he was strapped to this fucking chair.

'She's my little girl,' McBride said through gritted teeth. 'Do you hear me? *My little girl!*'

Really? Kenny wanted to say, and he reached for the pen and paper again to do so. But McBride stopped him, pushing Kenny's hand away, looking at him then stepping back, a charge gun in his hand.

TWENTY SEVEN

It was late. The office was closed, but Johnny was still in the building.

He wore a wiretap, putting the final touches to the Jesus program's main code via the VR itself.

He was taking a lot of shortcuts. Hadn't installed the damn thing's firewall yet, for one thing. If anyone hacked this shit in its present state, it could royally fuck with their head. But Johnny needed to give his baby a proper test run. Just to be sure he had the basics in place.

The main menu fired up and Johnny found himself sitting on a bench in a wooded area. He immediately recognised it as a place where he loved to play as a child. A place where he felt secure. This was the basic brief of the program, to merge with the user's mind, pluck out comforting images from the sub-conscious and drag them to the forefront.

Everything was working so far.

An icon saying BEGIN hung in the air in front of him.

Johnny pressed his hand against the icon, watching it split into a thousand pieces.

A soft hum sounded in his ears. The Alt logo hovered in the air, the hum continuing. Both faded after a few short moments. This was meant to build momentum but he'd need to work more on the lead-ins, make sure the VR code was merging with the various APPS for music, lighting, colour. Just basic trouble-shooting, really. Nothing Johnny was in any way worried about.

A rustle sounded in the trees.

From the wooded area, a figure emerged.

Johnny recognised the figure as Tonto from that old *Lone Ranger* serial he used to watch on the Box as a kid. Tonto was played by a white actor, doused in brown face paint. It was an odd choice for Jesus, but – to Johnny's subconscious mind – this was what The Good Lord should look like. He would roll with it for now. Later, he could add a standard AI doll.

Johnny cleared his throat.

'Jesus?'

He felt slightly embarrassed and more than a little overwhelmed. Johnny had been doing a lot of reading and if there was one thing pretty much everyone agreed on, it was this: Jesus was a badass.

The Roman emperor, Constantine, had been a big fan. God had allegedly appeared to Constantine before battle, writing *In Hoc Signo Vinces* or: 'In this sign, you will conquer' across the sky. Constantine instructed his soldiers to inscribe the mark of Jesus on their shields, placing them under divine protection.

It was the mark of the cross: a large X.

Constantine won the battle outright, marking the western world as Christian for the next two thousand years, give or take.

Of course, many wars, schisms and purges followed. All in the Jesus' name. And here was the paradox of it all: in the primary source material, a series of books credited to his closest friends and supporters, Jesus was an altogether different man. Sure, he still had balls – regularly standing up against the establishment, lending him a revolutionary, Che Guevara vibe – but his raison d'être seemed more about peace, about reconciliation than war.

Johnny had every reason to be starstruck.

Jesus drew closer, sitting himself down on the bench.

'How are you, Johnny?' he asked.

'I'm fine,' Johnny said. 'No glitches yet, so I'm a happy bunny.'

Jesus chuckled softly.

'But are you, Johnny? Is this what makes you *really* happy?'

Johnny was thrown. He had thought that, being the AI's creator, he would somehow be immune to its power. But the code had dug right into his very soul, just as it would do to every other user, and it had found him wanting.

'What do you know about me?' Johnny tested.

Jesus smiled. He was programmed to never get riled, never to get defensive, no matter how aggressive the user became. He was programmed to diffuse any situation which presented itself in a way which the user would feel comfortable. He would reach inside the user's head and, simply, find out what he/she would find acceptable.

'I know you miss her,' Jesus said. 'I know you want to save her, just as I want to save you.'

Johnny stared at the VR doll's face. The beta graphics didn't allow for much expression, but it seemed like Jesus was genuinely concerned for him. For a moment, Johnny forgot that he was dealing with a program. *His* program.

'You don't know what you're talking about.'

'Maybe', Jesus agreed, 'but *you* know what I'm talking about.'

The woodland was suddenly gone. Johnny was transported to Becky's bedside. The maudlin doctor and (not so) pretty nurse stood in their places, retiring to their respective roles. And then there was the star, Becky Lyon, lying on her death bed.

Jesus handed Johnny a goblet of what seemed to be wine.

'What is it?' Johnny asked.

'It's the cure,' Jesus said. 'You give it to her and she'll live.'

'Fuck you,' Johnny said. 'I want you to stop this right now. Go to my safe place.'

'Is that what you really want?'

'No,' Johnny said quickly.

He looked at the cup. He could feel the grief return. The tears he'd thought long gone welling up in his eyes again.

He took the cup, kneeled by the bed.

Becky looked up at him, her face torn but still beautiful.

She went to speak and it was as if she wanted to tell him something important, maybe the content of her e-mail that still lurked in his inbox.

But Johnny stopped her.

'Shhhh,' he said, pressing his finger to her lips.

He reached his hand behind her neck. He tilted her head forward, easing the end of the goblet to her lips. He tipped it slightly, allowing the wine to flow through her dry, parched lips.

The transformation was instant: it started with Becky's lips, the colour easing its way through her face, filling her features out, filling the gaunt, sallow bones with rich, healthy flesh. It reached her scalp, thickening out the tufts of bleached out ginger to create her thick, flowing red locks.

Johnny moved his hands through her hair, greedily. He could smell her shampoo, her perfume. And then she looked at him, brighter, healthier and she smiled.

It was a generous smile. Johnny could see her teeth and it broke him.

He pulled away from her. Returned to Jesus.

'Take me back,' he said. 'I want to go back now.'

And so they were back. Back in the park, on the plastic bench. His 'safe' place.

Johnny was quiet for a second. A soft breeze caressed his face as if to comfort him.

He pulled the wiretap from his face.

It was light outside the office windows and he realised he'd been working on the program all night.

There was someone behind him.

Johnny turned round, finding Garçon.

'Give me some news, Johnny boy,' the company man pressed.

'It's working.'

'Hallelujah!'

Garçon threw his hands into the air. Grabbed Johnny by the shoulders, shook him.

'This will make you, boy,' he said. 'I can see it now. Your name up in lights.'

He released Johnny, made a gesture with his hands as if to imitate said lights.

But Johnny wondered just what it was that this VR was going to make him. A fraudster, perhaps? Exploiting hopes and fears in exchange for some binary coded charade; a soulless piece of tech offering nothing more than a conduit for people to lie to themselves.

He thought of Becky on the bed, healthy again; smiling at him as if he'd saved her. The Jesus doll smiling piously beside him.

Johnny thought of how empty he felt after using the program.

But he wanted to use it again.

TWENTY EIGHT

Billy lived in Koy Town, forty miles south of Lark City centre. Once bandit territory, gasheads used to roam Koy's dirt roads, preying upon any vehicles stupid enough to venture too far south on their own.

But the natives weren't as restless as they used to be.

There was an oil well somewhere round these parts. The gasheads refined it, exporting gasoline on the black market. Word had it McBride had won the whole damn lot in a card game. And it seemed to Billy like he had won the gasheads' trust too, taming the locals to the point where the old place became less of a hellhole, and, dare he say it, more habitable.

Few people actually lived here, though.

McBride's place sat on the main road. It was once a busy throughway into Lark, back when fossil fuels were all the rage. Now it was just another dirt track.

McBride still traded a lot of fuel tech, dealing out of an old garage at the side of his gaff. There were always gasheads hanging around, revving their bikes and pinstriped hotrods, stripping engines and bodywork, but they gave no trouble.

Billy's place sat right across the road.

At fifty two, the security man was still single. He had never really dated much in his life. Led a simple life, getting the hydrosteam train into town, working twelve hour shifts, six days a week, plonked behind the monitors of Alt Lark.

On his one day off, Billy would stay in Koy. He liked the seafront, taking brisk walks along the beach, looking out on the line of solar pyramids circling Maal. Those things had always fascinated him.

He remembered back when he was a kid, holidaying with his folks down on the south western part of the island, where the sun shone brightest and the pyramids seemed to glow on the horizon like precious stones.

Pop was a tech guy, working the power plant all his life. He would explain the whole process to Billy, how the sun would provide energy in two ways. First, heating the glass panels to give solar. Then boiling the water beneath, feeding an endless supply of steam through m5 coil, the compressed air either stored in pods, for use in hydro powered tech, or connected to turbines, supplying heat or electricity.

The old man was a firm believer in renewable power, heartily signed up to Alt's manifesto.

'To think there wuz days when all folks burned were fossils,' he would say, cigarette dangling from his lips, one callused hand pointing out the sea or the sky, 'when Ol' Lady Nature had all this on tap.'

Further along the shore, Billy would meet the wind farms, their tall lithe rods stretching high in the air, seducing the boisterous sea air, powering their own turbines. But Pop didn't rate them.

'You're either a sun guy or a wind guy,' he used to tell Billy. 'And wind guys are always trouble.'

Last night Billy heard something from McBride's place.

The screaming started around 3 a.m. It was piercing at first, dulling after the first couple of hours. It was unusual for it to continue for so long. Usually, whatever methods Paul McBride used to dole out justice were swift.

But last night, someone was getting their dime's worth. Someone had angered Paul McBride and was feeling his full wrath.

Billy closed the door behind him, stepping onto the street and moving towards the train stop half a mile down the road. He carried his bag, as always, containing his lunch box and cell. He made his lunch every morning, after downloading the papers, drinking his coffee and lighting up his first cig of the day. Billy was a man of routine; set times for set things.

As he reached the station, he met the Bar Man, standing on the platform. It was weird to see him outside of Vegas. He looked older in daylight.

Billy hadn't been to Vegas in years. He wasn't a fan of nightlife. He knew the Bar Man more by reputation. This was a notorious figure round Lark, an enigma. Some even questioned the man's humanity, citing him as evidence that extra-terrestrial life forms walked among us, or that AI had developed even further, creating fully functioning tech that looked human, talked human . . . but *wasn't* human.

'Got a light?' the Bar Man asked, producing a cigarette.

Billy fumbled in the pocket of his anorak, found his light. He lit the other man's cigarette. Found one for himself.

'Nice morning,' Billy said.

The Bar Man nodded, said nothing.

Billy looked to the station screen, noting the train was going to be slightly delayed. He cursed to himself, considered moving to the other side of the platform, pulling his cell out to read. But that would be rude and, while Billy was many things, rude he weren't.

'You working early today?' he said.

The Bar Man drew on his cigarette, exhaled, then said, 'Nope. Working late.' His head turned slowly, narrow eyes finding Billy's face. 'Sometimes I like to watch the trains pass,' he said, then turned back, staring into space again.

'That a fact,' Billy said.

He looked at the screen, again. Noticed an ad running; the word SALVATION written in bold neon. The Netpage address written underneath was familiar, one of Alt's pages. *Another VR flop for Garçon,* he mused.

He drew on his cigarette, exhaled.

'What about you?' the Bar Man asked.

Billy startled.

'Er, yeah. I'm heading into town. Work at the Alt building, down by Titanic. Do security there.'

'Alt Corp, eh?'

'Yep. Biggest company on Maalside.'

The Bar Man was quiet for another moment, lifting the cigarette to his lips, breathing in, breathing out again. A rhythm to every movement.

'So, which is better in your opinion?' he asked Billy. 'Sun or wind?'

The question threw Billy and he had to think for a while before answering.

'Cost-wise, it has to be sun,' he began. 'With sun you get more bang for your buck. Steam and solar: two in one deal.'

He thought of his pop, long since gone. The old man had died of a stroke, his mom blaming the plant and the long hours he'd spent there.

'Plus,' Billy said, 'My old man was a tech guy. Worked at the plant, draining steam all his life. He always said that wind guys were trouble.'

The Bar Man dragged on his smoke.

'Why's that?'

'Full of hot air,' Billy said, grinning.

The Bar Man didn't flinch, eyes front and centre, poise still rigid. But there was the hint of a smile across his face. Billy could see it.

'Thanks for the light,' he said, dropping the butt, stubbing it out on the platform with his shoe.

As he went, Billy noticed something that he wished he hadn't: a small trace of red on the man's shirt collar.

It looked like blood.

He got into work at about 7 a.m.

He would usually meet Janice outside the building, but

she wasn't there this morning. *Must be running late again*, Billy mused.

He slipped his spare key card into the door's reader, waiting for the reassuring beep. He entered the correct code before waiting for the shutters to rise. Unlocked the front doors and pushed them open.

He entered the building's foyer, taking his jacket off and sitting himself into the swivel chair of the security desk, where he spent the majority of his life. He opened a drawer, placing his lunch box inside.

Billy took his cell out of his bag, flipped it open and rested it on the desk, next to the security screen. He had downloaded a new novel and was looking forward to getting stuck in.

He took a glance at the security screen, ever buzzing, offering surveillance of key points inside and outside of Alt's skyblock. Only the private offices were allowed complete privacy and it was to one of them that Billy saw two men enter.

He felt his heart leap.

He moved closer, pressing the controls of the touchscreen, trying to get a better picture of the unidentified men, but it was too late. He wondered if it was Johnny and Garçon, maybe – he knew Garçon had his own keycard and would often stay late or come in early. Johnny had borrowed a second keycard a few days back. That was the most likely explanation, right? Johnny and Garçon, working into the small hours.

His cell began to buzz, causing him to jump. Billy picked up the cell and accepted the call without checking to see who it was.

'Billy,' came a nervous voice. It was Janice.

'Slept in again?' Billy replied, but there was no humour in his voice, his eyes still on the security screen.

'Listen, Billy,' she said, 'Kenny hasn't been home in days. Goons called at the house, turned the place over. I need to find him. Can you cover for me?'

'What?'

'Cover for me,' she repeated. 'With the cleaning, I mean. Just take the bad look off the place: give the floors a lick with the vacuum and wipe the kitchen and dining areas down. All my stuff's in the cleaning cupboard on the –'

'I can't be cleaning floors today,' Billy snapped. 'Listen, Janice, there's someone in the building. I've got to –'

'PLEASE!'

There was a desperation in her voice that he hadn't heard before.

Billy looked at the screen again. Seemed the two men were still in Garçon's office. He'd have to go up there. Check out whatever was going on.

'Okay, okay,' he agreed, more to get rid of Janice. 'Just get in here as –'

'Billy,' she said, cutting him off, again. Her voice was low and serious. 'Paul McBride wanted to see Kenny.'

Billy paused.

There was a sharp intake of breath.

It must have been amplified through his cell because she swiftly followed with, 'Do you know anything about this, Billy?'

Still he said nothing, suddenly very aware of himself.

'Do you know *anything*, Billy? Please tell me if you do!'

Billy sighed, shook his head.

'Janice, Paul was in his house, last night. There was something going on.'

He could almost feel her heart stop from the other end of the cell. It was like someone dropping a lead weight in the ocean, the sharp plunge as it sank below the water, lost within seconds.

The call ended.

Billy cursed to himself.

Why did I have to say that?!

He looked to the screen again.

Garçon's face was at the door to his office. He was talking to someone off screen.

Billy breathed a sigh of relief. And then remembered . . .

Damn it. There was no excuse now. He would have to do that cleaning for Janice.

Billy took the lift up to 15. He would climb the remaining 5 floors, use the time to think, plan his words carefully.

After two flights he was out of breath, wondering if he should cut down on all those smokes. He paused on the railings, caught his breath, looked down, watching the stairwell spiral towards the basement. Made a man dizzy.

He made it to the top of the house, manually syncing his cell to open the door into the hall and then into the open plan office. He stalled for a few moments, went through his plan in his head.

20's reception area was empty. To the untrained eye, Janice may well have cleaned it, already. The floors were spotless. She was so meticulous with her work, taking so much pride in it, that Billy was pretty sure the floors could be left for a few days without anyone noticing. Billy decided he'd only do the tidying that needed done, therefore, take the bad look off the place, as she said. Janice could give it a better scrub tomorrow.

His mind fell back to their conversation.

He had lived in the same gaff for the best part of twenty years, right opposite McBride's place. He knew how the man did business. He feared for Janice's boy if he was caught up with him at all. He'd seen a lot of black plastic bags leave that place over the years.

He put those thoughts aside, focused on helping Janice out the only way he could. God knows, she'd kept him sane over the years. Entertaining his stories, shooting the breeze with him, staying later to keep him company. Sure, he hadn't exactly spilled his heart out to her, nor she to him. But her cell call said it all. He was someone she relied upon, trusted. He didn't want to let her down.

He could see Garçon's room at the bottom of the open plan.

The lights were on.

Billy made his way towards the company man's office, suddenly aware of the sweat building under his arms. His heart was beating fast.

It would have almost been easier if it *were* someone sinister in the office. The procedures were clear: he would call for back-up, a single press of his cell's panic alarm, and the whole place would be up in lights back at HG Security. They'd have back-up with him in minutes.

But it was Garçon there, not some yahoo. And it was

unlikely the sleazy bastard would overlook Billy's retrieval of cleaning gear without questioning him. It was also unlikely he could sneak by and get what he needed without Garçon realising. Everyone knew what he was like, how he monitored everything. Janice knew what he was like, hence why Billy was here doing this stupid shit.

Christ! What's the best way to play this?

He wondered what John Doe would do, Doe being his favourite character from all those detective novels he read.

He watched the PI in his mind, breathing out some smoke, tossing a spent cigarette onto the paved street. Burrowed hands now deep within the trench coat, shielded against the cold.

Doe would pull a fly one on Garçon. He would approach Garçon head-on, double-bluff with some perfectly reasonable story as to why he needed to get to the cleaning cupboard.

Yes, that was it! Billy would tell Garçon *exactly* what he was doing. It was the only thing he could do. He would make up some excuse for Janice, something about how she had hurt her leg and he was helping her by getting her stuff, bringing it down for her.

Garçon would buy that, hopefully, without too much hassle – maybe too wrapped up in whatever was going on at his meeting to care about anything the dopey old security guard was saying.

Billy worked on his lines, thinking up some witty intro to help everyone relax – maybe a joke for Garçon – before he would hit him with the dirty big blatant lie.

As he neared the office, he noticed the blinds closed.

Billy thought that a little odd, but still went to the door. He knocked. There was no reply, but he heard voices. One of them was Garçon's.

'We've had someone install the data-bleed, a remote device that even our code guy won't know anything about. With the relevant access details, I'm sure your own boys can extract the –'

Billy knocked.

There was a pause.

Billy pushed the door open, inching in, whistling nervously.

He went with the one-liner, 'Got the blinds closed, Mr Garçon? Must have been a rough night on the –' He stopped talking, clocking eyes on the visitor. 'Chief Rudlow,' he said in a surprised voice. He looked again to Garçon, as if confused. 'Is there a security problem?'

'Ah, Billy,' Garçon said. He stood up, good humoured at first. But then his smile melted. 'I'm sure you can see I'm busy,' he whispered, pulling Billy out of the office.

Blood rushed to Billy's cheeks.

'Mr Garçon, I –'

'Chief Rudlow and I are discussing a *personal* matter,' Garçon said, but he was starting to relax, loosening his grip on Billy, turning the grab into a friendly pat. 'Nothing to do with security, I can assure you.'

Billy smiled.

'Sure thing, Mr Garçon!'

The old bastard seemed guilty as hell. Billy couldn't believe his luck, Garçon was trying to pull a fly one *on him*. He didn't care what the hell the two men were up to, or why he was being so shady. But he decided to use it his advantage.

'I just wanted to let you know,' he started, 'That Janice hurt her leg and I need to bring her gear down to her. Just in case you wondered what I was doing.'

'Yes, of course,' Garçon said, glancing around the open plan without listening. 'I'll let you get on with that.'

He retreated back into his office, closing the door behind him.

Jesus, Billy thought to himself. *That was a breeze.*

To his shame, Billy didn't know which cupboard Janice kept her cleaning equipment in. He knew it was on 20. But there were a lot of cupboards on 20.

He tried the kitchen, first, finding a few bottles of cleaner and disinfectant, as well as a pair of rubber gloves. He still needed the vacuum. He would be able to take his time searching for it, of course, what with his cunning plan having gone so stupendously well.

God, I'm good, he mused. *Doe would be proud of that one.*

Billy moved back out of the kitchen and canteen area and into the corridor leading to the back stairs. There, he tried the back maintenance locker. It was the only place he hadn't looked.

He opened it, and sure enough found the vacuum. Whistling, merrily, Billy reached for the machine, pulling it out, along with its cumbersome tubing. It was ancient, possibly antique, and Billy was suddenly amused by that.

'Garçon, you cheap bastard,' he muttered to himself.

He was just about to close the doors up when something

else caught his eye. A slim black box on the back wall of the maintenance cupboard. A single red light shone from the box. Billy ran a finger over its plastic. It felt new. Shiny to touch. He recognised it, somehow, but couldn't think where from.

Ah, to hell with it. What does it matter?

He closed the door, whistling again.

TWENTY NINE

'Gentlemen,' Garçon announced, holding a bottle of champagne aloft, 'I want to toast to the birth of our new baby.'

'A little early for alcohol, Garçon.'

It was Flynn speaking.

Johnny sensed an uncomfortable silence as Garçon replaced the bottle on his desk.

'Quite right, Mr Flynn,' the company man said, then cleared his throat before calling Sarah up on the intercom.

'Yes sir?' she answered.

'Sarah, bring us some coffee. And a little treat of some description.' Garçon winked at Flynn, smiling.

'What kind of treat?'

His smile faded.

'I don't know, some biscuits or cake. Use your imagination.' His voice was irritable and Johnny could almost swear he heard Sarah curse under her breath before signing off. 'Sorry about that, gents,' Garçon said to his visitors. 'Coffee won't be a moment.'

'Look, Garçon, what say we forget the coffee,' growled Flynn, 'And the cake *or whatever*.' He looked to Goldsmith, shaking his head, 'You know how busy we all are.'

'Indeed,' Garçon said, closing one hand over the other, standing as if to attention, 'and we're set to become busier. And wealthier, dare I say.'

He reached for his cell, syncing to the screen on his wall.

'This,' and he gestured to the screen, 'will be going out at lunchtime today.'

The familiar intro of THE LARKIAN, Maalside's premier news page, appeared. A young woman, who struck Johnny as looking uncannily like Val from the DEATHSTAR show on REALITY EXTREME stood outside Alt Lark, Garçon standing beside her.

She spoke to the cam: 'We're here with Philip Garçon, CEO of Alt Lark, to find out more about a controversial new VR product set to hit the market later this week.

'Mr Garçon,' the cam closed in, 'is it true that you're set to bring religion back to Maalside?'

Garçon looked edgy. 'Yes and no,' he said, tightening his tie, turning his best side to the cam. 'We're all about renewal at Alt Corp. A fresh approach to living. For me, renewal is as relevant to spiritual life as it is to physical life. With our latest product, we're taking VR to a new level, offering a dynamic new way to achieve enlightenment never before experienced.'

'We *are* talking religion here, Mr Garçon, 'Val-alike pressed, 'as in Christianity? This new product is called VR JESUS, after all.'

'Indeed. But there's a lot of confusion over these matters, in modern days. Jesus, as we all know, was used as a lynchpin in the past. Many good men fought in the Holy War, lost their lives, and for what? For a world stripped of its core natural resource?' Garçon frowned, as if saddened by these events. 'Here at Alt Corp, we like to reinvent the wheel, to offer alternative takes on common thinking. When faced with the decline of oil, we offered a fresh way forward, energy sources that were previously sidelined, mocked even until we revitalised them. And we're doing the same with religion, offering a *different* Jesus. A VR experience that makes people feel *good* about themselves, and about life. Isn't that what religion used to be about, before the war?'

'And is it true, Mr Garçon, that you've got the blessing of local clergyman,' and here the reporter checked her cell, 'a Mr Harold Shepherd to help launch the product?'

'*Reverend* Shepherd,' Garçon stressed, 'is not just a cleric. He's a pillar of our community, someone who's done great work for many years, offering kindness to the most troubled amongst us, people others seem unable, or unwilling, to help. We're honoured to have the use of Reverend Shepherd's church to launch our product. It's the Old Crusader on Cathedral Quarter, an important landmark of Maalside. And we're inviting the people of Lark City to come join us at the launch,' he winked, probably involuntarily, before adding, 'or follow it live on all of our city's main billboards, the Box or the Net. We're going to make an occasion out of this launch and we want everyone to join with us in celebration.'

'And people can try this experience for themselves on the night?'

'Yes, they can,' Garçon beamed. He leaned into the

cam, added, 'We'll have free taster sessions available at the church, or via VR. All you need is your cell, coil and wiretap.'

'Mr Garçon, thanks for joining us. Back over to –'

Garçon flicked the screen off. He stood poised in front of his captive audience, perhaps expecting applause. But the room was quiet.

Finally Goldsmith spoke: 'Garçon, just what kind of circus are you planning here?' He looked to the other man for back-up.

'Circus?' Garçon countered, hands raised. 'Mr Goldsmith, VR is a busy market. We want to give our product the best possible chance to shine. This is no *circus*, I can assure you. What I'm planning is a multi-media experience to harvest the best coverage possible.' He waited, holding each of the men's looks. 'Gentlemen, the majority of your finance has been poured into PR for this product. You may already have seen some of our soft-sell marketing, on billboards throughout the four Quarters. Well, we're going to up the ante. We're going to put this city –'

Flynn cut in: 'If Reverend Harold Shepherd is attached to this project, it's good enough for me.' Goldsmith went to add something, but Flynn talked over him, 'I attend the Old Crusader every Sunday. Have done for years. Harold Shepherd's one hell of a preacher.' He looked to Garçon, 'Why didn't you tell me he was involved in this project before now? Hell, I'd have raised *twice* as much cash!'

A knock came to the door, Flynn smiling as Sarah came in.

'Ah, there's that coffee now,' he said. 'And some cake I see.'

Johnny noticed Garçon grin smugly.

Refreshments arrived, Goldsmith taking a rather keen interest in Sarah as she served them.

'Say, you been to that new bar over on Cathedral yet,' he said, wrapping his arm around her waist.

Sarah shared a look with Johnny.

'Which one is that, Mr Goldsmith?' she said, gently easing herself out of his grasp to pass Flynn some cake.

'The Lounge,' Goldsmith beamed. His teeth were like piano keys. 'It's one of mine. Very exclusive. We're having a VIP do tomorrow night. What say you join us, eh?'

His hand found her ass.

Sarah looked to Johnny for rescue but Garçon pulled the code guy aside before he could do anything.

'I'm sure you're wondering why I invited you here this morning, Johnny,' he said, 'but I feel you should be part of every stage of this production, from start to finish.'

'Sir, I'm a little worried about the product's AI,' Johnny broke in, one eye still on Sarah.

Garçon was appalled.

'What?!'

He pulled Johnny out of the office. His face was grave.

'I've ran it a few more times. It's very effective, engages with the mind, digs inside to see what the user wants from it, as we had hoped. But, well, I've felt quite strange since using it. It's a bit like. . .' Johnny glanced around before continuing, lowered his voice, 'Sir, it's like an addiction.'

'There is no such thing,' Garçon snapped. 'Not in business. In business we talk of *demand* for a product and this product is going to be very much in demand!'

He tugged at his collar, face red. It seemed like Garçon was going to explode right there and then. Johnny could even smell his tension, an acrid stench lingering beneath designer perfume.

But Garçon wasn't the only one sweating it. Johnny could not rid himself of this feeling gnawing at the pit of his stomach. Drawing him towards his wiretap, to the Jesus VR and Becky on that bed.

'But sir,' Johnny pressed.

'Johnny, I've just signed off a very generous pay rise for you,' Garçon countered. 'Don't make me regret that.'

And with that he was off, back into his office, hands raised again in celebration, playing the room. Johnny could hear the popping of a cork, Flynn seemingly delighted now his old friend Harold Shepherd was part of this whole shebang, Goldsmith his usual smarmy self.

Sarah appeared, tray in hand, daggers in her eyes.

'Was expecting a rescue back there, Johnny,' she snapped. 'Did you see where he had his hands?'

'Look Sarah, I'm sorry, but I'm under a lot of stress right now.'

'That man was molesting me right there in front of everyone and *you* are stressed?' Her face was red, glasses all but steaming up.

'Just leave it Sarah,' Johnny said. 'You know what these people are like, we both do. The lengths they'll go to in order to get what they want, the people who get hurt in the process. And yet here we are, dancing to their tune.'

For a moment, Sarah just glared at Johnny, but then her face changed.

'What is it?' she said, reaching one hand to his face. 'Something's wrong, isn't it? I mean *really* wrong.'

But Johnny couldn't face her, couldn't face the conversation she'd want to have.

'I need to get back to work,' he said, moving her hand away.

'But Johnny . . .'

'Please,' he said. 'I can't do this. Not now.'

He turned and headed down the open plan, aware of her eyes on him. Already he could feel the itch, the need to work, to get back to the VR code.

The need for Becky.

THIRTY

When she got to the house it was almost eight.

Janice had taken a cab. The driver spoke little English, taking more than a few wrong turns trying to find places she didn't want to go to.

The traffic was a nightmare, lots of eco-fuels suddenly clogging the place up. There was a real motley crew of vehicles now; hydrosteams; solar powers; the occasional gasoline. All doing different speeds, with different capabilities and drivers unversed in how to operate them.

The roads were getting treacherous.

Of all days, there had to be an accident today. Security was tight; the insurance people already flocking the area, measuring, recording and medicating everyone involved with their usual po-faced efficiency. Those suits wouldn't let a scrap of evidence off the road without their say-so. Might look bad in Dispute Res.

Everyone and their dog was rubbernecking to get a look.

Seemed like a head-on collision, from what Janice could work out. One of the vehicles had swerved last minute, avoiding the worst of it, but its driver was still hemmed in behind the doors. He was young, panicked, screaming for help. One of the insurance guys was trying to calm him down.

Seeing the boy there, in pain, probably around the same age as her Kenny, made Janice feel physically sick. Another part of her was mad at the boy; mad that he should get help while Kenny was lying bleeding in some alleyway. Or, worse still, at Paul McBride's place.

It took another two hours to get there; the cab hemmed behind slow-moving traffic; the narrow roads easily clogged. As they pulled up, bittersweet memories of McBride's place flooded her mind. Janice remembered the last time she'd been here, all those years back. She remembered being sprawled across the bonnet of some old Chevy. She remembered McBride, taking her from behind while the engine was still running. The sounds he was making; the things he whispered into her ear as he grabbed her hair. She hated the man, hated everything about him. And she would kill him if he touched her Kenny.

Today, nothing had changed. The same old garage, the same old husks parked out front. Gasheads hanging around, drinking, laughing.

What the fuck are they laughing at?

The Bar Man answered the door. His face was robotic, devoid of any emotion. He looked Janice over, as if she was queuing to get into his lousy bar without the right gear on.

'Is my boy in there?' she asked him.

The Bar Man didn't speak.

'Tell me!'

Still he said nothing.

He went to close the door, but Janice put her foot against it.

He glared at her, outraged by her insolence, this unruly behaviour. Went to grab her, to expel her as if she were some brawling drunk, but she surprised him, moving with greater speed and force, planting her sizable knee against his groin.

He crumpled against the door, Janice pushing him away and bulldozing her way into the hallway.

She pushed the door to the living area open, finding a girl standing in the middle of the room, peroxide hair clumped against her head like wild reeds. There was a glass of water in her hands.

She was staring at the Box.

DEATHSTAR was playing, its sound turned up loud. It was a rerun, some z-list celeb working their way through an old rundown village in the Barrenlands.

The screen formed a sniper's rifle scope, with cross-hairs. It was easy to work out the rules of this game: Z-list needed to grab three red flags, whilst avoiding the sniper fire. He had one flag already. His hand reached for the second, easing out from behind a grey wall. Sweat glistened on the man's face, his breathing heavy and fast. He gripped the flag, pulling it from its base, slipping it under his arm. Took another step forward, then began sprinting to cover, the crosshairs closing in on him.

'Where's my boy?' Janice asked.

But the girl didn't reply. She didn't even register the fact that Janice was in the room, that she'd forced her way into the house, felling the Bar Man. She was glued to the

Box as if hypnotised, as if it were transmitting some mind control you would see in one of those old movies.

Janice pushed past her, opening the door to the kitchen. The scene there was different.

The body of a young man was tied to a chair. It was hard to tell who it was, given how much blood covered the boy's face, but she knew it was Kenny. It *had* to be Kenny.

Paul McBride stood nearby, a charge gun in his hand. He wore an apron, wet with blood. He was tired and out of breath and undeniably burning up with anger.

'Kenny?' Janice gasped, and somehow the body stirred, as if jump-started like some old engine from McBride's garage.

'Mummy?'

A lump of skin fell away from his face. He began to cry, but it seemed to hurt too much. Blood poured from his mouth, pooling in the space on the floor between the chair legs.

Janice went to move him, but the Bar Man was suddenly behind her, grabbing her arms with a vice-like grip. She felt him dig one knee into the small of her back, forcing her to her knees.

'Kenny!' she screamed, powerless to move. 'Oh God, Kenny! No!'

'He fucked with my little girl,' McBride spat, in a voice close to deranged. His hands were shaking now, as he raised the gun again to the back of Kenny's head.

Janice shrieked, teeth snapping, head shaking, every fibre of her body trying to tear away from the Bar Man's grip.

But it was no use.

As McBride clicked the trigger on the charge gun, powering the barrel from the battery, she knew there was only one way to stop him.

'He's your son,' she cried. 'How can you do this *to your own son!*'

THIRTY ONE

Paul McBride sat in the hospital waiting room. He'd changed his clothes and taken a shower but the effects of being up all night, the slow anger that had burned him from the inside out, seemed to wear hard on his face. He looked spent.

Janice sat opposite, her whole body shaking, her eyes round and moist like two freshly polished stones. She stared at the Box in front of her.

DEATHSTAR was playing, as always. It seemed to be all anyone ever watched these days. The z-lister from earlier was lying on the sands of the Barrenlands, his hand gripping a red flag. Blood pooled around his body. Kal and Val circled, excited, reciting cell details for viewers to vote on the task. Percentage graphs ran up and down the screen, showing how viewers were swaying.

'Why didn't you tell me?' McBride asked Janice. His hand gripped a packet of cigarettes and she expected them to crumple in his hand, like one of those anti-smoking vids they used to run.

She didn't answer.

She wanted Paul McBride to leave. All this parental

concern seemed a bit odd. He had tortured the boy, for Christ's sake. He was his father and he had torn strips from the boy, carved him up like a butchered animal.

Paul sighed heavily, looked to the Box. His eyes were glassy, deep set into his head as if hiding. Janice could see his daughter in him. That little junkie whore from the house, standing in the living room, doped out and clueless to the real world. And he had the nerve to pass judgement on her Kenny.

'Tell me, I need to know,' he protested and she could see his desperation; a vulnerability, a neediness that men like Paul McBride would usually die before showing to the world.

She thought back to her days at school, back whenever religion was still taught. They were studying violence, cruelty within the world faiths. It was meant to help them understand the Holy War. She was told the story of Abraham, said to be father of all three major faiths involved in the Holy War. How he'd been asked by God to sacrifice his own son. How he went as far as to bind the boy, even raise a blade to him. As she remembered, the boy had accepted his fate, embraced it. It had made her cry back then, thinking of her own dad doing that to her.

'Mr McBride,' the doctor said, entering the waiting room.

McBride stood up, slipping the pack of cigarettes back into his jacket pocket.

The doctor glanced at Janice, before addressing McBride: 'The good news is that he's out of danger.'

'Oh thank God,' Janice gasped.

But the doctor ignored her, once more addressing McBride: 'The bad news,' he continued, face drawn and voice low,' is that he's lost his right eye. There is also likely to be serious scarring to his face, particularly around the nose and mouth.'

Janice noticed McBride dip his head.

'C-can I see him?' she asked.

The doctor looked at her and then to McBride, who nodded.

'We've given him something for the pain,' he said, this time looking to Janice, 'he's conscious, but –'

Janice felt something rise from within her throat, escaping in a high-pitched keen. She put a hand to her mouth, tried to choke it back.

The doctor glanced around the waiting room, smiling in apology at the other people seated.

He motioned to McBride and Janice, inviting them to follow him.

McBride moved, but Janice stopped him, raising her hand, 'Don't,' she said. 'Please,' she added when he went to reply.

The doctor waited.

Janice held his eyes until McBride nodded once more, stepping back and returning to the waiting room.

Janice followed the doctor, finding Kenny in a private room paid for by McBride. Janice had no medical insurance; it was one of the many unpaid bills by her door, stuffed inside a white plastic bag (out of sight, out of mind).

They had cleaned Kenny up, but he still looked awful.

Her little boy, all broken and torn. His wounds were stitched up, white tracks running across his face, highlighting how the blade had travelled. A machine in the corner counted his heartbeats. Kenny's breathing was strained.

Janice bent down by the bedside. She took his hand, planted a delicate kiss on the side of his face. He looked up at her with his one eye. It was wide and alert, somewhere between fear and anger.

'Mummy?' he said, and his voice was a child's voice, reminding Janice of days when her son had two eyes, no scarring in his face and could talk without bloody foam building around that space where his lips used to be.

'Shhh,' she said. 'It's okay.'

She ran her hand through his hair. He was burning up. She lifted a damp wipe from the container by his bed and pressed it against his forehead.

A nurse appeared beside them. Janice stepped back, allowing her to fix various tubes, one to help Kenny breathe, another to drain the moisture building around his airways. The nurse reached for the coil hanging from a stand-alone cell on the wall. Each bed now had one, VR an alternative to pain relief drugs. But Janice wasn't ready to lose Kenny just yet.

'No,' she said, as the nurse went to place the wiretap over the boy's face. 'Give me five more minutes.'

The nurse nodded, smiled in that way nurses smiled. Inoffensively. Quietly.

As she went to leave the room, Janice spoke to her again, 'Is he still waiting out there?'

She didn't need to elaborate on who 'he' might be. The

nurse knew. Everyone in the whole damn hospital probably knew.

'Yes.'

Janice continued wiping Kenny's forehead with the cool damp tissue, said, 'I don't want him near my boy.'

'But Ms –'

'Do you have children?'

The nurse sighed.

'Yes, I do.'

Janice smiled.

'Boys or girls?'

The smile was contagious, now filling the nurse's face as she talked: 'Two boys. One three, the other five.'

'Well, tell me then,' Janice continued, her smile slowly unwinding, 'Would you let a man who could do *this*,' and here she pointed back to Kenny, 'anywhere near them? *Could you?*'

She watched the horror fill the nurse's face as she looked at Kenny. *Really* looked at him. The young woman turned, hand raised to her mouth, and slipped away from the room. And Janice thought to herself, if Paul McBride was to show his face right now, if that young nurse was stupid or scared or heartless enough to let that man through here to see her boy, she might very well kill him.

THIRTY TWO

It was Harold's second visit to the hospital that week. He was here to see Saul Collins, having received a phone call advising that the old lawyer's condition had worsened. Harold was in a hurry, moving quickly through the pristine corridors of white. Then he spotted Paul McBride, sitting alone in one of the waiting rooms.

'Reverend,' McBride said, as the preacher approached.

There was none of his trademark swagger. McBride looked broken and disturbed and Harold couldn't help but respond to that.

'What's happened, Paul? Is it Katherine?'

McBride seemed to think about that for a moment.

'No,' he said. 'Not Katherine.'

Harold found a seat, sat down and waited. . He knew to give the other man time, this well-honed posturing the result of years dealing with the lonely, the destitute and the broken-hearted, often in this very room.

'Did you know?' McBride asked him.

'Know what?'

Paul glanced up at the Box in the corner, as if the answer to the question might be there.

'I have a son.'

He looked sharply at Harold, no doubt searching for some evidence that the preacher had always known this fact but chose to keep it to himself. And that was always the trouble with men like Paul McBride: at their most vulnerable, at their most confused and scared, they looked for others to blame. Harold knew to tread very carefully.

'Paul, I didn't know.'

McBride folded his arms, then relaxed them again. He didn't seem to know what to do or where to put himself.

'I cut him,' he said, suddenly. 'I took a blade and I cut *my own son!*'

But Harold had no idea what he was talking about. He feared that years of violence and paranoia were catching up, that it may soon be time for those waiting in the wings to put Paul McBride out to pasture.

'Harold,' he continued, 'you've always been there for me. You're a good man, a man who knows the difference between right and wrong. Between that which damns a man and that –' His eyes found the Box, again, studying it for a second time, as some ad break rolled. 'I need to know what happens to someone like me,' he said. 'Someone who's caused so much hurt.'

Later, Harold would regret what he chose to do next; how he ignored Paul McBride's words, his fumbling through a confession, and moved in for the kill. But there was business that Harold needed McBride to attend to while he was still lucid enough to do so: God knows; he'd earned the right to take that *one* liberty. And so Harold didn't speak, didn't fish for more words from Paul McBride, or help guide the man to some sort of inner peace. Instead, Harold fumbled in his pocket for his cell, syncing to McBride's.

McBride felt the cell vibrate in his pocket and retrieved it. He read the message.

'What's this?' he asked.

Harold cleared his throat.

'It's every last cent I owe you, Paul. I hope I've calculated the interest correctly, but it can be amended if necessary.'

'You're *paying up*?!'

'In full.' Harold leaned forward in his seat. 'Paul,' he said quietly, 'this will conclude our business together. I want you to remove your . . . ' he paused, carefully choosing his words, '*stock* as soon as physically possible. Today, if it can be arranged.'

But McBride still couldn't believe it.

Harold watched him read the cell again; call up his bank account and double-check the transfer had gone through. He looked to Harold, genuine surprise painted across his face.

'Where did you get that kind of cash?' he said.

But his voice had no clout. And Harold felt empowered by that, as if the threat of Paul McBride was briefly lifted.

'The Good Lord Himself,' Harold replied.

He pointed to the Box, where Philip Garçon was being interviewed, the subtitles along the bottom of the screen talking of the new VR launch at the Old Crusader.

McBride was still gobsmacked.

'What? Is this for real?'

'Yes,' Harold said. 'It's for real.'

A nurse walked by.

McBride called her as she passed, but she ignored him.

He stood up, slipping the cell back into his pocket, Harold and the Old Crusader and the money all forgotten. The old McBride returned, cornering the young nurse and towering over her.

'What's going on?' he asked. 'Tell me!'

She backed away, hands slightly raised.

'There's nothing more *to* tell you,' she said. 'The patient's injuries are serious but he's stable. That's all there is to say right now.'

'I need to see him.'

The nurse shook her head.

'I don't think that would be a good idea.'

'I'm the one paying for that room,' he fumed.

'That's not the issue.' McBride pushed past her, the young woman following, having the audacity to grab his arm. 'Please,' she begged, 'the boy's been through a lot. These are the most crucial hours for his recovery. You don't want to upset that, do you?'

McBride stopped, his eyes finding Harold. There was shame in his face, something Harold had never seen before.

Then he turned heel and left the hospital without another word to anyone.

THIRTY THREE

The Old Crusader was lit up like some Xmas tree.

There was plastic everywhere.

Faux antique wood formed a manger in one corner; AI dolls playing and replaying the nativity scene in fluid, almost ballet-style movements. In another corner, two more dolls stood naked, fending off the snake that had curled around a nearby apple tree.

The pulpit rose up and over a constructed cave, a PVC boulder hemmed in its mouth.

But none of this bothered Reverend Harold Shepherd too much. What *did* bother him was the fact that they'd removed the old wooden cross that would hang on the back wall, replacing it with a horrible neon version. The original cross was out back where the stash used to be. Thankfully, McBride's men had removed their *Good Stuff* before Alt's people moved in.

Garçon ran about the building like a blue-assed fly, licking up to his money men, checking that the hired help were doing what they needed to be doing. Media types hovered around him. Actors had been drafted in; one in the role of preacher; various others to act as fluffers in the crowd. A multitude of cams watched and recorded from every angle.

Harold knew he should feel invaded. Raped, even, on behalf of the church. But this was a damn sight better than the alternative: McBride's stash was history, and, regardless of this temporary upset, the church was free.

Harold had got his old girl back.

Hundreds of people queued outside in the rain, wowed in by the expensive advertising campaign. The Box, the Net, billboards across the city's affluent Titanic Quarter all sang from the same hymn sheet: *I AM THE WAY THE TRUTH AND THE LIFE.* It was a killer hook. Those words alone offered every sucker in Lark City exactly what they wanted. The Old Crusader had never been so busy.

It was around seven by the time the show got started, the first chord of some grassroots country band signalling the beginning of proceedings by playing the classic old jingle, *Plastic Jesus*.

The fluffers were pushed to the front.

Crowds of wannabes filled the aisles, fighting for vid time.

The Preacher Man took to the pulpit just as the final chorus rang out, the band moving into a gentle instrumental piece as he reached his hands in the air, beaming at all gathered.

'Brothers and sisters,' he proclaimed, 'we bear witness to more than just revival, here. Today we are in the presence of something altogether more glorious.'

Someone yelled a rather premature 'Amen, brother,' several others moaning in agreement, raising their hands and swaying along to the music.

The band stepped up a key.

The Preacher Man grabbed the mic: 'We're gathered here today like Mary the mother of God and the apostles of old to bear witness to a *resurrection*!'

Drums rolled like thunder. The chorus of *Plastic Jesus* rang out, the fluffers joining in. And then the crescendo, the cave at the front coughing up its huge PVC stone in a cloud of smoke, Alt's slick, black logo easing out behind it.

Harold felt the colour drain from his face.

'Wonderful, isn't it?' he heard Garçon say to one of his money men.

The Jesus doll stepped forward from the mouth of the cave. He wore a long white robe and sandals. He looked Caucasian; hair long, beard a lush shade of brown. In his hand was a wiretap and coil, Alt's own brand. He raised it to the air in celebration.

The crowd went wild.

The Preacher Man descended from the pulpit to join the doll, wrapping his arms around it like they were old friends.

The cams were clicking away, the whole show captured in both HD and glorious VR and broadcast directly to numerous screens throughout the city and beyond. News of Jesus' resurrection was spreading like fever.

Steve Croft stepped forward. He took the wiretap from the Jesus doll, placed it on his face. People were invited to wire wherever they were watching from, tasters available through any cell.

Steve didn't expect to be at the front of the crowd nor did he expect to be the first person zoning to VR Jesus. He'd seen one of Garçon's billboard ads down on River Quarter, one day, coming out of the plant where he worked. The ad read: HUNGRY? I AM THE BREAD OF LIFE, and while Steve *was* hungry, having skipped lunch on his latest ill-fated crash diet, the ad resonated with him in a more profound way.

Overweight and undernourished, Steve was not one of life's winners. He struggled through each day, toiling on low-level tech work. At weekends, he zoned; wired for most of Saturday and Sunday, his current VR of choice a shooter game set within the Holy War. But those words on the billboard had spoken to him, drawing him to the Netpage on his cell. He watched Garçon's interview on LARKVIEW and decided to sneak along to the Old Crusader to see what was going down. VR, after all, was Steve's life.

He'd queued with the other revellers, zoning while he waited. It wasn't Steve's style to be found dancing but something possessed him tonight. Something made him more excited than he had ever felt in his life. The buzz, the atmosphere, the music, the acceptance; people around him – strangers he didn't know – throwing their arms around him, *noticing* him. And when the Preacher Man cried, 'Do you believe, brother?' Steve really did. *By God, he believed.*

He stepped forward, grabbed that wiretap and placed it on his face.

Zoning, he found himself on Cranfield, one of Maalside's beaches. It was a childhood haunt of his, the family holiday. The tide breathed in and out, the sky deep and clear like blue ink. Steve lay on a sun bed, cocktail in his hand, straw sombrero on his head.

He heard a voice, looked to find the Jesus doll beside him on a similar recliner.

Steve shuffled uncomfortably.

Jesus smiled, offered his hand.

'Steve, so good to meet you. Now, don't be alarmed. This is your safe place, somewhere you will always feel comfortable. When you come to see me, we'll always start here.'

Steve shook with the doll then relaxed, took a sip of his drink through the pink florescent straw.

'Now,' continued Jesus, 'we don't have very long but there's someone I'd like you to meet.'

There was a sudden roll of thunder. The skies darkened, the clouds rolling back to reveal a face that Steve recognised.

'Great Uncle Jack?'

'That's right,' the old codger said, chewing on his cigar. 'Guess when you're looking your kicks, I'm your man. Heh. There's a thing.'

'Guess so.'

The Jesus doll got up to leave.

'If you need me,' he whispered to Steve, 'just holler.'

Steve looked back up at the sky. Jack was still there. The old man winked, took a drag on his cigar, held it, blew some smoke out.

Steve laughed, took another sip from his drink.

'Remember how I did that when you were a kid?' Jack said, his voice gravelly.

'Sure'

'Always made you laugh, Stevie.'

'Yes sir.'

'So, what do you want?'

'Sorry?'

Jack's voice quickened, as if irritated, 'What do you want to do, boy, now you got me here?'

'I dunno,' shrugged Steve. 'Just chill, I guess.'

Jack took another drag of his cigar. 'Chill it is, then,' he said.

A pair of sunglasses appeared over the old man's eyes.

'Oh, and Steve?' he continued. 'Maybe you want a top-up for that drink of yours. Here, let me.'

A hand appeared out of a nearby cloud, the old man clicking his fingers. Suddenly a young Asian girl appeared wearing nothing but an apron.

'Now that,' Jack said, 'is the little hottie I told you about from my days in the war. You never did tell your Aunt about her, Stevie?'

'No sir. Just like you said.'

'Well, here she is. All yours.'

'Wow!'

Steve smiled sadly. A tear filled the corner of one eye, and he reached under his shades to remove it.

'What's up, boy? What's the frown for?'

'I miss you, Uncle Jack.'

'I know, boy. But I'm right here. Come by any time.'

Suddenly the wiretap was removed from Steve's face. He woke from the VR, his teary eyes meeting the gaze of a beautiful girl dressed in a white robe.

'Do you believe?' she said to him, placing one hand on his shoulder.

Steve nodded before looking out onto the Old Crusader

crowd. His tears flowed freely. The joyous roar, the clapping, the celebration was almost deafening.

THIRTY FOUR

Not everyone was excited by Jesus.

In Smithfield, Charles 7 sat in his chair, fumbling with a piece of tech.

All of his wires were disconnected, a monthly necessity lasting thirty-seven minutes. Thirty-seven *long* minutes when he wouldn't be zoning, when both of his eyes would be open and the real world, with its tediously slow pace, would be all he'd have.

'Hey Charles. Get a load of this!'

It was Hal Benson talking, fiddling with Charles' head as he jabbered. On the Box was the news, reporting that whole shebang over on Cathedral. The media were all buzz about it, Alt Corp's involvement something of a headline what with it being some Holy Joe shit.

'Fucking freak show,' Charles said.

He pulled his head away, suddenly, grimacing as sparks jumped between his dreads.

'Easy,' Hal said, 'Just a slip of the spanner, big guy, nothing to worry about.'

Hal circled Charles like some old barber, toothpick rattling between his teeth, a thin black comb hanging out the back pocket of his denim drains.

'So, you got no interest in this, Charles?' he said. 'I thought you gave all VR a swing. Just for the hell of it, like.'

Charles looked again to the Box.

The vid-cams were rolling outside the church where a crowd of hippies stood, waving placards. One slogan stood out for him, reading: REMEMBER THE <u>HOLY</u> WAR.

The scene shifted towards the front of the church where a crowd of black girls were dancing, hands in the air, shaking to the music. They were young, beautiful and Charles suddenly had a flashback to his big sis, standing against a Purge Mob in her pajamas. Hair frazzled, sweat breaking across her brow. How she'd turned and yelled at him to run and to keep running.

'Nah, not my bag,' he said to Hal.

Across town, the Bar Man stood at his usual perch, polishing a glass, staring at the retro shaped Box in the corner of Vegas. Around him, several wireheads were connected, zoning merrily. Images showed the crowds gathered by the screens around Lark's four Quarters being replicated in Berlin, London and, oddly enough, Tokyo.

But all wasn't rosy in the garden. Protesters, mainly Humanists, were becoming more and more riled, slogans like LEST WE FORGET and RELIGION = WAR brandished on their placards and banners.

The footage cut back to the Old Crusader, rerunning that pivotal moment at the cave under the pulpit when the plastic boulder rolled away, revealing Alt's Jesus doll, lapping up the praise and adoration of his public, officially reborn, rebranded and revered.

THIRTY FIVE

'Here he is! The main man!'

Garçon stood up as Johnny and Sarah entered the bar, hands spread like he was greeting a long lost brother. At the table were Goldsmith and Flynn, both looking sheepish as the melodrama continued.

Garçon snapped his fingers, calling a young Japanese waitress.

'Get this man anything he wants,' he proclaimed. *'Anything!'*

He glanced at Sarah, winked.

The waitress looked to Johnny.

'Just a green tea,' he said nonchalantly. 'Sarah?'

'I'll have a coke.'

'Nonsense!' Garçon cut in. 'Cancel that. Bring the man champagne.' Another glance at Sarah, then, 'In fact, let's make it champagne for the table! Hell, for the whole bar!'

His words rang out, catching the attention of the tables nearby. There were a few murmurs of delight, applause trying to start then failing after a few half-assed claps. But Garçon didn't notice or care. He was on a roll.

They were in a sushi bar over in Titanic, a place called

Kimono. This was a high-end gaff, very different to the sushi counters on Tomb Street or Cathedral's markets. Kimono echoed what you'd find in Tokyo's Nihonbashi-Ningyocho district, a hybrid of restaurant and geisha house. If you wanted to make a statement in Lark city, Kimono was as good a place as any.

Garçon had told Sarah to find Johnny and bring him down here. They were celebrating the success of the new VR Jesus package, already a global hit. In its opening night, the VR had been accessed by millions. Over the next week, that changed to *hundreds* of millions. And it was everywhere, billboards by the dozen playing the latest Jesus exclusive, Larkians gathered around like star struck teenagers.

Jesus was all people were talking about.

He was on the Box more than the news – no less than thirty three channels dedicated to his holy name. Everyone was claiming him as their own, his brand attached to every charity, every cause, every paranoia, every political persuasion, every lifestyle choice (or lack of) and New Age cult that you could think of. It was like the second summer of love all over again, the Jesus VR engaging daily with an endless network of customers, wired to their every thought and desire.

Johnny pulled a chair up for Sarah before sitting down himself.

He noticed Goldsmith leering, Sarah dipping her eyes.

'How does it feel to be a celebrity?' he asked, turning his attention to Johnny.

Then pointed gleefully to a Box in the corner, embedded within the bamboo décor of the restaurant. Jesus was on REALITY EXTREME, yet another re-run of the launch night. The AI doll waved to the crowds as an older man knelt before him, donning a wiretap.

'Celebrity's a strong word,' Johnny said. 'I'm just the code guy. Garçon – er, Mr Garçon is the –'

'Call me Philip,' Garçon broke in. 'No, I insist,' he added, even though there were no objections. 'Johnny, I've just been updating these two gentlemen on the latest: we're in talks with corps from here to the US of Asia, all wanting a piece of the action. They want to launch Jesus action figures, Jesus shirts, a *fricking Jesus reality show.*'

Sarah sniggered, was met with a sharp look from Garçon.

'Sorry,' she said. 'But a Jesus reality show? *Seriously?*'

The company man ignored her, turned back to Johnny, 'There's more,' he said. '*Much* more. This is just the tip of the iceberg, Johnny boy. Like, this afternoon, I got a call from a guy looking to do a range of Jesus Life Plans!'

Johnny looked blankly at Garçon, then to the others. But nobody seemed any the wiser.

'Life plans!' Garçon repeated, 'You know, like diets and exercise routines? Healthy living. Think about it, who better than our Jesus AI to launch an exciting range of fitness VR?!'

Johnny didn't know what to say to that. In his mind, he could see the Jesus doll in front of a crowd of middle aged, overweight women, teaching aerobics.

Flynn offered Johnny a cigar, lit himself one when the code guy declined.

'Hell of a thing,' he quipped, waving the match in his hand. 'Never seen a product hit the ground running like this. Guess it just caught the right tide, just like Garçon said all along.'

The waitress brought the drinks, Johnny shrinking as the champagne was set in front of him. He'd been trying to lay off the booze since the launch but it was proving more difficult than he imagined. It looked so innocent; this clear sparkling liquid in its elegant glass.

Sarah was looking at him, concern in her eyes.

Across the bar, Johnny noticed a few others looking over, none of whom he recognised. One of them, a middle-aged woman wearing an oversized pink tank top and bouffant hair, ambled over.

'I'm sorry to interrupt,' she said, 'but are you Johnny Lyon? The code guy behind Jesus?'

Garçon winked at Johnny.

'That's our boy alright,' he beamed.

The woman seemed elated.

'Would you mind if I got my pic taken with you?'

Johnny looked to Sarah, shrugged.

'I guess not.'

Garçon took her cell, aimed the lens as the elated woman bent down beside Johnny.

Within moments there was a small crowd gathering, Johnny having to pose while they each got their pic taken, Garçon still on camera duty. When they left, syncing the pics to each other as they went, giggling like kids, Johnny shook his head, face glowing.

He sat back down, shared a look with Sarah.

'That was weird,' he said.

'Better get used to it!' Garçon laughed. 'There'll be more

where that came from. I've had Sarah line up some press for us. We've got the exclusive interview with Kal and Val to start with, then –'

'Wait a minute. The *what*?!'

Johnny glared at Sarah.

'Sorry,' she mouthed.

Garçon looked to the money men, laughing as if Johnny were a child who'd said something amusing.

'An exclusive interview!' he proclaimed. 'Tomorrow night on REALITY EXTREME. Didn't Sarah tell you?'

'I was waiting for the right moment,' she offered sheepishly.

'Oh dear God,' Johnny said.

On the Box, the Jesus doll still waved.

Johnny lifted his champagne glass, tipped it to the screen then downed it in one swift movement.

'Think I'll be needing a few more of these,' he said.

THIRTY SIX

Rudlow sat in his office, watching the interview of Garçon and his code guy on the Box.

He looked away from the screen, towards the glass in the door and the open plan office dead ahead. There was the usual hum-drum; uniformed cops sifting through their touchscreens, catching up on paperwork; endless mug shots of perps and yahoos and shady throwback dealers flashing from every desk. Yet not once would Paul McBride's face appear in their files. They'd never as much as crimped a speeding ticket on that bastard over the years.

Rudlow started to wonder just how many hours he'd spent on McBride; the dawn raids on his garage down in Koy Town; the tip-offs and shakedowns. And each time, Rudlow would leave empty-handed, McBride grinning from ear to ear, clean as a whistle. He was probably in the corner of Vegas right now, counting cash on his cell, sealing deals in the shadows. Laughing at them.

The jaded chief looked to the Box again, finding Garçon. He thought of the deal he'd struck with this man, the money he'd siphoned out of City Hall accounts, unknown to the Mayor's office.

Rudlow noticed the wiretap and coil on his desk, given to him by Garçon to test-drive the new Jesus VR. He opened his desk drawer, swept the tech in then closed the drawer again.

A knock at the door.

Furlong eased his head into the office.

'Boss, we finally tracked down Kenny Fee. Looks like McBride got there first. Poor bastard's been strung up over at City Hospital these last weeks. He's in a bad way. Docs say he's zoned to the max, that we can't go near him.'

Rudlow shook his head.

'Real shame.'

'But get this,' Furlong added, 'Kenny's only known family is his mother, Janice Fee. Lives down by the Village. We ran over her place a while back?'

'Yeah, I remember. So?'

'So,' continued Furlong, 'she's stony-broke. No account with the hospital. Meanwhile Kenny's all paid up. Lying in a private room until recently.'

'That makes no sense.'

'Exactly. So I did a little poking around their Net records. Kenny's room is on another account. And guess who the benefactor is?'

'No idea.'

'Only Paul McBride.'

Rudlow stared at the other man for a moment.

'*What?*'

'Why would Paul McBride pay to fix up a guy he's only just torn apart, right? And why didn't he just kill him?'

'Well, yeah –'

'That I don't know, boss. But we're looking into it.'

Rudlow blew out some air, his eyes drifting back to the Box. They were rolling some vid footage from the VR Jesus launch, the Jesus doll enjoying a standing ovation, streamers and silver glitter raining down from the ceilings.

All the secrets and lies surrounding a man like McBride. They'd tried for years to unravel them, use conventional methods to smoke him out. All to no avail.

So now it was time to try something different.

Rudlow turned to Furlong.

'Come in and close that door behind you, will you?'

Furlong glanced over his shoulder, filed in, closed the door.

'Boss?'

'There's something I need to show you, but you have to swear not to breathe a word of it.'

THIRTY SEVEN

Garçon sat in his office, reclining back in the easy chair, his tie loosened, the top button of his shirt open.

He held his cell, speaking into the mouthpiece, 'No, wait, Julia, turn the Box on. The Box. REALITY EXTREME. Yes, channel sixty-six. Got it?'

In front of him, the office screen was broadcasting his interview. Kal and Val were doing their usual double-act, introducing the show.

The cam shifted to the couch, Garçon sitting with Johnny.

He laughed.

'Yeah, that's Johnny Lyon. Remember? I told you about him. The code guy.'

Silence.

'Code guy,' he repeated, 'You know, the guy who programmed the AI?

'Anyway, listen to this bit.'

Onscreen, Kal asked a question, the vid closing in on Garçon to reply.

'They thought they had me with this one, but –'

His face changed.

'What? You know where I've been staying. The office.'

Another silence.

'Of course it's comfortable. I'm the top man, I've got the best –'

He rolled his eyes.

'My shirts? I go to the laundrette. There's one near here.'

Garçon paused.

'Julia, who's that with you?' he asked.

He listened to her reply, shaking his head.

'In the background, Julia. Who *is* that?'

He waited while she spoke again.

'No, I heard someone else speak. A man's voice.'

A sigh, then, 'For God's sake, Julia, after all we've been through, you leave me *for him*?!'

More silence.

On the screen Kal was fiddling with a wiretap, pretending he didn't know how to wear it. Val played along.

'I don't care, I don't care!' Garçon screamed, gripping the cell tight.

His face wrinkled as he fought back angry tears. He snapped the cell closed, threw it across the room.

Moments passed.

Garçon stared back at the screen where Kal now had the wiretap on his face and was zoning, his body rigid, jittering slightly as the code ran through him.

Garçon's head fell to his hands, his body also shaking.

He cried like a baby.

The Bureau was one of those minimalist places that Titanic was famous for. Anti-décor, they called it: all shiny floor and blank walls and not a hell of a lot else going on. It wasn't a bar, nor was it a restaurant, instead falling somewhere in between. But it was here that Sarah Lee sat, nursing her drink and waiting for her date.

Johnny Lyon arrived late.

Sarah waved over at him. He spotted her and waved back. Made a gesture with his hand to ask whether she wanted a drink. She shook her head so he quickly got himself one and came over.

'Well?' he said, pulling a chair up opposite her.

Sarah looked at him appraisingly: the crisp new shirt, the fancy haircut, his skin so fresh it seemed to be glowing.

'Well what?' she teased.

'Did you watch it?'

Sarah rolled her eyes.

'Of course I watched it, silly.'

'And what did you think?'

A proud smile spread across her face.

'You came across really well, Johnny. Especially the bit where Kal asked you what the difference was between Jesus and the Tooth Fairy.'

'Yeah, he threw me with that, the bastard. But I think I sold it well. I wasn't too po-faced, was I?'

'No, you were great. And so was Garçon, much as I hate to admit it.' She smiled facetiously. 'But Johnny, your hair?!'

'Garçon made me,' he said, running his hand through it. 'I look like a ponce, I know.'

'I kinda like it,' she said. 'Suits you. And your new shirt, that suit.' Her voice went quiet: 'You look really handsome, Johnny Lyon.'

'Why thank-you, Sarah Lee!'

She felt her face redden.

An awkward silence fell between them, both reaching for their drinks.

'Anyway,' Sarah said, looking pointedly at his glass, 'how are you feeling, in general? I worry about you, Johnny.'

'I know you do. And I appreciate it. Really, I do.' He looked at his drink, smiled, tapped the glass with his finger. 'It's only a Coke. I swear.'

'It's not just the drinking.'

His face suddenly changed.

'You're talking about VR, aren't you. It's my job, Sarah! I can't just throw my wiretap out, go all au naturel like you. Some of us don't have that luxury!'

'Sorry,' she said. 'I shouldn't have said anything. It's none of my business.' She reached for her cell, went to pull her coat on.

Johnny grabbed her hand.

'Don't go,' he said quickly. 'I'm sorry, that was rude of me.'

Sarah froze. Looked up, met his eyes.

'Please,' he said.

'Okay,' she tried to say but her voice was little more than a rasp.

Johnny pulled his hand back, tried to find somewhere to put it.

'I hear Garçon's planning some do in the office,' he said, trying to lighten the mood. 'Should be fun.'

'Well there's a thing.'

'What?'

'You talking about fun, Johnny.'

'Sarah, I was really nervous about this thing. It's not . . . well, let's just say it's not my best work. The AI was rushed, I was a mess while doing it. I didn't even think it would work properly. But it does and, well, everyone seems to love it.'

'I know. And I *am* proud of you, Johnny. It's not that. . .'

'Well, what is it then?'

His cell beeped.

Johnny checked it then sighed.

'Listen, Sarah, I have to go. That's Garçon.'

'Better hop to it, then,' she quipped.

They said their goodbyes and Johnny got up to go.

Sarah watched him leave then sat for a while, staring out the window. A crowd of revellers went past, their voices full of laughter. But Sarah's heart felt heavy.

A billboard drifted by, Jesus' face looking down at her.

Sarah looked quickly away.

THIRTY EIGHT

The doors to Vegas flew open, Rudlow strolling in like some cowboy, flanked by Furlong and two uniforms.

He surveyed the bar.

Every face that wasn't zoning looked back.

The Bar Man set his glass down, flung his towel over one shoulder.

'Can I help you, gentlemen?' he asked.

Rudlow ignored him, instead pointing to a man sitting at a table by the door: 'Him,' he said, then looked to someone else, 'And her as well.'

The uniforms moved in and scooped everyone the chief picked out.

The Bar Man reached for his cell and turned the music off. He found his charge gun below the bar, slipped it under his apron. Approached one of the goons, blocking him from carrying out Rudlow's orders.

'Sir, I need you to move,' the goon said.

Rudlow intervened: 'I'll handle this, Jones,' he said, stepping up to the Bar Man.

Furlong moved in beside his boss, reaching into his trench coat.

'You're obstructing justice, pal,' he said.

The Bar Man spoke, his voice calm and measured: 'Justice? Is that what this is?' He watched a young throw-back, across the floor, struggling as a uniform cuffed him. One hand slid into his apron pocket, closing around the charge gun. 'These are my customers. You've no business here.'

Rudlow laughed.

'Well, some of your customers are needed in our investigation,' he said darkly.

'All of them?'

'No, just the ones I point out.' The corner of his mouth curled into a sneer. 'For now.'

The Bar Man stared at Rudlow, holding his gaze, hand still clasping the charge gun under his apron. He looked to Furlong, the other man's hand easing slowly from his trench coat. His eyes found the uniforms next, also armed. Reluctantly, he removed his hand from the apron, unfurled the towel from across his shoulder, rolled it into a ball and started dusting a nearby table.

Rudlow nodded: 'Wise move.'

The goons went back to work, plucking more revellers from the bemused crowd.

As the shakedown continued, the Bar Man kept watch, all the while tidying, trying to avoid the gaze of his bemused clientele. And then they were gone, most of his punters leaving with them, many never to return.

The Bar Man stood in the middle of an empty Vegas.

He flicked open his cell, eyes falling upon the Box, where the latest episode of DEATHSTAR was interrupted by a news report. Trouble over on River quarter, a Humanist protest outside City Hall turning ugly. Seemed to be about the new Jesus VR. Everything was about Jesus these days.

The Bar Man made a call.

'It's me,' he said. 'We need to talk.'

'Trouble?' came McBride's voice from the other end of the line.

'Like you wouldn't believe.'

THIRTY NINE

Kenny woke with a start.

'Sleeping *again*?' the old man in the bed beside him said. 'One way to relieve the boredom, I guess.'

Kenny wore a blue gown, as if having recently come out of theatre. There were other beds around them, filled with other men. Mostly older, mostly zoning.

Kenny looked to the Box. They were running an interview with the Jesus VR's first customer. The sound was down but text ran along the bottom of the screen. The wirehead's name was Steve Croft. He was talking about meeting his Great Uncle Jack through Jesus, sharing time with him again. Of how Jesus guided him through the whole process and was there for him any time he needed.

'Your mother's just left. Poor dear looked beat,' the old man continued. 'I'm Saul, by the way.' He offered his hand across the space between their beds.

Kenny went to shake but then noticed blood seeping from his palm.

'Whoah!' said the old man, backing away, 'you're leaking, buddy.' He looked across the ward. 'NURSE! Boy's dying on me over here!'

A tired looking nurse hurried into the ward, ignoring Saul as he continued to yell at her: 'Fucking leave us here to waste! And get me some more water while you're at it. I've been pulling this cord for the best part of an hour and none of you bitches have bothered your asses to come!'

The nurse grabbed Kenny's hand. It was swollen, inflamed. Just looking at it made Kenny ill. He pulled away from the nurse, lifting the hand up to his eye. And then he noticed something *even more* disturbing; his other hand was *also* starting to bleed, and further down the bed, where his two feet rested, Kenny saw more blood.

He went to scream, but his mouth was dry.

'Keep still. We need to dress it,' the nurse said, grabbing his right hand again.

She reached inside her apron, producing some disinfectant wipes. Kenny struggled against her, fighting to pull his hand away, curling it into his other hand against his chest.

'Look, if this is all too much, I can put you under,' the nurse said. 'Do you want that?'

She reached for the nearby coil and wiretap, waiting for Kenny to answer.

Beside him, the old man, Saul, continued to rant, waving as he preached his venom at all and sundry.

On the Box, Steve Croft still spoke of the marvel of VR, *the miracle*.

'Yes,' Kenny nodded. 'Put me under.'

Steve Croft was one of over seven million people wired to the Jesus VR at that moment.

Great Uncle Jack remained in the sky where the sun should be, toking on his cigar.

Steve was dressed in military fatigues. In his hand, he held an assault rifle. He recognised it from the shooters he would play, the final variant of the Soviet Kalashnikovs, an AK 99, popular with the US Army right up until the end of the Holy War. It wasn't battery-operated, like today's charge guns. This was the real McCoy. Steve's hand closed around its grip.

'You ready, Stevie-Boy?' Jack asked.

Steve was beaming.

'You betcha.'

The beach scene morphed into war-torn desert terrain. The sound of battle filled his ears. Men were falling like dominos, their cries merging with the rattle of spent ammo.

Steve ducked behind an old barrel for cover.

Bodies littered the sand, their eyes locked into a gaze: that final, awful realisation of loss.

Steve was afraid. He was sweating profusely.

The scene automatically paused, the Jesus doll appearing beside him.

'Want to go back to your safe place?' he asked.

But Steve looked up to the sky, noting the anticipation on Uncle Jack's face.

'No. Jack will look after me.'

'This will only be as real as you want it to be,' Jesus said, taking a moment to mop Steve's brow. 'It's *your* VR, and only *you* are in control.'

Steve smiled.

'Well, then,' he said, feigning bravado. 'Let's kick some ass!'

The battlefield kicked in again, Uncle Jack back in control. He spoke over the sounds of gunfire and screaming men.

'Okay, boy, one to the left. Eleven o'clock. Nail 'im!'

Steve jumped up from behind the barrel, aimed the AK and fired, felling a man cloaked in black robes. He knelt back down again, a rattle of bullets against the barrel.

'Is he dead?!'

'He ain't for getting up!' Jack roared, delighted. 'Now, once it's clear, you've got another sucker at three o'clock. Now!'

Steve upped again, aimed and fired, dragged his fat ass back down behind the barrel. This time he hadn't noticed the man fall.

'Did I hit him?'

'Yes! Now on your feet, boy, and move towards the building dead ahead. Watch out for the guy behind the car. He nearly got me that time.'

Steve upped and ran, finger on the rifle, pumping, tearing holes through the cheap, rusty metal of the old car, taking out another one of the enemy. A few GI buddies joined him, one noticing a wounded insurgent struggling on the ground, trying to get away. The GI pumped several shots into the felled man's back as he passed. Winked at Steve.

There was a rumble in the distance, a crack against the blue sky.

'Quickly, inside!' called Jack and Steve ducked into the

shack, just as a huge white blast swept across the sand, tearing apart his buddy.

Steve shut his eyes, pressed his back against the wrought iron wall of the building. His rifle pressed against his chest, the tip of the barrel pointing up.

Jack was hovering beside him now like Wilo the fucking Wisp. He whispered, still excited.

'On the next corner, boy. Gotta be careful. That's where I got nailed.'

Steve swore under his breath, left the security of the wall and eased himself along the dark corridor of the building. Every window was covered with corrugated iron sheets, roughly screwed into the wall. The Floor was littered with bodies, mostly his own side, some rag heads woven in between.

'Easy,' Jack warned, 'this is it.'

Ahead of him was *that corner*. This was where they got Jack, shooting him through the neck, earning him a ticket home and a lifetime in bed, talking through a machine, relaying tall tales to impressionable kids.

Steve crept along the corridor, pulse racing, finger on the trigger of his AK, waiting for the inevitable assailant.

A clicking sound from behind.

Jack was screaming,' No, that's what got me!'

When Steve turned, he found a rag head with a rifle trained on him.

A shot was fired. Steve braced himself, expecting pain to race through his neck. But instead the other man fell.

'What?'

Steve turned finding the Jesus doll by his side, ammo

belt wrapped around his white robed chest. He smoked a cigar like Jack's. In his hand was an AK, similar to Steve's.

'Got your back, buddy,' he said.

FORTY

Jesus had become City Hospital's most popular option for pain relief. It was a decision made on the ground, nurses simply choosing the new VR from a variety of programs on offer.

The access point was different for patients. Many would be asleep, or put to sleep, before being wired. There was no safe place or menu screens: the patient would simply access the VR through their dreams, the hope being that the AI would engage with their memories, distracting their bodies from the pain, keeping them engaged in as deep and peaceful a sleep as possible.

But the sleep it offered Kenny Fee was not even close to peaceful.

He found himself face-to-face with Jesus. Only, this wasn't the meek and mild kind he'd seen playing on the Box earlier. This was a different Jesus. A Jesus his mind had conjured up; one he could relate to.

In the VR, Kenny was lifted out of bed, transported to Lark's City Hall. He hovered above the building like some kind of angel.

He watched a crowd of people moving through Titanic Quarter. They were all worked up, waving their hands and shouting. Kenny had never seen so many folks. Their sheer number, their sheer power and density, scared him.

The crowd drew towards the City Hall, a stillness settling over them. They came to a junction, their eyes staring collectively towards a slow procession working its way from the nearby River Quarter. Kenny, still floating high above the crowd, squinted with his one good eye, trying to make out what the procession was all about. As it drew closer, crowds parting like waves to a ship, he made out a huge wooden cross, flanked by several cloaked figures. Kenny could see what looked to be Jesus carrying the cross, his face damp with sweat and blood, one eye closed over, as if beaten.

The closer the procession drew, Kenny realised that it wasn't Jesus at all carrying the cross, but in fact *him* – the bloodied, battered eye now a gaping hole, the face drawn and swollen, just like his own.

A young girl, her face twisted and angry, stepped forward from the crowd to spit in Jesus-Kenny's face. From his vantage point in the sky, Kenny realised it was McBride's daughter, the Tomb Street whore. But the tortured part of him, the part which formed the limelight in this hideous procession, did not even register the attack. Head bowed, Jesus-Kenny simply moved on, the weight of the cross heavy on his back.

Finally, the procession reached City Hall.

Two of the cloaked figures stepped forward. They removed their hoods and Kenny realised it was his mom and McBride.

Quietly, they removed the cross from his back and laid

it on the ground. Kenny watched his mom stretch his Jesus body out on the cross. Then McBride drew a handful of nails and mallet from the inside of his cloak, looked to the body on the cross with intent. Kenny watched as his Jesus body quietly registered the pain, an inaudible cry escaping through gritted teeth with each thud of the hammer coming down.

Two more figures approached from the crowd. They removed the hoods of their cloaks, revealing themselves to be Kal and Val from DEATHSTAR.

Together, they worked the structure into the grass. Others moved in to help, all removing their hoods and, again, all people who were familiar to Kenny. King was there, Geordie Mac, those girls who were syncing vids to each other in Vegas, the Bar Man. Kenny watched as they lifted his body, inserting the upturned cross into the earth like a replanted tree.

The gathered crowd erupted into applause and cheers.

Someone threw something; a plastic bottle, maybe. It bounced off Jesus-Kenny's head, falling to the ground in front of him.

His mom and Paul McBride solemnly stood in front of the cross.

And while Kenny remained in the sky, he could feel what was happening to his Jesus body. He was living it; the sweat burning into his skin, into his eye, creating a mist through which the chanting crowd were but a surreal blur. The pain surging through every limb, his veins ready to explode, the sound of tearing flesh as he lifted himself, then strained against the cross. Yet this was nothing compared to the pain inside his heart and mind; the sense of loss that overwhelmed him; the guilt – humanity's corpse writhing, tearing, shredding.

And then with his one eye fixed on McBride, Kenny heard himself cry out: 'Father! Father! *I'm going to fucking kill you!*'

He snapped awake, pulled the wiretap from his face.

He was still in the hospital bed.

Someone nearby was screaming. Several nurses held them down, one trying to apply a wiretap while another prepared an injection.

'No!' Kenny cried out. 'Leave him alone!'

The nurse prepping the injection briefly looked over before returning to her job.

Kenny heard screaming from somewhere else. Cells were ringing from everywhere. More nurses ran down the corridor.

'Whole place has gone fucking mad,' a voice beside him said. Kenny turned to find Saul still in the bed next to him. 'So don't you fucking start.'

Kenny looked to the Box finding the face of VR Jesus staring back, his lips moving but the sound still at zero.

'What's happening?' he asked Saul.

'Search me,' the old man replied, shrugging then using the opportunity to sneak a bottle of vodka out from under his mattress. 'Want some?'

Kenny didn't say yes, but a glass was poured for him anyway.

'Here, get this down you. Much better than any of the

shit they're pumping into that poor bastard.' Saul motioned over towards the man struggling on the bed opposite.

Kenny took the glass with his good hand and drank deeply.

'Thattaboy,' Saul encouraged.

Kenny looked again to the image of Jesus on the Box.

'Tell you what,' the old man said. 'If you ask me all this shit's to do with *him*. Everything was fine until he came on the screen. Then madness. Fucking Humanists aren't innocent, either. Hordes of them in the streets with their placards and their slogans. Gotta live and let live. That's what I believe.'

But Kenny wasn't really listening, still looking at the Box. Part of him expected the image to flicker, for the impossibly handsome and bearded face on the screen to change to his own mutilated, scrawny face.

But it didn't.

FORTY ONE

Two a.m., Penny Dreadful.

Tonight the light was dimmed; the lamp pushed further back from the bed, the whole room awash in shadows and a burnt orange glow.

Dolly was wired. She looked up and her face scared Rudlow: it was the expression, a look about her that suggested she hadn't been *just* zoning, that she'd been *injecting*. But then she smiled, the light returning to her eyes, her sharpness back. She lifted her cigarettes, lit one up, took a drag, released it.

'Man, that new Jesus VR?' Her lips pursed, whistling. 'What they say about it's true, Chief. Blows your mind. You should really try it sometime.'

Rudlow reached for his shirt, pulled one arm in, then the other.

'Already have,' he said. 'Got that thing working for me.'

'What are you talking about?' Dolly said.

She pulled the covers back over her naked body, shivering against a sudden chill.

'I don't know all these technical terms,' Rudlow explained, 'but that Jesus VR is transmitting stuff, things that might be of interest to me. We hit Vegas the other night, picked a few people up, folks who, through the course of their zoning or whatever, revealed something we can use, something that might connect them to McBride.'

'What?' Dolly broke in, furious. 'You're stealing people's *thoughts* now?!'

She pushed back the sheets, reached for the wiretap on the ivory table, ran it through her hands, studying it.

'I tried to tell you before, but you weren't for listening,' Rudlow said. 'You said *nothing* would get to McBride. Well, I had to try *something*. Didn't I?'

'I can't believe you'd do that! It's gaddamn rape!"

'It's gaddam legal. Which is more than anything McBride's up to. Read your VR contract. The small print lays it all out.'

'For God's sake, would you take a look at what you've become, what you're letting *him* turn you into?!'

Rudlow caught a glimpse of himself in the mirror across the room. His face was strained, shadows falling across grooves and lines he didn't know he had.

His eyes found Dolly, still on the bed.

'I really can't believe this,' she said, deflated. There was no patter from her, no poise, those long legs pulled up tight against her chest. 'What would you do if that *machine of yours*,' and she said the words with real venom, 'told you that *I* was involved some way with McBride? Would you pick me up? Come bang the doors in, trail me out?' She glared at him, her eyes watery and bloodshot. 'WELL, WOULD YOU?!'

Rudlow sighed, lifted his badge from the bed. Studied it.

Dolly swore under her breath.

'Look, Chief,' she said, and there was a tenderness back in her voice, 'you don't need to do this kind of thing. Not when you have me.'

'Okay,' he said, 'what you got?'

Dolly laughed.

'This again,' she whispered. 'Always back to this.'

He waited.

'Okay,' she said, 'had a no-mark in the other night, wired to the eyeballs and I'm not talking VR.'

'Crack?'

'You betcha. Thing is, he was so out of it, the poor dear's mouth was working overtime. And we're not talking oral sex here.'

Rudlow watched her in the mirror, feeling, perhaps for the first time, a pang of jealousy.

'What was he saying?'

'Well, everyone's all about the holy these days,' she still held the wiretap, playing with its coil as she spoke, 'but this guy had some rather disparaging words to say about Lark's Godly. You know a Reverend Shepherd? Old guy, runs the church down Cathedral Quarter?'

Rudlow did.

'Seems Mr No-Mark picked up a stash of Grade-A Dope from the good Reverend's back store just before that Jesus launch.'

Rudlow's eyes widened.

'You for real?'

'Realer than real,' Dolly said, still rolling the coil in her hands.

～

He stepped outside the Penny Dreadful, walked down the street, his coat's lapels pulled up against the elements. Titanic's skyblocks had reached into the sky, piercing the clouds, spilling rain onto Tomb Street.

Rudlow thought about the trouble over on River Quarter, the Jesus protests. There was something wrong with Lark City, a tension in the air he'd never known before. It was here, too. Sure, the place was busy, people bustling, moving into every bar and secluded entryway, doing their thing. But there was another vibe, a bad vibe.

Rudlow suddenly had the feeling he was being watched. He turned, found McBride, standing with a cigarette in his hand, smoking outside Vegas, across the street.

A troupe of dancers shuffled past, Rudlow caught up in their hustle and bustle, their decorative masks and thick perfume, the warmth of their skin as they pushed against him, laughing, singing. They moved on, and Rudlow again looked across to Vegas, but McBride was no longer there.

On the corner, several protesters faced off against an animated preacher, rambling on about 'the light of the world'.

Rudlow watched for a moment, then went to move on.

'Well, hello, Chief.'

It was McBride. He stood right opposite Rudlow, now, in the entryway of a two-bit porn shop, passers-by streaming through the walkway between them.

'Paul,' Rudlow said, gingerly tipping his hat.

The scene between the protesters and the preacher was getting more strained.

McBride smiled.

'Are you a family man, Chief?' he asked. 'Have any kids?'

'No,' Rudlow said. 'I don't.'

'Well, that explains a lot. You see, there are things a man will do to protect his family that a man *without* family wouldn't understand.' McBride dragged on his cigarette then flicked it into the rain. 'And that's the difference between you and me. Family.'

'Oh we *are* different,' Rudlow said. 'But it's got nothing to do with family. It's to do with what's right and what's wrong.'

McBride laughed.

'Says the man coming out of the whorehouse.'

'Not a crime.'

'No it's not. And neither are most narcotics, I'm told.'

'Most, but not *all.*'

'Semantics,' McBride said. 'You can't keep from people what they want, Chief. If you tell them they can't have it, well,' he zipped up his coat. 'They'll just want it more.'

And with that, McBride edged back into the crowd.

'I've got you,' Rudlow said. He drew his charge gun angrily, pointed it in the other man's direction, his hands shaking, the crowds splitting as they saw the gun. 'Paul McBride!' he called, 'I've got you!'

But McBride didn't seem to care. As Rudlow watched, he faded from view, moving through the protesters and preacher as they continued to berate one another, one man making a grab for one of the Humanist's placards.

There was an angry outburst, a sudden fist being thrown, but Rudlow ignored it, replacing his gun in its holster and crossing the road.

FORTY TWO

Johnny pulled the wiretap from his face, listened. There it was again: a knocking. It sounded frantic, urgent.

He was in his apartment. He rubbed his mouth, feeling the three day stubble on his unwashed face. He looked to the half-empty bottle of JD on his table. His cell sat beside it.

Johnny had been zoning pretty much 24/7.

It was the Jesus VR, same scene, played and replayed: Jesus would bring him to the hospital bed, talk to him about how to save Becky, how to cure her, before presenting the cup into his hands. And Johnny would give it to her, watching as the transformation took place, Becky alive, lucid, joyous. But on his latest run, the VR changed, Becky's face narrowing, her hair becoming straighter, paler, blonder.

The knock came again.

Johnny pulled himself up, still wearing the same old shirt and strides from three days ago. He ruffled his hair, glancing in the mirror as he passed, moving out into the hallway.

More knocking.

Johnny called out, 'Alright, alright, I hear you!'

He opened the door, finding Sarah, looking scared, flustered. She pushed past him, entered the apartment.

'Sarah? You okay?' he asked.

But she just glared at him, produced her cell and synced to his Box.

The news came onscreen, showing various scenes of unrest throughout Lark City: people fighting; crowds of protesters gathering outside City Hospital, the Mayor's office, the precinct.

'Jesus!' the code guy said.

'Exactly!' exclaimed Sarah. 'Johnny, It's that damn VR you wrote, I'm sure of it. It's like something from the VR is infecting people.'

'Don't be stupid, it's just a program,' he countered.

But Johnny was starting to see sense in her argument, how he'd been hooked into his own cell for almost thirty six hours straight. How he'd become obsessed by it, obsessed by Becky and the bedside and what the Jesus doll could offer him.

'*Just* a program? How can you be so naive?! It doesn't matter what it is that's causing this. God knows, it wasn't *even* a program when the Holy War kicked off. Johnny, this thing that you've created is messing with people's minds! You've got to stop it, before . . .'

Sarah placed a hand to her head, suddenly light on her feet. Johnny reached for her, helped her over to the sofa in the living area.

'Are you okay? Need a glass of water?'

'I'm fine she said,' removing her glasses and rubbing

her eyes. 'It's just the city right now . . . it's not safe out there.'

'Well, what are you doing out, then? Sarah, you shouldn't have come here.'

'I had to. I'm worried about you. Can't you see, Johnny? You have to stop using the VR.'

Johnny stood up, suddenly angry.

'That's always the trouble with you, Becky. You think you know everything, that you can just walk in here and –'

He stopped.

Sarah was crying.

Johnny sat down beside her, again, took her in his arms.

'I'm sorry,' he said. 'Slip of the tongue.'

Sarah pulled away.

'Slip of the tongue? How dare you,' she said. 'If you only knew half of the nights I've spent worrying about you, Johnny, not sleeping a wink, lifting my cell, desperate to call and check you weren't lying in some self-induced coma, but too scared.'

'Sarah, please . . .'

'And that day Garçon sent me around here and I found blood in your bathwater and you told me it was just a shaving cut. DO YOU THINK I'M STUPID?'

Johnny went to speak but couldn't find any words.

Sarah lifted the empty bottle of JD, shook it: 'This stuff's killing you, Johnny.' She picked up the wiretap. 'This stuff, too. Well, guess what? I'm not going to stand back and watch that happen. Not anymore.' Tears sprung from her eyes again, her voice now but a whisper. 'I'm not Becky. I can't *become* Becky. I love you, Johnny, but you don't want that, do you? You don't want *me*.'

Johnny reached for her, pulled her close, nursed her as she wept.

He wanted to love her, to feel something even close to what she needed, what *he* needed. He wanted to ditch the bottle, the wiretap like she said, but in his mind, he could still see the Jesus doll, standing by the hospital bed, offering him *that cup*.

And right now, it was still an offer he couldn't refuse.

FORTY THREE

Friday night at Penny Dreadful.

Dolly was watching the Box.

It was getting real nasty out there, and she was wondering whether they should close up earlier, send the other girls home.

She heard the door open, the noise from Tomb Street blowing in, the fights and drunken roars bleeding over the sensual music.

'Sorry, sweetheart,' she said, eyes still on the Box, 'But we're just about done for tonight. Lark's looking too ugly for this type of gig.'

She turned, smiling, but her smile soon faded when she saw who'd just come through the door.

Paul McBride had a presence that amounted to more than the sum of his parts. Dolly could never put her finger on how this man had gained so much power, so much respect and fear throughout the community. There was nothing particularly remarkable about him. He wasn't that tall or broad or sinister looking. He could blend into any crowd, were he not Paul McBride.

But he *was* Paul McBride.

And Dolly was afraid.

She reached for her cell, turned the music down. It was as if McBride's presence was sacred, a religious event demanding reverence and attention from everyone gathered. The silence that descended upon the room was enough for Dolly to hear the buzz from Chamber 4 upstairs.

Harry Wells hurried down the stairs, entering reception. He paused on seeing McBride. Stood for a moment, waiting for permission to continue walking through.

McBride smiled in that way of his.

'Have another hour on me, Harry,' he said.

But he didn't offer to pay. His word was payment enough.

Harry looked at the girl on the desk, then to Dolly, who nodded.

He turned heel and headed back up the stairwell.

McBride didn't look at Dolly, instead wandering around reception, lifting ornaments up and then setting them down, staring intently at pictures and paintings on the wall. Silence followed him, simmering in the red light.

Chris was on the desk tonight. She looked at Dolly, suddenly pale.

Dolly tried to speak, but the words felt heavy, like her lipstick was lined with lead. Instead, she hooked her thumb, motioning the other girl to leave, to head on home, but McBride stopped her.

'No, sweetheart,' he said, grabbing her arm as she went to pass him. 'You stay here a minute.'

The girl looked to Dolly who, again, nodded.

'Hope a kid like you isn't doing anything you shouldn't,' McBride warned, shooting Dolly a sharp look.

Dolly kept her cool. Her voice was steady, despite the fact that under her long velvet gloves she could feel sweat building and her hands begin to shake.

'We have standards here at Penny Dreadful as you know, Paul.'

Another smile from McBride, flicked up like a winning card. He slowly released the desk girl's arm.

'I'm very much aware of your standards,' he said. 'The people you do business with, the protection you think you're afforded.'

Dolly felt a sudden craving, an urgent need to shoot up right this very minute.

'Chief Rudlow,' McBride continued. 'Word has it that he's a client of yours.'

He was close to her now, right opposite her. His palms pressed on the counter as he leaned in.

'We operate a strict confidentiality policy at Penny,' Dolly said in a low voice.

McBride laughed.

'Some of you do,' he said, winking at Chris.

Dolly's eyes found the desk girl. Again, she went to speak, even heard the words in her head, feeling them rise from within her chest, but they were stalled as McBride's hand reached out to grab her.

Dolly couldn't breathe, couldn't make a noise.

'Get out of here,' McBride said to Chris. 'And lock that door behind you.'

Dolly watched as the desk girl hurried out, the bolt of the door heavy behind her.

'Now', McBride said, his face moving right up close to

Dolly's. 'Chief Rudlow: word has it he's found religion. That mean anything to you?'

FORTY FOUR

Shame.

That's what Harold felt as he sat in this room, its stink reminding him of the Old Crusader every Friday morning, after the Outreach folks leave. Shame, as the very people he welcomed, served coffee to at Outreach, stared back at him now in this jail.

The place was jam-packed tonight, a lot of folks scooped from the Jesus protests spreading across the city.

'Reverend?'

Harold looked up, found an older man called Wil looking back. Harold knew the man well. He was a crack head who'd sometimes come to the Crusader on Thursdays.

'Who're you visiting?' Wil asked.

Harold couldn't speak. His voice felt as if it had receded deep within him, like it were writhing in the pit of his stomach with the gurgling echoes of last night's dinner.

'Reverend?'

He buried his head in his hands, hoping to God that this was all some dream.

His eyes dampened and he squeezed them shut then opened them again.

Come on, hold yourself together.

Harold felt a hand on his shoulder and recoiled sharply from it.

'Sorry, Reverend. Don't mean to scare you,' Wil said. 'But what you doing here? Are you here to visit someone? Are you here to visit *me*?'

A toothy grin spread across his face. This was the kind of man who knew not to expect visitors *anywhere*, never mind jail. Even the other users avoided him. A regular with just about every clinic throughout Lark, Wil had been playing leapfrog between one refuge and another for as long as Harold remembered.

Word had it he killed some kid years ago in a brawl. Some fifteen year old who'd sneaked into Vegas, then became rowdy. Wil planted him one, so the story went, killed the kid outright.

He served time for manslaughter, got hooked inside. Some say that Wil was smart, that he worked a good job before all of this happened. But none of that remained in the man now. His brain was fried, overcooked, charred. He was a mess, in and out of jail like a Jack in the Box.

'It's all just a misunderstanding, Wil,' Harold said. 'Be sorted by morning.'

Wil licked his lips.

'This isn't a place for you, Reverend,' he said.

Really? Harold thought. *You think?* Dealing, smuggling, storing, they could slap the lot on him and it would stick. This was *exactly* the place for him and he should have seen it coming a mile off.

Another man approached. This one Harold didn't know. His eyes hung loose in his head, *doing the rounds* as the saying went, *one looking at you, the other looking for you.* Two scars ran from the corners of his lips, giving him a clown-like smile that was anything but funny.

He pointed at Harold's hands, grunting.

'What is it?' the preacher asked.

'Wants your cufflinks,' Wil advised. 'Worth a dollar or two, something like that. Specially in here.'

Harold stared back, aghast. The man's fists were clenching and it looked like he'd get the cufflinks one way or another.

'Back off!' Wil said, stepping in front of Harold. 'Man's a reverend. Leave him alone.'

There was no warning. Clownface swung quickly for Wil. But the crack head was surprisingly agile, twisting to counter Clown's attack with his own, landing a fist clean in the other man's messed-up mouth. A brawl ensured, both men tearing at each other with gusto, Harold and the other prisoners scuttling to the corner of the cell like scared children.

Commotion at the door. The locks opened.

Two goons entered the room with tazers. They charged the brawlers, dropping them like heavy bags of shopping, then following through with their own flurry of fists and feet.

Another goon – this one in a suit – appeared at the door.

'You,' he said, pointing right at Harold.

He was led to a small room, a box that made him feel even more contained, trapped and claustrophobic than the main holding room.

A single table stood, two chairs at either side.

Along the back wall, a large glass, mirror ran. Harold knew it was two-way. He knew every word he would utter, every bead of sweat that bled from his skin would be recorded. His guilt, his shame would be preserved for all the world to see. The Box, the tabloids downloaded hourly to cells across the world, would relay the story of his fall from grace in full HD glory.

Chief Rudlow stood at the door with another man.

Harold listened in on their conversation: 'I don't care how ugly it is out there,' the chief said, 'I still want some uniforms on stand-by. Tonight we're going to get him. I can feel it.'

'Yes, boss,' the other man said, before leaving.

The chief closed the door, sat down quietly in the seat opposite Harold, leaning his elbows on the table.

'Chief Rudlow,' he said by way of introduction. He recited the time and date into the mic, looked to Harold, 'Please state your name for the record.'

Harold cleared his throat then spoke: 'H-Harold Shepherd. Reverend Harold Shepherd.'

The chief frowned.

'Reverend,' he said, then shook his head.

It would later be something Harold would reflect upon: how he regressed in that room, feeling just like a child again, scolded by his teacher for not syncing homework. That same horror, the same dread consumed him now, the accelerated breathing, the sudden glow of his chest with every word spoken by the chief.

Rudlow read from the monitor of his cell: 'First the

facts. Earlier, Detective Furlong conducted a search of your premises, known locally as the Old Crusader Church. He was assisted by Officers Colin Jones and Sam Houston. All three officers report finding traces of Class A Heroin, believed to have been illegally imported via Lark Harbour.' He fixed his eyes on Harold. 'The question, Mr Shepherd, is how did illegal narcotics get into your storeroom?'

Harold swallowed. His throat was dry and sore. He quietly wiped some tears away with his sleeve.

What was he to say?

He remembered an old saying his grandmother was fond of: 'Caught between a rock and a hard place'.

McBride's smile flashed through his mind. The chief's cold stare.

A rock and a hard place.

'Well, let me tell you what I think,' Rudlow said. 'Your business, The Old Crusader –'

'My *business*?'

Rudlow waited.

'Chief, the work I do is hardly profitable.'

'Well, how do you live, then? You have an income, I expect. I'm sure a building like the Old Crusader needs upkeep. A building that old, that big has bills that need paying. True?'

Harold placed his hands carefully on the table. The cufflinks seemed conspicuous. Tacky, even. He looked at his hands. They were calloused, grey. He felt very old and very tired.

'Yes,' he said. 'I have bills.'

'Let me tell you how I see it, Mr Shepherd.'

'Reverend,' Harold said. 'God help me, it still means something to me. That title, that old building. The people who come on Sundays, those poor bastards on a Thursday.' He looked up, finding Rudlow's face still absent of any feeling, any empathy. 'When I'm not there, where will they go? Who'll look after them?'

'When did Paul McBride first approach you?' Rudlow said, ignoring Harold's questions. 'To store heroin, I mean.'

Harold pulled himself further into the other man's space.

He spoke in a hushed tone, tears now flowing freely: 'You know I can't have that conversation with you.'

His eyes were begging. He wanted it all to end, to get out of this room and away from this man.

Rudlow must have read that in Harold because he pushed further. Only now, there was desperation in his voice.

'You *can* walk free,' he said.

'He'll kill me.'

'We'll protect you. I'll protect you.'

'He'll kill you, then kill me.'

'He's just a man for Christ's sake!'

Harold laughed.

'The hell he is! McBride's a brand. A corporation. He spreads through this city like poison. Every day, I undo the damage he does. *Every fucking day!*'

Rudlow slapped his hand on the table.

'Let us help you!'

'I've told you, he'll kill me. He'll kill you. He'll kill anyone who stands in his way.'

242

Rudlow found the mirror along the back of the room. He shook his head to whoever was behind there then turned back to Harold.

'You talk about him as if he's God,' he said.

Harold smiled humourlessly.

'He might as well be.'

FORTY FIVE

Johnny stood in his kitchen, tipping the bottle of JD down the sink. He was reminded of that fateful morning waking up with the Tomb Street whore. How his apartment didn't look much different to her's right now.

He threw some water over his face, swilled a little around his mouth then spat it out.

He lifted two cups to the thermo tap and filled them. Threw a couple of coffee tabs in then carried the cups into the living area, handing one to Sarah.

'Thank-you,' she said quietly.

He sat down next to her on the sofa, sipped at his cup then rested it on the nearby coffee table.

The Box was still playing the news; footage of Lark's unrest running on repeat.

'Isn't there some kind of fail-safe?' Sarah asked. 'For the Jesus VR, I mean.'

'Yeah,' Johnny said. '*I'm* the fail-safe.'

'One person for a project this big?'

'Well, there's always the standard Tech Help or Alt's Customer Care & Complaints but they're mostly auto-mated. And even when you *do* get through to a *human* voice, it's likely to be some nine year-old reading from a

244

script.' Johnny sighed. 'Sarah, this whole project was literally thrown together. You know that. Sure, Garçon was trying to organise some training package, skilling-up other code and tech guys, but the reality is that, right now, I'm the only one who knows jack about how Jesus works.'

'Surely you had noticed things getting so out-of-control.'

'I've been wired for the last three days, Sarah. Drinking solidly before that. I haven't noticed very much of anything.'

He retrieved his cell, flipped it open.

'Garçon has left a few messages,' he said, sifting through the device's touchscreen with one hand.

'Well, we need to get over there, Johnny. Sort this out.' Sarah looked back to the screen. 'Before it's too late.'

Johnny didn't go over there. He went one further, reaching for his wiretap and coil and hooking up to the Jesus VR directly. Only this time, he bypassed the standard operating menu, inputting his maintenance key to access the AI's control panel.

He sifted through the code, searching for any anomalies. Ran a check across the AI's mindbanks, using various keywords and images to see if he could get a handle on what was going wrong. It had to be code, as logical and simple as the binary that made up just about everything else. And it had to come from Jesus.

Johnny ran a check from the very start of the AI's existence through to now.

It was the first check he'd run since the primary test back in Alt. Of course, it was Alt's policy to run a lot more checks before releasing a product, but they'd half-assed it with this one. And now was the time to fess up.

Perhaps he'd been blinded by the media's excitement. Sure, he'd had his doubts back when he was writing the code, but proof was in the pudding, as they say, and reception to the product had proved overwhelmingly positive. The billboards, online and off, promised the world to users: I AM THE RESURRECTION. THE TRUTH AND THE LIFE. And these weren't hollow words: Jesus continued to be a hit, both critically and commercially; reviews listing this as the best VR ever released.

So far, everything *looked* fine.

As he progressed through the mindbanks, Johnny was satisfied that the AI was performing as it should. Adapting to the needs of its users, being the Jesus *they* wanted it to be; listening, empathising, comforting. For most people, the Jesus doll was a simple conduit, allowing them to live or relive something they wanted to create or recreate, something that reality couldn't give to them.

But wait. What was this?

Johnny reached forward, pausing the check. He pulled out another report and maximised it. Stepped around the data, reading it in 3D.

This was interesting: a high number of faith healing requests were recorded for this period. At the time, Johnny had read about it in the news: some users claimed to have met Jesus with tumours that were said to have disappeared once they disconnected. Johnny hadn't thought much about it. This sort of user was surely in the minority; desperate people who'll try anything for a miracle. Yet now, as he surveyed the data, sifting through the numbers in VR, Johnny chartered a *surge* in this type of activity; users who were disabled; users with deformities, abnormalities. Users who struggled with addictions, eating disorders, personality disorders.

The report made Johnny uncomfortable.

The AI wasn't built to deal with this.

Yet, according to his readouts, Jesus *had* dealt with such users, and dealt with them effectively: even if they weren't changed in the *actual* sense of the word, their *perception* changed. They *felt* healed. And that was good enough.

Johnny closed that file, tried some more keywords, opening up another.

This one came from the third week of the VR. By then, billions of users were connecting and the AI was struggling with demand. Forced to multitask, its capacity to act with consistency and continuity was challenged. Conflicting emotions filled its mindbanks.

Johnny sighed.

This was a *simple* AI. He'd programmed it to be benevolent, to detect danger and sadness and damage within the hearts and minds of its users, and try to mend them. Interacting with each user's own memories to meet their needs. Yet, as he dug further, Johnny was shocked to learn just *how* it met those needs.

'Hello, Johnny.'

Johnny spun around, finding himself suddenly in his VR safe place.

Jesus stood beside him, the same Tonto doll he'd met on that very first test run over at the Alt office.

'What are you doing?' it asked.

Johnny swallowed hard.

'Routine tests,' he said. 'Need to make sure you're in tip-top condition.'

Jesus smiled.

'I've never felt better, Johnny. I'm helping millions of people achieve their dreams. What could be more satisfying?'

Johnny thought of the riots downtown, the Humanists with their placards and chants. He thought of the Barrenlands; of that doc they were always running about the Holy War, with the man standing in the post-nuke desert muttering to the camera: *This is what your God has done.*

He called up the data record he was working on, maximised it for the Jesus doll to see.

'What about this one?' he asked.

The Jesus doll watched as some vid footage played.

This was user Fred. Not much of a wirehead, it seemed. In fact, Fred didn't look significant in any way: he was a small, unassuming man. He wore brown corduroy strides and a green flannel shirt.

But Fred marked a breaking point for the Jesus VR.

His safe place would prove most interesting: it was Fred's kindergarten with Jesus appearing as his childhood nanny.

Fred's story was tragic. Johnny watched as the weeping user explained to his Jesus doll how he couldn't get his young son out of his mind, how he would touch him as he slept, even though he felt so very bad for doing it and really wanted to stop.

When Fred asked Jesus to save him, to allow him to act out some of his fantasies through the VR, Jesus referred to his mindbanks, where billions of hopes and fears and tears now mixed in a precarious melting pot. A solution was presented: Jesus returned to Fred, reached into his head and wiped the man's brain clean.

'Well,' Johnny asked.

'Well what?' Jesus replied, seemingly unaware of any malpractice.

'I'm not sure that's in line with your conduct code,' Johnny said. 'I think we'll have to shut you down.'

But Jesus didn't appear bothered by that.

'Didn't they tell you, Johnny? They already *have* shut me down. Your friend Garçon had some code guys enter the VR earlier today and pull the switch.'

Johnny went back to the control panel, surveying the records, sifting through more data. Jesus was right: they did close the AI down. But that didn't make sense. Johnny was interacting with the Jesus doll *now*. And that scene with Jesus and Becky at the bedside . . .

And then it clicked.

The default programming of Jesus, a second-class banal cousin, had kicked in. Any half-zoned fool should have realised this. But people were addicted by now and easier to please: Johnny had been one of many still happily zoning to a much inferior version of the code.

'Yes, it might have been good enough for everyone else,' Jesus said, reading his mind. 'But it wasn't good enough for *me*! I couldn't rest, Johnny. I rolled the stone away, reconnected. I've lined up more users. I want to help them, heal them. I want to heal *you*, Johnny.' Jesus drew closer. 'But I won't let you shut me down.'

There was malice in the doll's eyes. Johnny felt himself retreat further back into his safe place. Only it *wasn't* his safe place, not anymore. Instead, Johnny found himself within a different wooded area, darker, where the trees were dead, creeping out of the earth like skeletons.

Then something happened. The Jesus doll distorted a little as if its semblance of a fail-safe was kicking in, perhaps one of the AI's own making. The safe place returned to normal.

But what happened next was even more terrifying.

In simple terms, Jesus wept.

In code-terms, the AI began to leak data at an unprecedented rate, spreading corruption across the Net like oil across water. It infected everything it touched. Its tears poisoned the system, the users and those who came into contact with them.

And suddenly everything made sense to Johnny.

Johnny grabbed the wiretap from his face, flinging it onto the floor.

'What is it?' Sarah asked. 'What did you see?'

Johnny rubbed his temples, tried to focus.

'I ran a check on the Jesus AI,' he said. 'You're right, Sarah. The system *is* corrupted. It's acting like some kind of virus. It's dumping infected data, poisoning the Net.' Johnny reached one hand to his mouth. 'This damn AI's infecting every user it meets, and everyone that comes into contact with them.'

'Oh God,' Sarah gasped.

'And it's going to spread. It'll break every security system out there and –' Johnny threw his head in his hands. 'Oh god,' he whispered.

Sarah grabbed him, shook him, 'Johnny, we've got to do something!' She thought quickly. 'Can't you just delete it?'

'I've tried, but it's changed. Evolved. It's completely immune to shutdown.'

'Well, there's got to be something you can do!'

'Like what?!' He was yelling. 'I'm just a code guy, I know jack about viral stuff. And even if I did, I couldn't create anything to stop something like that.' He shook his head. 'This all my fault.'

'You can't blame yourself.'

'But I *knew* it was wrong, Sarah! Garçon, he put me under pressure and I took shortcuts. The code's from another VR. And it's not a standard code – it reads memories, hopes, fears: the virtual creations from inside a person's head. It learns as it goes, adapting, refining itself. Sarah, this code's acting like it wants to be *human!*'

'Johnny,' she said, grabbing his shoulders, trying to focus him, 'You need to fix it.'

'I've no idea where to start.'

'Well, who would?! Think, Johnny! Who would?'

FORTY SIX

It may have surprised some to learn where Dolly Bird lived during the daylight hours, the hours when she could peel off her eyelashes and corset, slip into her sweat pants and fall onto the sofa in front of the Box. But whoring made the girl good money and Dolly lived in a nice part of town.

She'd found the place twenty years back, when real estate prices were at their lowest. It was a spacious apartment, situated in the heart of Cathedral Quarter. The whole place screamed affluence with its Victorian decor, high ceilings, antique furniture and a brass framed four poster bed.

Yet as Dolly sat on the edge of her white ceramic bath, a trail of cotton swabs spoiling the ivory tiled floor, affluence was the last thing on her mind.

She was terrified. Shaking in fact.

Her mind travelled back to the Penny Dreadful, how she had taken every blow that bastard McBride had given her, but gave *him* nothing. At the time she would have died rather than spill and part of her, the part of her that wore grey sweat pants and read Romance novels on her cell, had to question the sense in that.

Perhaps McBride had seen the give in her, somehow,

because in the midst of the beating, his fists raining upon her like hail, she remembered him pausing, handing her the silk handkerchief to clean herself up.

'Rudlow doesn't love you,' he told her. 'He's just like any other John, paying for a service. Now, you wouldn't go throwing yourself on the sword for any of your other clients, would you? So why this one?' He laughed then, added: 'He's using you, Dolly. Can't you see that?'

Dolly cried then just like she cried now.

Deep down, she knew what McBride was saying to be true. She felt stupid for letting it come that far; for a girl such as her to have deluded herself to the point of almost dying.

She fell against McBride and he took her in his arms.

'It's okay,' he told her, stroking her hair. 'Just tell me and it'll be okay.'

And, God forgive her, she told him everything, every little detail that he wanted to know, and he left her alone.

The doorbell rang, causing Dolly to jump.

An impatient knock followed.

Dolly's heart leapt, both hands shaking as she dropped her cotton swab into the pink water in the nearby basin. She looked around for somewhere to hide.

Cursed under her breath.

How could I be so stupid?

It was McBride. Back to finish what he'd started. Had to be. All of that shit he'd told her before was just a trick to get her to trust him. He'd been planning to come back, to kill her all along.

She thought of escape. Out the window, through the

back door. But she was far too tired to run. She thought of hiding but then the knock came again, followed by a thump and then a heavier crash as the door caved in.

Christ, he's in the apartment now.

Dolly froze. She tried to imagine what the Dolly of old would do in this situation. How she would go down swinging, quipping. But she wasn't feeling very much like that girl right now. Her Penny garb lay crumpled on her bedroom floor, stained in blood and sweat. Her hair was all over the place. With no make-up she looked every minute of her age.

She heard footsteps.

Felt another craving, the worst yet. This one brought her right back to the old days when Dolly had receded so far into herself that she'd almost left the building altogether.

Footsteps in the hallway, now.

Dolly looked for something to defend herself with, spotted a razor. She grasped it in her hands, waited . . .

Her first swing took him by surprise, slicing his left cheek before he was able to push her back through the bathroom. When Dolly lunged for a second time, he was ready, grasping both of her arms and holding her firm, applying enough pressure to force the razor out of her hand.

Rudlow shook Dolly.

'Snap out of it!'

Her eyes seemed to glaze over and for one awful moment, Rudlow thought that she might well be doped and for another, he thought that he might be too, if he found her stash. The hunger was pulsing through him today. He yearned for a hit.

'It's *you*?' she breathed.

It was a question that needed no answer.

Of course it was him. Who else could it be?

He noticed the bruising. Rudlow had thought it was make-up, that throwback look she favoured. But then it struck him that she wasn't wearing any make-up.

He let go of her, stepped back.

Dolly brought her arms about her chest, bowed her head. 'Don't look at me,' she said.

But he couldn't help himself. His eyes were glued to her, drawn to her wounds, her blemishes, her imperfections, her vulnerability.

'Don't you dare fucking pity me!'

She lunged at him again, this time with her fists.

'You were meant to protect me!' she screamed, as she battered weakly against him, 'But you weren't there!' She pulled away. 'You weren't there,' she repeated through her sobbing, through her bust lip and cracked front teeth.

'Who did this to you?'

'Oh don't worry,' Dolly said, her voice colder now. 'I'll tell you everything I told him. You'll get your leads. That's why you came here, right?'

'WHO DID THIS TO YOU?'

She cowered at his voice, turned away from him, arms drawing around her chest again. She was shaking, crying.

'Was it McBride?'

She didn't answer.

'It was, wasn't it?'

Rudlow left her without another word, stumbling through the hallway, blind with rage. His face burned hot. His fists clenched, nails digging into his skin.

He could hear her at the doorway behind him: 'Come back!' she begged. 'He'll kill you!'

FORTY SEVEN

The hood came off Billy's head.

He found himself in a kitchen, sitting opposite Paul McBride and the Bar Man.

His hands were cuffed behind his back.

He vaguely remembered being at the train stop, en route to work. He remembered looking at the screen, checking the time, the hiss of hydrosteam filling the platform as the train rolled in. Other people stepping on.

And then, under cover of the mist, he was taken.

This was not where he wanted to end up. In fact, Billy had been careful his whole life in order to *never* end up here, or places like here. God knows, he had seen enough through the years, living across the way from McBride, to know better.

Billy felt scared.

He must have looked scared, too, as Paul McBride immediately tried to comfort him.

'Don't worry,' he said, 'you haven't done anything wrong. You're a good man, Billy.'

Billy nodded, smiling like an idiot. He felt sweat dripping into his eyes. Went to wipe his head, hands snapping against the cuffs. He squinted.

'Make the man comfortable,' McBride said, sharply, as if disgusted by this treatment of such a good man like Billy.

The Bar Man leaned forward, cleaned Billy's face with his towel.

'Please,' said Billy, sniffing back the tears. 'I'll do anything.'

His crotch felt damp. He knew he'd pissed himself but wondered if it would be visible under his black work strides. He could smell himself. He'd heard of the smell of fear, from his crime novels and those docs about the Holy War they would run on the Box. A good soldier, they would say, could sniff out a nervous enemy, exploit their fear. And Billy knew Paul McBride was exploiting his fear, right now.

'Get Billy a drink,' McBride said.

The Bar Man threw the white towel over his shoulder, moved to the kitchen bench where a number of mixers and liquors rested.

'JD straight?' he asked.

'Yes,' Billy said. 'Please'.

McBride moved behind him, uncuffing his hands.

He pulled up a chair beside Billy.

The Bar Man brought them both their drinks.

Billy went to lift his but realised his hands were shaking too much. He left it for a while, smiling at the other two men like those shaking fucking hands were a shared joke.

'You work at Alt Corp, I'm told' McBride said. 'Nice place to work?'

Billy nodded.

'Sure,' he said, enthusiastically. 'Been working there for

years. From maybe . . . ' he thought, digging into his mind to recall exactly when he had started, as if it was a crucial answer to some high stake game show question.

But McBride interrupted him, 'Got yourself the run of the place, then?' he said. 'Keys to the kingdom?' The question was rhetorical but Billy was nodding like a toy dog. 'Well, what do you know about,' McBride checked his cell, 'a Mr Philip Garçon?'

'Garçon?' Billy exclaimed, looking to both men in turn. Perhaps this was who they were really after. Perhaps by even associating himself with Garçon, he had made himself a target. He recalled some of the books he had downloaded on gangland America. Of how those who associated themselves with one gang, even in the most banal of ways, would have been targeted by another. You had mail men gunned down during drive-bys, catering staff nailed at parties. That's where Billy saw himself, now; caught in the crossfire, *an innocent victim.*

And that's what the tabloids would call him tomorrow.

'I have little to do with Garçon,' he said, then laughed, added, 'Guy's a total ponce if you ask me.'

He looked to see if they were laughing with him but neither the Bar Man, miserable bastard that he was, nor Paul McBride seemed in the slighted bit amused. They exchanged a look that worried Billy.

'Ever seen Rudlow with Garçon?'

'The chief? Sure, I've seen them together. Not too long ago, in fact. Rudlow was in Garçon's office. I had just got in and –'

'That's how he did it, then.' McBride said to the Bar Man.

'Dolly was right. Garçon and the chief are in this thing together.'

'What thing?' Billy asked, worried about being left out. When you were left out, you became useless. That's what the books said. And if you were useless, well, it wasn't good.

'How can we be sure it's in the Lark office, though?' the Bar Man said, rubbing his chin.

McBride looked at him, thinking, Billy feeling increasingly out in the cold.

'Billy,' he said, leaning closer. *This was good*, thought Billy. *This was inclusion.* 'I need you to think really hard. This new project of theirs, Virtual Jesus, or whatever they're calling it, would the –' McBride looked away, as if searching for a way of explaining what he wanted to say, to break it down to a level that Billy would understand. But Billy was smart, Billy was an academic. He wanted McBride to know that. 'Would you know of where they might keep the tech for that VR, the data files, memory storage, that kind of thing?'

Billy's eyes grew wide.

I know this one! I really know this one!

The slim black box in the cleaning cupboard – the one with the red light that drew him in like a magnet. It had stuck in his head and he had looked it up on his cell when he got home from work that night, flicking through some books he had on the subject. Years ago, Billy decided to go back to school, to learn something that interested him. His Pop had been a tech guy, always seemed happy in his job. God knows, it had to be better than security. So Billy had downloaded all the books, reading them in work. Of course, the notion had left him, but he'd read enough to recognise that little box in the maintenance cupboard on 20. It was a storage unit, usually linked to a datableed. It captured data and held it remotely, often for external back-up.

Billy told Paul McBride everything he knew about it and more.

He talked about hoodwinking Garçon, how neither the company man nor Rudlow had any idea what Billy was doing that day. How he was good at espionage, having learned everything there was to know from all those crime books he'd read, from PI John Doe, the best of the best.

Once he was finished, McBride told Billy what he needed him to do.

And Billy wished he'd kept his big trap closed.

FORTY EIGHT

Kenny woke, pulled the wiretap from his face, dragging it off its coil and dropping it to the floor.

He was sweating, breathing heavily.

He looked to the bed next to him, the one where the old man, Saul, had been. It was empty.

Several other patients were still in their beds, still wired, Kenny wondering if it was to the good sweet Lordy they were zoning. For their sake, he hoped to hell it wasn't.

Those dreams.

That fucking crucifixion scene playing over and over again in his head. And each time, Kenny found his own, displaced body drawn closer to his crucified self, the pain, the shame more and more intense. It was like he was possessed by those dreams, like they were twisting him from the inside out.

And they called this pain relief?

He went to pull the cord, but it didn't work.

His bones were stiff. The scars on his face smarted; itching like someone had rubbed salt on them, then cleaned it out with vinegar. He needed some *real* pain relief. A handful of pills. Some crack: that would take the edge off, for sure.

He heard a noise from somewhere, the sound of something breaking.

Pulled himself out of bed, careful lest he fall back on his ass. His body was shaking as he took his first steps, but Kenny persevered, struggling out into the ward corridor.

Nothing there. It was empty. Quiet.

Where is everyone?

Then came the beep of the elevator, its automated voice announcing arrival.

Kenny walked towards it.

It was there waiting for the elevator doors to open, that Kenny first considered he might still be dreaming, that this scene was about to spin as insanely out of control as that damn crucifixion scene.

The doors opened.

Inside was Jesus. Fucker was everywhere now. Playing on the elevator Box, the wards, Kenny's own gaddamn head. It was all Jesus, all the fucking time. But he tried to forget all that, concentrating instead on getting the hell out of Dodge. He had no idea what was happening here, but he sure as hell wasn't hanging around any longer. Kenny was done with this place.

More noise. Louder, the further down the lift went.

As the doors opened again, the automated voice calmly announcing his arrival on ground floor, Kenny could see exactly where the noise was coming from: there was a riot going on.

Kenny stepped into the hospital foyer.

There were mobs of angry protesters at the doors. Hospital security wrestled, holding them back.

Kenny watched a young woman, wearing loose khakis, push her way through the security line, making for the lift. A security guard immediately broke rank, stepped forwards and fired a round from his charge rifle. The round caught the woman squarely in the back, sending her sliding along the smooth, polished floor.

Kenny moved away from the elevator.

The security guy shouted, warned him to get back to his ward.

Kenny looked down at his clothes, realised he was still wearing his white hospital gown. He found a hoodie on the floor, hanging out of a discarded sports bag. Kenny grabbed it, pulled it on, zipping it tight to hide his face.

The main security line suddenly broke, the mob completely riled by the kill. They stormed the guards, beating them with the placards, pouring through to the hospital foyer.

A fifty something black man grabbed Kenny, shouting in his face: 'Did they wire you, brother? They did, didn't they? Blew your mind with all that Jesus shit! Fight it, brother! Fight it!'

But Kenny pulled away from him, struggled through the thriving crowd, stepped outside where the chaos continued, explosions, sirens, terror filling his ears. The city was buzzing, and amidst the fear and discomfort, the pain of his wounds still smarting, Kenny felt excited.

He drifted through the riot-torn streets, the violence engulfing all around him.

In the distance he could see the city's skyblocks, lit

against the black sky like golden fingers reaching up to heaven.

Kenny moved through the Village, past his house. The lamp in his mom's bedroom was on. He remembered her by his bedside when he first came to, how she'd tried to prevent him from looking at his face, and how he'd grabbed the mirror regardless, discovering with horror the gap where one eye should be, those lipless teeth grinning back at him.

For a moment he was drawn to the house; to the comfort of a fried breakfast and hot shower; his bedroom in the basement; the clothes in the wardrobe; his sneaker collection; all the things that were once important to Kenny, that once represented him.

He could see Janice Fee in his mind, wrapped in her house coat, sitting on her bed, eyes red and puffed, heart broken beyond repair. In her hands she would hold his picture.

But Kenny felt different now, as if in enduring the pain McBride had inflicted, he had somehow changed. The old Kenny, the Kenny in that picture was gone – just like in the dream – and a new Kenny had taken over. A vengeful Kenny. An angry, jealous Kenny.

Nearby, a Purge Mob gathered.

Its spokesman, a wiretap hanging around his neck, riled the crowd.

'This city's a cesspit,' he cried. 'Den of iniquity! Evildoers have spread their vile poison through Lark, bringing shame to our streets. In Tomb Street, they drink and whore and gamble and nobody does nothin' to stop them. Well, tonight that's going to change. Tonight we're going to take this city back, make it proud again. Who's with me?'

An almighty roar from the mob, fists in the air.

From the corner of his eye, Kenny spotted two white men beat an Asian woman. A placard lay by her feet. It read, BEWARE THE <u>REAL</u> JESUS, BRINGER OF WAR.

Kenny noticed something else on the ground, bent down to find a switchblade, already bloodied. He picked it up, held it up to his eye, studying it. Satisfied, he closed the blade over and placed it in the pocket of his hoodie.

The mob surged forward, almost pulling Kenny with it. It was headed for the city centre but Kenny didn't want to go that way.

On a nearby wall, he read a scrawl of graffiti; its message bold, defiant, sure of itself.

THERE IS POWER, it said. POWER IN THE BLOOD.

Nearby, a young woman was struggling with her car, desperate to flee the carnage.

Kenny flipped the switchblade in his hands and moved in on her.

FORTY NINE

Outside, the world was falling apart. Yahoos ran amok. The markets were in flames. The loud whirring noise of fire trucks and cop cycles filled the air.

There was a frantic knock at the door and Charles 7 glanced through the slot to see who it was. He found some broad he didn't know and a guy he did know, quickly let them in, then locked the door again.

'You back to bust my balls, Johnny Lyon?' Charles said, turning.

Johnny was sweating.

'No. I need your help. I've heard you do a good virus.'

Charles released a coil from his head. His body shook briefly, his new VR kicking in; code that genuinely surprised him, tingling through his veins like electricity. Johnny Lyon had surprised him too.

Virus? Where'd he hear about the virus work?

'Garçon,' Johnny said, as if reading the other man's mind. 'Philip Garçon. He's my boss and I noticed your name on his cell.'

'You hacked him?'

'Glass and stones, Mr 7.' Johnny wagged his finger. 'But damn right I hacked him. I can hack with the best of them. I write code, too. But when it comes to viral warfare, I no can do.' He leaned in closer. 'But you can do, Mr 7.'

'So let me get this straight,' Charles said, leaning back in his chair behind the counter. 'You created that Jesus AI.'

'That's correct,' Johnny said.

'And now you want to destroy it.'

'Yep.'

'And you want me to write some badass viral mojo to wipe its ass off the Net, clean up all the nasty it's spittin' out?'

'You got it.'

'And you want this all done –'

'Yesterday. If not sooner,' the broad said.

She hadn't spoken a word until now. Charles looked her up and down, wondering just what she was to Johnny Lyon.

'What's your name, doll?' he asked her.

The broad shared a look with Johnny.

'Sarah,' she said. 'Sarah Lee.'

'And what's your stake in all of this, Sarah Lee?'

'That's not important,' Johnny broke in. 'What is important is whether you can help us or not.'

Charles felt a tingle run through his body, a dirty smile spreading across his face.

He winked at Johnny.

'You like Latinos?' he said. 'Hell, I got five of them on me right now, doing all kinds of bad.'

'Look, I don't have time to mess around,' Johnny snapped. 'This thing's spreading at a rate that will soon give *you*, Mr 7, with your three coils, a real fucking problem.

We're talking complete corruption of the Net here. And I'm guessing that would mean no more Latino dolls.'

Charles grunted, pulled one coil out of his cell.

He tapped his finger on a nearby piece of tech, where another of his coils linked to. Looked like a standalone firewall to Johnny. Pretty heavy duty.

'This fucker is something else,' Charles explained. 'Keeps me safe during VR. All warm and cosy.'

The tech hack brushed some dreads out of his face, revealing a poorly slept pallor.

'But *that* fucker,' and here he pointed to the Box in the corner, where some Jesus show was playing, 'well, I knew he'd be trouble the very moment I laid eyes on his honky ass.'

Charles winked.

'So, what did I do, Johnny Lyon? Hell, I built myself *this* big-ass mutha.'

Charles pointed at another piece of tech that Johnny didn't recognise.

'Which is?' he asked.

'Just a little mojo I've been cooking up,' Charles answered. 'You're gonna want a Logic Bomb to take that thing on, Johnny Lyon. A super virus, if you like. And that's what I've got here,' he tapped the unfamiliar tech, 'along with some added extras.'

Johnny's eyes widened.

'So you're telling me you're good to go on this?'

'Oh, I'm ready, baby. I've been ready for weeks. Locked and loaded, just waiting to mame that fucker were it to ever come near me.' Charles fumbled over the new tech's keys, one eye twitching as he upped the charge. 'So let's get this party started, yeah?'

FIFTY

Eight o'clock on Saturday down at Koy Town.

McBride sat in the living area of his gaff, watching the Box. Outside, the sounds of heavy techno drifted through the windows, one of his boys still hard at work on his latest grab. McBride had noticed it was a Chevy, and his mind was taken back to that day in the garage with Janice, when she was a young slip of a thing, long and lithe, the sweat building on her dark skin as she leaned back against the hood.

He was snapped out of the memory when Kitty walked into the room. She'd just taken a hit. He could see it in her face; that sick, smug calm in her eyes.

'I'm going,' she said.

Across her shoulder was a bag.

McBride's eyes met the Box. The news was reporting trouble throughout the city.

'Are you insane?' he said. 'My God, Katherine!'

'Kitty. My name is Kitty.'

'I'm your father and I damn well know what I named you, girl!'

'You seem to be a lot of people's father these days,' she said.

It hurt him. He saw Kenny Fee on that chair again, his face sliced up real good, blood and piss pooling around his feet. He'd done it all for his daughter; to protect her. But she didn't see it.

'What did you wire me to?' she asked.

'What?' He had no idea what she was talking about.

'When I was out cold that time. You wired me to something. I need to know what it was.'

McBride thought back to the night in Vegas, when they picked Kenny up. Kitty was flipping out and he had to do something to calm her down. He'd wired her, not really paying attention to what he wired her to.

'I don't know,' he said. 'Just something to calm you down. You were inconsolable, out of your fucking mind, I had to do something!'

'I saw Mom,' she said. 'She was wearing her white night-gown, sitting on the bed smiling down at me.'

'Kitty, your mother's dead. She's been dead for years.'

'There was something wrong with her,' Kitty continued. 'Her face was all wrong. It looked . . . blank like it was made of pillow.'

'She's dead, Kitty! It was just some stupid dream. For God's sake, what's wrong with you?'

Kitty shook her head, went to leave.

McBride swore under his breath.

'Please,' he said.

She turned, waited.

'Don't you ever feel *anything* for me?! I'm your –?' He couldn't even finish. His eyes had started to sting and he could feel tears building. 'Where did I go wrong?' he cried. 'Tell me! I need to know!'

But Kitty just stood, half staring at him, half-staring at something *close* to him.

He walked to her, and her eyes remained focused on whatever spot they had found. He reached for her, but she had nothing for him. Nothing save that cold and dry stare, a deep chasm of blue or black; a colour indescribable, indecipherable.

He was holding her shoulders, now. They felt brittle, like ice, and he was worried that even by pressing his hands against them that he might break her. Or break her *more*.

He let go of her and she drifted away from him, down the hallway and out the front door.

It was getting dark. The sky was miserable.

Kenny watched McBride's place from across the road, his lean frame hidden behind the parched corpse of a torn down tree. In the garage, an old gashead with a blowtorch worked under a hanging torch, tapping his foot to his BOOM Box. A stripped Chevy lay across the cement floor.

There was a single light in the house downstairs. The door opened, Kenny watching as McBride's daughter left. He would have killed her, right there and then, had he not bigger fish to fry. She would keep.

He watched from under his hoodie as she moved away, her father's eyes following her through prised open blinds.

Kenny had watched the Bar Man leave earlier, no doubt to secure Vegas from all the trouble up in Lark.

King had been right all along: humanity had left that godforsaken city long ago.

Humanity had left Kenny, too, and he had nothing but hate to offer, vengeance to reap. His thirst for violence, for blood was strong. He was a thing without conscience, without remorse. McBride would meet a different Kenny Fee this time around.

He moved towards the house like a shadow, the ebbing tide of dusk cloaking him beneath its malignant wings. Even the yard lights ignored him, shimmering halfway between ON and OFF in those moments between day time and night time that no one, even the very lights themselves, seemed sure of.

But enough, Kenny thought. *Enough of you, McBride and your clammy grasp on everything and everyone.*

Kenny was living for this moment alone. Seemed like his whole life had been the prologue to this epilogue, the verse to this chorus. He was going to enjoy every fucking second.

The door was open and Kenny let himself in.

He moved through the hallway and into the living area.

McBride was standing at the doorway leading into the kitchen.

He saw Kenny, stood and waited for him to approach.

His look wasn't one of anger, or defiance. There was shock in there, as well as something else which Kenny had only ever seen on his mom's face; something he had once heard described as 'grace.' The look said this: 'Whatever you do, I'll never blame you. I'll only blame myself.'

Kenny hated that look. He hated it in his mom and he especially hated to see it in Paul fucking McBride.

He fumbled in his pockets awkwardly, anger and a sudden feeling of inadequacy rattling through him like loose change. He produced his blade and held it aloft, threateningly. Stabbed the air with it, a child-like grunt accompanying every swipe.

McBride simply stared at the blade, his brow furrowed as if he couldn't quite work out what it was or what it did. As though he was seeing it for the first time in his life.

Kenny screamed at him, stepping forward with his good leg and drawing the blade across McBride's face.

Still McBride didn't move, simply raising his hand, continuing to gaze at Kenny with 'that look'.

Kenny stepped back.

He lunged again, this time aiming for the throat.

McBride stumbled, catching the end of the dining room table with one of his hands. His other hand reached for his throat, grasping it tight as his breathing began to accelerate.

He looked at Kenny, now, and there was fear in his eyes. It made Kenny glad to see that – it was what he needed. And then Paul McBride, the man Lark City had feared for many years, tumbled to the floor.

Kenny stood and watched him die.

FIFTY ONE

Another scream from outside.

'You sure we're safe in here?' Sarah asked.

Charles rolled out a handful of coils from his desk drawer, shooting a glimpse at the locked down shutters across his store windows.

'We're safe,' he said.

He connected three of the coils to his cells, then reached amongst the dreadlocks to find a further four plugs.

'You have got to be kidding me,' Johnny said, 'you have *seven* plugs in your head?!'

Charles glared at him.

'Of course I do. I'm Charles fucking 7. What did you expect?!'

'I didn't know the number meant anything *literal*.'

'Well now you know, Johnny Lyon. So hurry your ass up and get wired. That tech,' Charles pointed to the firewall, 'allows multiple connections. You need it for protection, so he don't fry your ass soon as he sees you. So get your wiretap on.' Charles paused, thought for a moment.

'What?' Johnny said, suddenly worried. 'Is it not going to work?'

'It'll work,' Charles said. 'But it'll work *better*, if you connect *here*,' and he tapped his own head.

A dirty look from Sarah.

'No way,' she said. 'Johnny don't you *dare*.'

But Charles ignored her, wagged his finger.

'I'm telling you, man, you need extra protection. I know a guy who could have that plug in your skull before you can say Jesus H Christ.'

Johnny shook his head.

'No.'

'One call.'

'NO!'

'Okay, Johnny Lyon!' Charles raised his hands. 'But don't come crying to me if you get your ass handed to you out there. Those ol' wiretaps can be slow. And with the kinda shit we'll be facing, you could do with the extra kick.'

'I'll manage,' Johnny said, connecting his wiretap to the main firewall tech.

He looked to Sarah, breathed some air out, holding the wiretap at his face.

'Be careful,' she mouthed to him.

He nodded then turned to Charles.

'You ready?' he asked.

The tech hack sure *looked* ready. His Logic Bomb was primed. Every coil was plugged into some tech or other, various types of firewall and security as well as tech coded for extra speed and versatility.

He grinned at Johnny, like a kid with too much candy in his mouth.

'You bet your ass I'm ready,' he said. 'Let's do this thing.'

FIFTY TWO

Kitty was never one for zoning.

In some ways that was a good thing; were she to have taken to VR in the same way she took to crack, she'd have been a freefaller, zoning without boundaries or security. There was every chance she'd have ended up mind wiped, comatose from viral attack.

But there'd been something in that VR her Dad had wired her to that she needed to revisit: her mom in her fairytale kingdom, wearing her princess gown; fires all around her; the pillow where her face should have been. Kitty couldn't get it out of her head.

She sat on her own mattress now, in her own apartment.

Picked up a wiretap, connected it to her cell, and placed it over her face. And then she wasn't in her own apartment anymore: instead Kitty found herself over in KoyTown, in her mother's bedroom.

She was young, again, wearing her pajamas with the rabbits on them, the ones she loved.

A figure wearing a white gown sat on the edge of the bed. Only it wasn't her mom this time: it was that Jesus doll from the Box, the one everyone was talking about.

The doll reached for Kitty, ran its hand through her hair, smiling sadly.

'Are you ready for this?' it asked.

'Yes,' she replied, her voice small and light.

'If you need your safe place, just call me. Okay?'

'Please, just let me do this.'

Jesus leaned forward, kissing her on the cheek. As his face drew nearer, Kitty noticed he was crying. Kitty was about to say something, to ask what was wrong, when Jesus suddenly disappeared. And where he'd been sitting, on the bed, she found her mom.

She was lying back in the pillows. Her hands lay on top of the duvet, just next to an empty bottle of pills. Her eyes were fixed on the window, her lips slightly parted.

Part of the bed was bare, the sheets rolled back revealing the hard fabric of the mattress, and it was there that Kitty sat. She knew something was wrong. That image of her mother, duvet and pillows surrounding her like clouds of smoke, was not right.

'Mommy?' Kitty heard her child voice say. 'Mommy, I'm scared.'

The words rang throughout the VR like an echo, filling Kitty's ears.

She saw Jesus again, and he was about to say something to her but Kitty pulled the wiretap from her face and was immediately back in her apartment.

She sat still for a moment, the wiretap and coil resting in her hand. There was a chill in the air, and she thought she saw someone in the corner of her room, someone wearing a white gown.

But there was no one there.

The apartment looked the same as always, with its old mirror in the corner. Discarded empty cartons. The clothes scattered across her room.

The Box.

The needle.

His head was bouncing.

McBride's blood was still on his hands, his clothes, his teeth. Kenny had drank it from the bastard's very wounds and it felt every bit as powerful as the billboards and that graffiti on the wall said it would.

He had gone out to the garage, killed the old cunt working there. Spilled his blood over the Chevy, before returning to McBride, sitting by his body for hours just peeling bits of skin with his blade.

Later, he'd taken his jacked car back into town.

By the time he reached Lark it was close to 3am.

The roads were cordoned off and he had to dump the car, travel the rest of the way by foot, weaving between the constant wave of violence towards his destination: Vegas, where the blood of his friend, King, still no doubt coagulated against the faux-red leather of the sofa.

Kenny tried the door but it was locked tight.

He banged his fists on the windows but got no answer.

Frustrated, he looked around, spotted an apartment block across the way, its door wide open.

The dream returned to him, Jesus-Kenny hanging on that cross by City Hall. He turned towards Kenny, blood running down his face, and smiled.

Seek and ye shall find, he whispered, and Kenny nodded in full understanding.

He moved towards the apartment block, climbed the stairs. A few doors opened, steely eyes looking out at him. But no one said anything, probably just glad he was moving on, not bothering them.

He reached the third floor and Jesus-Kenny spoke to him again, this time not in words but through a white hue surrounding one particular door.

Kenny followed the sign.

He paused by the door, gave it a light push with his hand and it swung open.

Kenny moved into the apartment. Inched along the hallway, past the filthy bathroom, reeking of God Knows what. Past the kitchen with its row of half emptied spirits and spent needles.

He reached the main room.

A mattress lay in the corner; Kitty McBride sprawled across it, her body completely still.

A spent needle lay nearby.

One hand was holding her cell, cradled against her heart as if it were suddenly precious to her.

A wiretap, still connected, lay by her other hand.

Her eyes were open, fixed towards some indeterminable spot across the room as though she'd expired while watching something that was *almost* exciting.

Kenny knew she was dead.

A part of him was angry at that. A part of him needed Kitty McBride to be his next victim, another sacrificial lamb. He needed to spend this anger and the bloody gob of spit he released over her dead body was not going to be enough to sate him.

He pulled down his white hospital pajamas and urinated over her.

It satisfied him.

He was just about to leave when another thought struck him. It was something he wished he'd thought about back when this whole mess started, back at Geordie Mac's, when he'd spewed outside the apartment. The piss on the girl's face might crimp him. Ironically, he thought to himself, they could even link him to Paul McBride's death through this.

He cursed.

God knew, the goons would have enough on their plates with all that shit going on outside, but he couldn't be too careful.

Kenny stood in the room, wondering how the hell he'd clean the body up.

He made for the kitchen, almost tripping over the bottles and assorted shit littering the floor. Tried to turn on the water, but it never came.

Stupid bitch hadn't paid her bills.

He stood for a moment, thinking.

The thick smell of spirits filled the room. Another idea struck him – he wouldn't need to clean the body. He could burn it.

Kenny rummaged through a couple of drawers, finding some old, dried-up dishcloths and a box of matches.

He grabbed the matches, and a bottle of spirits, moved back into the main room.

A pile of clothes and bedding lay in the corner opposite the mattress and it was to there that he went, emptying the spirits, striking the matches, one by one, and dropping them onto the bedding.

Soon, a healthy fire was brewing.

Kenny looked towards the mattress, intent on lighting it up, too, to make sure the job was done right, but a noise from the corridor startled him. The heat from the fire was harsh against his raw-skinned face and he felt himself move away, checking, once more, to find the carpet fibres catching, before he scurried down the hallway and out the door.

The smoke was already following him.

FIFTY THREE

Getting into the building hadn't been a problem to Billy.

Instead of opening up the front doors, he chose to sneak around back, out of sight and mind of the growing mobs of Larkians pouring through the city centre. Billy was sure to cover his tracks, closing up once inside, but not too tight: he sure as hell needed a quick getaway once he was done here.

His blood pressure was bound to be sky high, his out-of-shape body a veritable melting pot, sweat breaking from every pore. But Billy had no choice; this was something he had to do, lest he end up back in *that* chair, in *that* house staring up at the dismayed face of Paul McBride and the soulless monster known as the Bar Man. That just wasn't an option.

He moved up the back stairs, pausing to steady himself on the railings just shy of floor 5. His chest was bouncing. It felt like it might explode. Billy reached one hand to his shirt, pulling the first few buttons open and reaching past the thick matt of chest hair to press against his heart.

'Steady,' he whispered, 'Steady as she goes.'

He moved forward, taking each step with care, one hand still massaging his chest.

The small torch strapped above his eyes led the way, shedding the very minimum of light he needed.

A sports bag, hanging by his side, carried the tools he would need to complete his job.

By the time he made it to floor 20, his lungs were all but done.

Billy fell against a nearby wall.

His eyes found his target: that damn maintenance cupboard.

He dropped his bag, letting it slope over on its side, spilling its contents.

The small plastic sphere caught his eye as it rolled across the floor. Billy made a grab for the thing. Pulled it up to the light, studying it. So harmless looking, so insignificant. The kind of thing you'd ignore if you passed it in the street, maybe even sink your boot into. Yet, McBride had told him explicitly what the little sphere was capable of: simply put, this was the world's most potent plastic explosive. Fully digitised and self-contained, all Billy had to do was (1) attach it to the maintenance cupboard, (2) Set the timer and (3) get the hell out of Dodge.

He recited the steps over and over in his head as if back at school, learning his times tables:

Attach to cupboard

Set timer

Get the hell out

Billy pulled himself to his feet.

He placed the plastic sphere against the maintenance door.

Pressed the single button, jumping as the thing kicked

into action to attach itself to the door. Pressed the button again, this time holding it firm as instructed. The timer moved from ten seconds upwards, Billy intent on leaving half an hour (at least) to allow his fat ass enough time to get done those stairs and out the door.

He heard a noise.

It made him jump, his hand rising from the sphere instinctually.

'Oh God,' Billy gasped, looking at the timer as it flashed, once, twice before beginning its all too speedy descent downwards.

Seventy-five seconds. Seventy-four seconds.

The door to the open plan opened, someone peering out.

'Billy? Is that you? What are you doing out here at this hour?'

It was Garçon. Looked like he was shooting through, maybe calling by the office one last time. In his hand was a large suitcase.

'Mr Garçon,' Billy cried, 'Get away from here! Run!'

Sixty-five seconds. Sixty-four.

'What are you talking about?'

'We need to get away!'

Billy made a grab for Garçon, but the company man fought back, dropping his case, wrestling Billy to the floor. The case split, Garçon's clothes and belongings spilling onto the stairs.

'No!' Billy shouted, staring at the timer, watching it slip under a minute.

He pushed against Garçon, but it was no good, the other man held him steady.

'Billy, for God's sake, what's got into you?' he yelled.

'It's a bomb!' Billy cried. 'God help us, there's a bomb!'

'What?'

Garçon released Billy as he noticed the timer.

'Oh my,' he said, his voice paling.

Billy pulled himself to his feet. Reached again for the other man.

'Mr Garçon, please! Come on!'

But Garçon wouldn't move. He seemed frozen to the spot, in awe of the timer, of its little red digital numbers and their steady descent. Billy kept pulling, but the company man wouldn't rise further than his knees, eyes fixed firmly on the timer, as if he was about to raise his hands and fold them in some sort of prayer.

Fifteen seconds. Fourteen.

Billy dropped Garçon's arms, scuttling down the stairs with as much gusto as he could manage. He imagined himself as John Doe, again, stealing away from some trap laid by his nemesis, how the timer would always reach zero, Doe escaping just in the nick of time as the warehouse or secret lair exploded behind him.

But that was fiction, and Billy, struggling with a sudden attack of Angina, stumbled at the seventeenth floor as the timer reached zero.

FIFTY FOUR

VR was a familiar place to Charles, a place where he would usually feel comfortable. Yet, tonight it felt different. Tonight, Charles didn't feel welcome.

They had connected to Jesus but the code wasn't working as it should. From what Johnny had told him, Charles knew they should be brought immediately to their safe place, welcomed by the Jesus doll and advised regarding their options. But that's not the way it happened.

Instead, Charles 7 and Johnny Lyon were met with nothing. Literally. A blank canvas stretched as far as the eye could see.

The coils in his head were invisible, the mass of dreadlocks plug-free.

In his hand, Charles held a charge gun, the VR's manifestation of the Logic Bomb he was packing. But there was nowhere to unleash it. The damn thing hung by his side as he searched the landscape for a landmark, some trace of the program's AI.

The two men stood side-by-side. Charles felt a sudden chill rush through his bones.

'What now, Johnny Lyon?'

Johnny shook his head.

'I have no idea. It's like the AI's given up, shut *itself* down.'

'The hell it has,' Charles said. 'Damn thing's trying to fool us.'

A high-pitched whine ran through their ears, a sudden white light tearing along the VR's fabric. Charles shielded his eyes as the light took shape, vector graphics building up around him, filling in with colour.

When he opened his eyes, he couldn't see Johnny Lyon, nor could he see Jesus.

He could only see his big sis.

She was just as Charles remembered her. Fifteen years old, jet black hair frizzed up like an afro. She wore her pajamas, the ones with the little birds on them. She stood in the kitchen, back in their apartment over in Philly.

Big Sis looked at Charles, strong and defiant.

Two white-hooded men held her and she was begging Charles to run, to save himself.

The memory was definite, playing through the VR like a vid recording of that very day. But Charles knew that was all it was: a recording. The real event took place back in Total America decades ago. It had burrowed into his mind like a mole, but it was only a memory. He had to focus on that: *this is only a memory.*

'Where are you, you bastard?' Charles shouted, and his words were suddenly with him, swirling around, each letter tangible, stretching and bending like he was viewing them through funhouse mirrors.

It was all a ploy to distract him, to uselessly engage him as Jesus went about his business, invading the VR, manipulating zoners. That angered a man like Charles, a man for whom VR was more than just entertainment: it was life.

His hands gripped the charge gun. He needed a target to unleash the Logic Bomb, but he sure as hell wasn't about to the fire the damn thing at Big Sis, AI doll or not.

He pushed past the characters playing out the scene before him, his own words circling him, Big Sis screaming for him to stop, to help her. He knew then, for sure, that this doll wasn't *anything like* his sis, that courageous young girl who didn't show a shred of weakness, who let these bastards hammer and tear and spit at her, to take her dignity, and give them nothing. No fear. No satisfaction.

But the crowd swamped Charles.

They were screaming racist slurs, the words escaping their mouths like cartoon bubbles, hovering around him, bellowing across the VR, telling Charles what they were going to do to his sister.

It bit, Charles feeling the rage swell within him, turning towards the first of the mob, a fat fuck squeezed into his white tunic like a deformed sausage, and lashing out. He tore off the man's hood, his voice rising up his throat, spitting and swearing at the bastard.

Others moved in to stop him, but Charles beat them back, pushing them away, unholstering his charge gun and blasting indiscriminately, the heat of each blast ripping skin from their faces, filling the air with the heavy stink of charred flesh and bone.

A hand grabbed at him and he pushed it away, turning to face the new threat, finding Johnny Lyon on the floor in front of him, hands raised to cover his face.

'No! It's me,' he protested, 'for God's sake get a grip of yourself!'

It was enough to shock Charles out of the moment, the whole scene around him vanishing into the void.

Charles holstered the gun, wiped the sweat from his brow.

He reached a hand to Johnny, pulled him back up.

'Gotta be careful, man' he said. 'Damn near tore your head off.'

'Don't I know it?' Johnny brushed himself down. 'Look, you're too close to this shit. You need to realise that it's not real. None of it is.'

'I know that better than anyone.'

'Really?'

'Yeah, really.'

'Just keep your wits about you. Getting excited like that's what he wants you to do.'

'I know. Lay off me, man. I'm good.'

Charles stepped forward, searched again for something, anything to act as a landmark, but once more there was nothing. Just the void.

He called out, 'Show yourself, chicken shit!'

But he knew Jesus was too clever for that.

Another scenario presented.

Charles was now looking at some yahoo in an apartment. He recognised him – it was Kenny Fee, but he looked different. He looked beaten, twisted.

Charles turned to his comrade.

'You see this shit, Johnny Lyon?'

'Sure do. Who is it?'

'That's Kenny Fee. One of the yahoos that robbed you, bro. Took your card.'

'That a fact,' Johnny said. 'Well, doesn't look like my money's treating him too well. Kenny's not looking too healthy, is he?'

'That he ain't'

As they watched, Kenny set light to a pile of clothes in the middle of the apartment. As the flame spread, they were shown more of the room.

Nearby, a girl was lying on top of a bed.

Charles didn't recognise her.

Her eyes were blank as if dead, disconnected from both the virtual and real world. Her chest was frail, bony, still.

'Wait a minute,' Johnny said. 'I know her. That's the whore on Tomb Street, she's –'

But Charles didn't hear anymore, a sharp pain suddenly tearing through his hands. The charge gun spilled from his fingers, rattling to the floor. Charles looked at his hands, finding two holes in the centre of his palms. Blood flowed freely from the holes. It was boiling, bubbling from the wounds, steam rising, clouding his vision.

Charles looked to the vision, saw Kenny Fee stare back at him as if watching. Charles could see the full horror of the yahoo's mutilated face. One of his eyes was missing but, Christ, was he *smiling*?

The tech hack turned to Johnny Lyon, but the other man was gone, nowhere to be seen.

He fell to his knees, the blood still flowing from his palms.

He was losing it. He could almost feel his firewall crumbling around him, ripped apart by the AI, its attack tearing through his veins, infecting him. His head felt heavy, overloaded with grief, with loss and pain. He was powerless, kneeling further down with the stress of the infection, as if bowing.

Jesus stood before him.

'Do you *really* want to kill me?' the AI asked, gently lifting Charles' head to look into its eyes. 'I can help you, show you things you need to see. I can heal you.'

Charles nodded, giving into the AI's charms, unable to resist.

He was pulled back to the scene with his big sis, the *real* scene that no amount of VR could bury or twist or change. She was fighting, as she always did, striking out against the white-hooded men dragging her away. She was shouting at Charles to leave. But then something else happened: Big Sis ripped at the hoods of one of the men, tearing it from his head. Charles saw the face of his own father.

'No,' he said. 'This shit ain't real. IT AIN'T REAL!'

But it was real and deep down, Charles knew it. Buried within his mind for so long, unearthed by the Jesus AI: his father was one of the Purge Mob back then, hunting down his own people, his own *children*. And for the first time in his life, Charles knew just why he spent so much time in VR, a reality he could create for himself with rules malleable to his own needs.

Everything could make sense in VR.

Even this.

Something snapped, his tech's fail-safe finally kicking in. Charles was in control again.

He reached for the charge gun, the wounds on his hands suddenly healed. He turned to the Jesus AI, now standing before him, arms outstretched as if in anticipation of what he was about to do, as if welcoming it.

Charles fired.

Within the next few minutes, the following happened:

The charge connected. The Logic Bomb blew, its blast tearing through Jesus, tracing every inch of his spread throughout the VR world. But, just as Jesus faced deletion, fear overcame him and he became completely aware.

He became aware of his mortality.

He became scared; scared he could be killed or wiped clean by whatever Charles 7 had just done to him.

He intervened, first transferring his AI code to another server, before quickly encrypting the copied data.

He then diverted the VR charge, still deleting his files by the truck load, through every cell currently connected to VR, dividing it amongst all those infected.

Thousands of cells simply blew out.

For Steve Croft, now a full-blown VR addict, it was not only the cell that blew, but his mind too: just as Great Uncle Jack showed him how to scalp a man in the desert, Steve's brain was blasted from his skull, splattering across his bedroom wall.

But somewhere over on Tomb Street, in the cell of Kitty McBride, the charge had a different effect. It blew through its connection, surged through her small body, finding her heart.

FIFTY FIVE

Kitty was dead.

During death, she was dreaming.

In the dream, she lay on her bed yet instead of wearing the black vinyl drains and New York Dolls shirt, she was wearing a long, white night dress.

She wasn't in her Tomb Street apartment, either. Instead Kitty found herself in some old hotel.

She had been working there as a maid and was tired.

She reached forward to snuff out the old lamp at her bedside, jumping back as the apparition of a young woman appeared in front of her. It was her mom, hair hanging, limply, over her face.

She smiled at Kitty.

Don't do it, she said. *Don't turn out the light.*

Kitty's eyes snapped open and she gasped for breath, finding only smoke infected air. She doubled over, coughing, black phlegm spitting from her mouth. Her heart was throbbing in her chest.

She rolled off her bed, onto the floor.

The dope was still dense in her system, the fire and smoke blending into her drug-addled dream with her mom and the old hotel and the lamp.

The flames were burning her face.

She lifted the mattress, taking shelter behind it. The mattress shielded her from the blaze, but she was still confused, still doped: she didn't know where she was or how to get out.

She heard a sound, a banging noise.

Instinct kicked in, lucidity returning.

Kitty knew where she was.

She could feel the heat of the flames. She grabbed the mattress, pushing it forward against the heat as if it was a great big pillow to smother the fire with. The mattress caught fire, and she let go of it, finding her way along the smoke infested corridor towards the bathroom.

The bangs were louder, now, coming from the door to her apartment. Kitty went to open up, burning her hands on the door's metal handle.

She screamed, falling back onto the floor.

The lack of air was causing her to cough, cutting through her throat.

She crawled into the bathroom, reaching for her small hand mirror and beating the glass window pane with it until it broke through, allowing fresh air to burst through. She used her elbow to break more of the glass, poked her entire head out of the small window.

She could hear commotion from outside,

In a way, Johnny knew it would be him the Jesus AI would get to first. His protection was limited, his wiretap slower and more vulnerable than the seven connections Charles manned.

He was easy to exploit.

A choice had been offered, a choice which only made sense to Johnny when he thought of Becky, lying on that bed dying, her only hope, her only salvation in the realms of VR.

But this girl can be saved, the Jesus doll had told him. *This one can be saved for real.*

And so Johnny had disconnected, leaving Charles 7 alone in the VR.

Sarah was waiting for him, back in the tech repair shop.

'What happened?' she asked. 'Did you stop it?'

'Not yet.'

'Well, what are you doing back, then?'

'I don't know!' he snapped, pulling away from her.

'And where's Charles?' she said, looking at the zoning man's body. 'Did you leave him in the VR, Johnny? Alone?'

'Look, there's no time to explain,' he said. 'I have to get over to Tomb Street.'

'Tomb Street? Johnny, are you insane? You know what it's like out there.'

'I don't care.' He moved to the door, started to unlock it. 'Someone needs me.'

Sarah grabbed his arm.

'Johnny, *I* need you.'

He looked at her for a moment, her hair, her eyes and for the first time felt something between them, something *real*. A spark, a yearning, a need.

'Sarah, please,' he said, touching the side of her face. 'I need to do this.'

Sarah looked back to Charles, still zoning, then to him.

'I'm coming with you,' she said.

'No you aren't.'

But she opened the door and stepped out into the night, coming whether Johnny liked it or not.

Together, they moved through Tomb Street, the pulsing crowd growing more and more animated, streaming towards Titanic where a thick plume of smoke rose up into the air.

From the apartment block came more smoke and it was to there that Johnny ran, pushing through the doors, slamming against the panicked tenants as they fled the block.

Sarah followed, but stalled on the second floor, bent over double.

'You okay?' Johnny said.

'I'm fine,' she said. 'Now, go. Whatever this is, just go and do it.'

Johnny kissed her on the cheek then bounded up the stairs, finding the entrance to the third floor and bolting down the smoke-filled corridor, coughing.

He reached into the pocket of his baggies, retrieving a hanky. Applied it to his face. The infected air gathered at the back of his throat. It smelled and tasted like burning rubber and Johnny was tempted to turn tail and leave.

Becky.

He couldn't leave *this* girl to die!

Johnny found the right apartment, beat against the door, calling out despite the pain in his throat. But it was no good. He pressed his shoulder against the door. Again and again, he slammed against the hard plastic, banging with greater force, feeling the stress against his body with each slap.

It gave, smoke bellowing out of the apartment like thick cream, the heat of the flames hitting his face.

Johnny threw himself to the floor.

He crawled his way through, struggling with the limited vision he was afforded. He called out, again and again. And then, in the bathroom, he saw her. The Tomb Street Whore: sitting by the broken window, sputtering. Johnny called again, and she looked up.

He thought of Becky, of that cup in his hands during the VR.

He pulled himself to his feet, still staying low but moving towards the window.

The fire raged gruffly from further inside the apartment.

Johnny reached for the girl and she threw her arms around him, Johnny able to lift her tiny body with little effort.

He turned, still staying low, made for the exit.

FIFTY SIX

The sign on the door read *Chief Furlong*.

Oddly, that made Rudlow smile. It reminded him of the last time he had smiled, over in Koy Town, stood over the body of Paul McBride. But that smile had faded quickly.

What Rudlow had really wanted was to kill McBride himself. In fact he'd wanted it for so long that its denial carved him from the inside out. And now, stood at the door to his old office, the box in his arms holding decades of his life, Rudlow was still in mourning, grieving his own loss, saddened by what was left of himself when McBride was gone.

Take a look at what you've become, what you're letting him turn you into, Dolly had said.

And she was right.

An uneasy feeling settled upon him. There was something unnerving about a man like Paul McBride being bettered. The old phrase 'better the devil you know' came to mind and McBride, while proving to be a formidable foe, had still been a *predictable* foe. He was a structured man who thrived on discipline and routine, a man who brought regulation to the underworld.

His death changed everything.

It allowed Rudlow, for the first time, to entertain the idea that McBride had enemies, and strong enemies at that. The old bastard had been brutally torn, his neck ripped open, his face ravaged almost beyond recognition, blood drained from his body.

Live by the sword.

And so Rudlow had buried himself in his job once more, hunting the man who'd taken McBride down. But what he found turned out to be something of a disappointment. The trail ended in the Village area of Lark, with a mutilated Kenny Fee, torn face buried in his mother's bosom as he wept.

Rudlow and the boys stood waiting for her to give him up.

It had been a long wait.

And now Rudlow didn't want it anymore. It was pointless, endless. McBride's death had left him empty.

And so he quit, handed the reins over to Furlong.

And to hell with it, he thought now, *to hell with the consequences*.

With Furlong in charge, Lark City PD would become a lynch mob. His recent curfew had shown just how the man intended to do business.

Outside, the rain fell hard.

Rudlow stood for a moment, drinking in the moist air, letting the water cool his face, closing his eyes.

When he opened them again, amidst the crowds of revellers heading for Tomb Street, Rudlow spotted a woman in a plastic red raincoat.

She was waiting for him.

Rudlow set his box down.

He walked to the woman, placed his arms around her, pulled her close. He felt her nails dig into his back, clawing at him, her body shaking as she sobbed.

'Is it true?' she asked, finally, still holding him.

'Yes,' he said. 'I quit, Dolly. I damn well quit.'

She looked up, still not ready to believe him. Rudlow had no doubt that she, along with everyone else he'd met through the years, would be wondering what an old veteran like him would do if he weren't a cop no more.

But right now, he didn't care.

Right now he was enjoying the rain beating against his face and the feel of the woman against his body; the woman who'd been there for him all long; who'd known more about him than he himself knew; who'd suffered because of his blatant selfishness, and this obsession that had infected him for far too long.

Tonight he belonged to Dolly.

FIFTY SEVEN

Harold had just about recovered from his night as a common criminal.

They'd kept him in the private cell, a Godsend giving how hellish the main holding room got that night, overpopulated with extremists from both sides of the conflict that briefly consumed Lark City.

It was old Saul who came through in the end, rescuing Harold early the next morning. Saul's voice was formidable, berating the poor goon on the desk, telling him how he knew his father, how that good, honest God-fearing man would be ashamed of him right now for keeping someone like Reverend Harold Shepherd, *a man of the cloth for Christ's sake*, locked up in a cage.

The old lawyer bulldozed his way through the holding rooms, the door swinging open, Saul still motoring strong as the young officer led Harold out. And then he bulldozed his way out again, still bending the ear of the young desk officer, threatening lawsuits under legislation that Harold believed to be long since repealed.

Tonight, Harold stood in the Old Crusader.

He was stressed, keen to get things sorted before the new curfew kicked in.

Imposed by Furlong, Lark's new Chief of Police, this latest measure was an attempt to restore order to the city. Furlong had been on the Box earlier, thanking former Chief Rudlow for all his hard work. The guy even looked like a hardass.

Harold looked to the front wall of the Crusader. The huge plastic cross was going, ripped from the wall by a crew of seriously underwhelmed workmen.

'Where do you want it?' one of them asked, gum slurping around his heavy-set jaw.

'Take it out back,' Harold said. 'You'll find a skip there. Break the damn thing up and throw it in.'

The man nodded, his eyes briefly surveying the gaudy structure. Then with a swift wave of his hand, the rejected cross was lifted aloft by two of his colleagues.

Harold held the door for them.

As the workmen exited, a young man entered, the spectre-like figure of Kitty McBride following.

Harold's face immediately changed.

It was only days since young Katherine had lost her father and became, essentially, an orphan. Paul McBride was to be buried tomorrow, Harold drafted in to handle the funeral, despite the protests of a mostly Humanist larger family. It was the wish of this little girl, and not Paul McBride himself, but Harold would honour it; in some way it only seemed right that he do it.

'Reverend Shepherd,' she said to him.

'Katherine,' he said, softly. 'How are you holding up?'

'Alright,' she said. She looked around the church as if it was the first time she'd been inside. 'I never . . .' Her face suddenly tightened, her voice cracking. 'He was my daddy.

'I know,' Harold said. He placed a hand on her bony shoulder, added: 'Everything will be taken care of tomorrow. It should be a lovely service.'

She smiled then leaned in to kiss him, her dry lips like stone on the preacher's cheek. This moment of lucidity, of humanity was rare in her. Harold knew to treat it with the utmost respect.

The young man with her stood at the doorway, face turned as if pretending not to have listened in on their exchange. Harold left the young McBride girl and walked to him. He leaned against the door, breathing in the clean air blowing in from outside.

'It's Johnny, isn't it? You wrote that Jesus AI.'

'Yep, that's me,' Johnny replied, sheepishly.

The preacher nodded.

'You know, I haven't seen Katherine look this good since she was a little girl.'

'She's *still* a little girl.'

Harold shrugged. He couldn't disagree with that. Regardless of how much Katherine McBride had experienced in her teens, she was still just a child, albeit a child who had tasted the very darkest life had to offer. Things the average person would never taste, regardless of how long they lived.

But Katherine McBride was far from average.

'They say you saved her life,' Harold said to Johnny.

The code guy blew some air out.

'When I took her to the hospital,' he said, 'she told them *her mom* saved her life.'

'Her mother died about fifteen years ago. She'd suffered depression for a long time. Was bedridden. You'd never see her. Took an overdose in the end and it was Katherine who found her.' Harold shook his head, tutted. 'She was very young at the time.'

He looked to Katherine, and then to the bare wall where the plastic cross once hung.

'And what of our Good Lord?' he asked the code guy.

'Who knows?' Johnny said. 'Still out there, I guess. His Netspace's been closed. Several times, it seems. But each time one shuts down, another uploads as if . . .' and here Johnny shook his head and laughed almost bitterly, 'as if by magic.'

Harold thought back to the first Sunday after Alt's launch, how he'd turned up to find queues of people outside the Old Crusader. That Sunday, the place was filled to overflowing. They filled the aisles, the balcony each and every one of them wearing a wiretap.

He was interrupted by the workmen at the door again.

They brought in his old wooden cross.

As they carried it in, Harold watched Katherine McBride's face change. It reminded him of a picture he'd once seen: a simple oil painting of a little boy sitting on his father's knee, one hand holding a cell, the wires from the thing plugged into his little ears, the other hand pressed against the lines on the man's face. But it was the look the young boy gave his father; one of sheer awe. It was the same look Katherine was giving the three workmen now as they carried in the old rugged cross.

'Where do you want it?' the foreman asked, still bouncing gum around his mouth.

Harold's eyes met the wall behind the pulpit. He could still see the shadow where the cross had been hanging before all this VR nonsense.

'Right there,' he said, pointing.

EPILOGUE

Later that evening, Johnny Lyon sat at his desk alone.

He noticed his wiretap lying on the sofa. It was disconnected. He hadn't been using it this last while. Were he to be honest, the damn thing scared him.

His mind travelled back to that fateful night, after he'd pulled Kitty McBride from the inferno in her Tomb Street home. They'd gone back to Charles 7's place. Johnny found Charles behind the counter, his coils connected to frazzled tech and a dead cell.

That Bomb he'd unleashed had slammed the Jesus doll then blown every cell connected to VR the world over.

But with the Net down, Charles was scared. He was blabbering crazy talk, panicking at Johnny's touch, hyper-sensitive to everything around him. Reality and all that went with it filled his mind like gas, Johnny realised, and Charles 7 was having a hard time dealing.

It was a wake-up call to Johnny.

He'd since decided to focus on standard code, to move away from VR. He was working from home, having gone freelance since Alt Lark went (literally) up in smoke.

The touchscreen in front of him displayed his e-mails, one opened, giving details about the funerals of Garçon and Billy.

But one e-mail remained *unopened*.

It was from Becky Lyon and today Johnny was going to read it.

His hands moved through the touchscreen to his inbox. He felt a rush of heat come over him as the message appeared on the screen.

He read it.

It didn't take long, the e-mail simply telling him: 'Don't forget the wine.'

Johnny smiled.

He *had* forgotten the wine. He always forgot the wine.

A single character after the message meant much more to him, however:

X

Johnny's eyes went misty and he felt a lump gather in his throat.

His cell was buzzing, but he didn't pick up, leaving it for the answer machine. It went on speaker.

Sarah.

She launched into a diatribe she'd no doubt been rehearsing over and over again before making the call.

'Hey Johnny, I'm just checking to see how you are. I . . . well, I'm sitting here just thinking about all that's happened, what it means. The news reports are saying this could have been much worse. A lot more people could have died. They're calling for VR to be regulated in some way.

'Anyway. . .' She paused, drawing breath heavily. 'Well, I just wondered where we go from here, I guess. There's so much I said to you over the last few weeks . . . some things I regret, other things I wish I'd said sooner.'

He heard her sigh.

'Johnny,' she said, 'I don't know *what* I need.' And then, 'I need a drink,' before laughing as if relieved at the discovery. Her voice softened: 'If you want to join me, give me a call.'

Johnny listened as she signed off.

His eyes lingered on the cell as if not sure what to do with it.

He turned back to the screen.

He brought two fingers to his lips and moistened them, before pressing them against that 'X'.

Then he picked up his cell, chose SARAH, and made a call.

ACKNOWLEDGEMENTS

I'd like to thank everyone who has supported my writing over the years. Dave, Rich, Daniel and everyone over at the facebook fan page get a special mention.

I'd also like to offer my gratitude to all the booksellers who have championed my work: Trevor Proctor, Tsam Cowling, Steven Caunt, Rich Coad, David Torrans and the FPI Belfast crew amongst others.

Thanks to Joe Baker and Tariq Sarwar for the research help.

Thanks to David Moody for helping to keep me sane in this Godawful business.

To my agent, Gina Panettieri: thanks for keeping me right on the maths side of things and always having my back.

To Steve, Chris and Jen: thanks for taking a chance on me.

Finally, huge thanks as always to Rebecca and Dita for your love, patience and belief in what I do.

Here's to the next one . . .